The Power of Rain

The Power
of Rain

A DIGGER DOYLE MYSTERY

Rosalie Rayburn

Landscape cover photo: Albuquerque, New Mexico (USA), captured from the volcanoes west of the city. Istock.com | viennetta. Title page illustration: line engraving by T. de Leu after M. de Vos. Wellcome Library no. 15557i. https:// catalogue.wellcomelibrary.org/record=b1164100.

Publisher's Cataoging-in-Publication Data

Names: Rayburn, Rosalie, author.
Title: The power of rain : a Digger Doyle mystery / Rosalie Rayburn.
Description: Rosalie Rayburn, 2022.
Identifiers: LCCN: 2022907912 | paperback ISBN: 978-0-578-29637-1 |
    ebook ISBN: 978-0-578-29638-8
Subjects: LCSH Journalists—Fiction. | Hispanic Americans—Fiction. |
    Lesbians—Fiction. | New Mexico—Fiction. | Mystery fiction. |
    BISAC FICTION / Mystery & Detective / Women Sleuths |
    FICTION / LGBTQ+ / Lesbian | FICTION / Political
Classification: LCC PS3618 .A93 P69 2022 | DDC 813.6—dc23

To
the memory of
my beloved son
Max

Acknowlegments

I'D LIKE TO thank all of the people who made this book possible. The members of my writing group; Susan Stiger, Talia Freedman and Donna Olmstead, who provided the valuable encouragement and criticism that propelled this story from a simple sketch to a full-fledged novel.

My journalist friends who read and gave me feedback, corrected some errors and suggested some good plot twists; including Stephanie Hainsfurther, and my former *Albuquerque Journal* colleagues Ellen Marks and Mike Hartranft.

My lifelong British friends Julia Molony and Janie Clarke who overcame the peculiarities of American spelling and grammar to provide useful perspectives on the story arc.

My former college roommate Andy McKee who suggested the idea of incorporating a mysterious legend.

Sarah Jane Herbener of Savvy Communication who provided valuable advice and suggestions as she edited the manuscript.

Sara DeHaan of DeHaan Arts who did a superb job designing the cover and text and who guided me through the self-publishing process.

To my brother Bob and my son Patrick and the rest of my family for always being supportive.

Finally, to all the journalists at small newspapers everywhere, who keep the faith, shining a light on public officials so they can't get away with fooling the public.

The Power of Rain

CHAPTER ONE

TEN STRAIGHT DAYS of near 100-degree temperatures and still the rains didn't come. Digger couldn't remember the last time it had rained, two months, three months, probably more. In Bernalillo, and the little towns where the old families lived, they held rosaries praying for rain. Still, the heavens did not answer their prayers. Each time the deceitful clouds loomed over the land they lingered there, descending teasingly close to the parched earth before vanishing. The air and the earth remained so dry it shriveled the skin.

Drought spawned anxiety, and always the fear of fire. But fire wasn't the only thing to fear. In the high desert, rain isn't always a blessing. Sometimes when the monsoons finally arrived, the rain came like a vengeful lover, clawing and violating the earth. Digger knew what the rain could do. She'd seen those cruel claw marks and she'd written a series of stories. One of them had even won a press award. But nothing made a difference in a town where people came to live out their sunshine fantasies.

Digger always stopped at the top of the hill on her morning trail run. It was the halfway point and there was a convenient rock where she could sit and look down to where the drought depleted river bled feebly among the sand banks. Beyond it, the land rose sharply and atop the escarpment a line of fancy new homes crenelated the ridge line, windows glinting in the morning sun. Los Sueños, The Dreams, the city's newest subdivision. A hundred more toilets hemorrhaging water from the near exhausted aquifer.

Digger squinted at the development, studying the way the land dropped sharply to the wooded area below. All through her run, she'd been puzzling over last night's anonymous email and now it came to her. This is what it was all about.

The message had popped up in her inbox last night just before she'd left the newsroom. The subject line had jolted her: STOP THE ROAD! She'd opened the email and quickly scanned the text: "We will not have our rights trampled on again. We have our dreams too. We will not let this road destroy the sacred place beneath the cliff. Enough, is enough! We will take action. You will hear from us again soon!"

Digger had stared at it, frowning. No name, no contact information. Probably another scam. She trashed it.

Now, as she looked at the glinting windows of Los Sueños, it all made sense. A new section of road was supposed to connect the street that skirted the base of the escarpment with Los Sueños at the top of the cliff. So, the cliff held secrets. Weird. Nothing she'd read—and she'd scoured a ton of city records—said anything about sacred or historic sites. A whiff of controversy would have lit a fire. But there had been nothing, not even a hint of smoke.

Suspicion stirred like a tiny irritation, like a piece of grit at the bottom of her running shoe. Somebody in Las Vistas must have made sure the information never got out. The developer was Johnny Raposa. Hmm, that name. Grandpa used to tell a story about a Portuguese fox, *raposa*, quick, clever and elusive.

On the other side of Las Vistas, Mayor Jack Kimble stood at the edge of his patio staring at the gray-green sandy mesa that stretched west from his back yard for seventy miles to Mount Caballo. Clouds had been building all afternoon and now formed a billowy white tower that rose over the mountain ridge. Its underside loomed a dark, ominous gray, and the sky beneath was brown like an old photograph. The air, still until then, suddenly came alive. A gust beat against Jack's face, whipping his loose shirt around him like the robes of an Old Testament prophet.

Wind slammed the patio chairs against the table. A desert willow by the fence bent, its wispy branches shaking violently. Great thick thunderclouds roiled above him. Just then, a wall of brown sand-filled air blew toward him. He put his hands up to shield his face. Eyes shut, he smelled rain just before the first drops hit. They felt icy cold against his arms. When he opened his eyes, he saw big, fat drops splatting into the sandy earth like soft-nosed bullets, gouging deep ragged-edged holes. Within minutes, the air all around him was filled with sand and rain. Sluicing water bored into a tiny crack in the dirt beyond the fence, and suddenly the crack was a foot deep and a foot wide and still growing. Brown water foamed and gushed through the sand, carving its way past his house.

He staggered under the shelter of the patio, half blinded by rain and wind. The phone in his pocket buzzed and he fumbled for it.

"What?" he bellowed.

"Jack!" Linda Raccaro, the councilor from the southern side of the city, screamed in his ear. "You gotta get over here now! The whole place is flooding. People are gonna be mad!"

Kimble winced. Always something with these people. He'd been dreading a problem like this. Half the residents of Las Vistas were so new they didn't even know it could rain in New Mexico. They didn't know what rain could do here. He looked at the turbulent sky. Maybe it was a sign from God. The election was just months away. If he handled this right, it could boost his sagging popularity. An answer to his prayers.

"I'll be there!" he snapped. Yes, he would show them! God was on his side. He was sure of it. He hurried inside, rummaged in the hall closet for a raincoat.

"Is that you dear?" His wife's whiny voice twanged like a curb alarm. "You're not going out in this storm, are you?"

Kimble exhaled through clenched teeth. "Yes, dear. People are having a problem. I am their mayor. They need me."

He grabbed the keys to the Buick from the hook next to the refrigerator. The old car grunted like someone straining to defecate. Finally it rumbled to life. Kimble mashed it into reverse and sped out of his driveway. He squinted, trying to make out street names through the rain-drenched windshield. The directions Raccaro had babbled over the phone were worthless. Good God, the woman was clueless! How had she ever managed to get elected? No wonder people in her part of Las Vistas were always whining. Well, he would put a stop to that! He would be the one to turn the rainstorm into a blessing for Las Vistas residents. This would be his mission.

Fifteen minutes later he turned onto one of the gravel roads that led into the subdivision. The old Buick's engine strained through a foot of raging storm water. Halfway up the street, the Buick stalled. Kimble climbed out. A man in a Yankees ball cap come running out of a nearby house, waving.

"Help!" the man yelled. He pointed at the ground.

As Jack watched, the surging water blasted into the soft sand, creating a gaping chasm wide enough to swallow a truck.

"Look at this!" The man waved his arms helplessly as he glared at Kimble. "I moved here to be in the desert. My realtor said it never rains."

Kimble rolled his eyes.

➤

Digger was thinking about the email as she got ready for work. Who sent it and what did they want? What was at the base of the cliffs and why would anyone want it kept secret? Dressed, she picked her favorite pair of cowboy boots from the rack, rubbed the toes on the back of each pant leg for a quick shine. She was halfway to her car when she noticed the gray-white pile of clouds on the western horizon and ran back for a rain jacket.

Fifteen minutes later she pulled into the newspaper's parking lot. The *Daily Courier* occupied a downtown building a few miles from the new city hall. She nodded at the security guard as she entered the newsroom, then hurried to the city editor's desk.

"Hey Jim, I've got a story for you—"

"Not now!" he snapped, his eyes on his computer monitor. "We've got a fast-moving storm. I need you for a weather story."

Jim Swenson sounded as if he'd left rural Wisconsin last week, not twenty-two years ago when he'd joined the *Courier*.

Damn, thought Digger, he wasn't going to pay attention. Swenson didn't even look around. He pointed at the screen, frowning. "You can see here. It's coming in from the southwest with a lot of rain."

"Jim!" The police reporter yelled from across the room. "I just heard on the scanner, they're responding to an emergency—"

"Ugh—wait!" Swenson had gone pale. He held up a hand, pressed the other to his sternum and grimaced. He rummaged in a desk drawer, pulled out a bottle of Maalox, and took a swig. He wiped white residue from his lips and groaned. Digger waited. Lately the heartburn episodes were occurring more often. Swenson exuded stress like a personal form of body odor.

"Okay." He rubbed his chest.

"Jim!" The reporter shouted again. "There's flooding in that high-dollar subdivision, Vale de Oro."

Swenson groaned. "Shit! Those people are going to be pissed." He eyed Digger. "Go find Rex from photo and get out there as fast as you can."

Rex was in the photo department, lurking behind his over-sized monitor, consuming the remains of a donut.

"We've got a weather story," she announced.

"Yeah, I heard." He popped the last bite into his mouth and licked the sugar off his fingers.

Outside, Digger waited for Rex to load his camera gear into the back of one of the *Courier's* Jeep Cherokees. Here the asphalt was bone dry but to the south the sky was lawyer-suit gray. Rex took a last drag on his Marlboro and glanced at her.

"You got any rain gear?"

She waved the jacket she'd brought. Rex looked at it skeptically. "That'll be good for about ten seconds out there. Come on." He crushed the cigarette under his hiking boot and jerked his head toward the vehicle.

About a mile south of the office they hit the rain belt. The Jeep's sun-rotted wiper blades creaked and thumped, smearing brown dust streaks across the windshield. Rex hunched over the steering wheel, his jaw muscles clenching.

"Crap! I can't see worth shit," he said. "You know you the paper's in trouble when they can't even replace the wiper blades."

Digger shot him a look. Rex had such a negative attitude. She switched attention back to the directions she'd scribbled in her notebook and tapped a street name into her phone. She had a rough idea where to find the flood area. It was in a part of Las Vistas blooming with Tuscan-themed houses featured in "parade-of-homes" ads. Subdivisions there popped up so fast there was no time to put in stuff like paved roads, and no money to pay for them. It was all about the mountain views.

Today the mountains were obscured by a wall of dust and pounding rain. Rex turned off the paved road at the entrance to the Vale de Oro subdivision and made it about fifty yards along the sandy side street when half of it suddenly wasn't there. One lane had caved in and was now a crevasse.

Rex parked and they sat in the Jeep for a moment, surveying

the chaos. Rain streamed down the windows, drumming hard on the roof of the vehicle.

"Man, I've seen some storms," Rex said, raising his voice to be heard above the din, "But this one's a mother! There's going to be hell to pay."

"Like what?"

Rex looked around at her, eyebrow lifted. "You know what they call this area? The Valley of Entitlement. Says it all, doesn't it?"

Up ahead they saw people bunched together in front of an oversized ranch house with faux-Tuscan roof turrets. A lot of arm-waving and shouting was going on. The road ahead was a gaping crevasse with water sluicing over the sides. In the distance, beyond the houses, the sandy earth was dark with rain but undamaged.

Digger stared at it recalling the environmental reports she'd read. Every one of them warned that the soil was unstable because the sloping terrain was a precipitation catchment area. When there was rain, the reports said, natural water courses—arroyos—carried the accumulated runoff down to the river. Building on the slopes would create spillways that would collect and accelerate rain runoff. Without mitigating measures, such as drainage ponds and culverts, any significant rain events would result in flooding and erosion. City councilors approved the new subdivision anyway, without requiring drainage ponds or culverts.

She looked at Rex and shook her head. He gave her his seen-it-all-before shrug.

"You know how it is in this town," he said, "Come on, it's showtime."

He jumped out, loaded his gear, and began to snap shots of the arroyo, the water surging down the street and the noisy crowd.

Digger followed him trudging through the wet sand, rain pelting her face, water dripping from her eyebrows and trickling down the side of her chin. As Rex had predicted, water soaked through the flimsy rain jacket within seconds.

Up ahead a tangle of voices pierced through the hiss of the rain. "This is unacceptable!" shouted a short lady with shelflike hips and a grating New York accent. "I wanna know why the city isn't doing something about this."

"Yeah! The mayor oughta see this. Whatta we pay taxes for?" said a man in a Vietnam veteran's baseball hat.

A big flashy Cadillac swerved round the corner and barreled toward Digger and Rex, tires spinning, sashaying from one side to the other. It jolted to a halt a few yards short of the where they stood. Digger recognized the woman who climbed out as Councilor Linda Raccaro. Her springy grey curls sagged in the downpour as she sloshed across the road, mud smearing her white tennis shoes.

"Oh my gawd! This is terrible, terrible!" Her shrieks were barely audible above the surge of rushing water, the rain, and the angry complaints from home owners.

Another car ground up the road, transmission whining, tires slipping on the wet surface. Mayor Jack Kimble' s tall frame emerged from the vehicle. He strode toward them, heedless of the mud, shouldering his way through the throng until he reached the end of a driveway. He stepped on top of a boulder and stared round at the bedraggled crowd.

Digger slogged toward him, feet sinking in the soggy sand. "Mayor," she shouted, "Isn't it true the city knew this could happen? Why did the city ignore reports about the flood risks?"

Kimble towered above her, his long arms outstretched, his brush-cut hair bristling from his head, his turquoise eyes blazing.

"Mayor!" she yelled again.

Kimble ignored her. Instead, his eyes were fixed on the sky. He raised up his hands.

"I am listening," he boomed. "I will save you from this affliction!"

CHAPTER TWO

DIGGER SAT NURSING a Corona at Frankie's, exhausted after the frantic afternoon. The bar was her favorite place when she needed to decompress. Every now and then a rumor circulated that the place was closing. But who knew?

To Digger, the slightly run-down atmosphere of the women's bar felt like an old jacket, something you slipped into to feel comfortable and keep out the harsh elements. There were always people she knew, at least by sight. Tonight the place was buzzing. She was glad to see none of her old girlfriends were here. She hated running into women she used to date, especially the emotional vampires who made a point of flaunting a new girlfriend as if to say, "Look at me now—and you're all alone."

Tonight she just wanted to hang out at the bar and chat with Lexi. Some said if it weren't for Lexi, the place would probably have closed like a lot of other women's bars had. Lexi, with her buzz-cut hair, sleeve of tattoos, tank top, and cynical sense of humor, was the soul of Frankie's.

"So, what's up in your life, Digg?" Lexi asked in her throaty smoker's voice.

"Same old, same old. Working crazy hours, watching crazy people." Digger shook her head. "I don't know why I keep thinking what I write will make a difference. Lately I've been thinking I should give up and find something else."

Lexi shook her head slowly. "Hate to tell you, girlfriend, but people don't read newspapers like they used to. Maybe you oughta get another kind of job."

"Yeah. I hear you," Digger said, "but really, this is all I wanted to do since I was about thirteen. It kind of gets in your blood. Take today, when we had that storm. I was out there on one of the flooded streets: water everywhere, people sloshing, complaining. All of a sudden the mayor shows up. He climbs up on this rock, stretches out his arms, and he looks like that guy in the Bible parting the Red Sea." Digger flung out her arms. "It was the Red Sea, wasn't it?"

"Damned if I know. I flunked out of Sunday school. Want another?" Lexi gestured at the empty Corona bottle. Digger nodded.

"What about that woman you were seeing?"

Digger shrugged. "Oh, you know. Things didn't work out. Six weeks and she starts talking about moving in with me, wants to get inside my head. I don't do that stuff."

Lexi shot her a shrewd look. "What is it you want? You're cute, you got all kinds of women interested in you. You want a reputation as a player?"

Digger shook her head. "I'm not a player. I just don't like being smothered, I don't like drama and I'm not a U-Haul girl."

Lexi gave an exasperated sigh. "Sometimes you gotta open up. Can't hold the world out all the time. I mean, look at me and Susan. We've been together twelve years now. Got married as soon as it was legal. Never thought that'd happen, but I'm sure glad it did." Lexi folded her arms across her ample chest and beamed.

Digger shot her a cynical look. "Lex, stop trying to fix me up."

Lexi pouted. "Well, you can't blame me for trying."

She turned away to serve a couple of women at the other end

of the counter. Digger swiveled on her stool, beer in hand, letting her gaze drift around the bar. A figure on the far side of the room caught her eye: a tall Hispanic woman was handing out leaflets to women at the tables along the wall.

Digger studied her for a while.

"Hey, Lex, who's that?" she asked at last, cocking her head toward the woman.

Lexi leaned over to follow Digger's indication. "Oh, her? Don't know. She used to come in here a while back with some real butch-looking woman. The butch was a possessive type. Haven't seen either of them for a while. You interested?"

"Maybe." Digger eased down off the stool. "Guess I'll find out."

She walked slowly around the edge of the dance floor, keeping her eye on the woman, noting her long hair, tight-fitting jeans, a silver cuff bracelet on one wrist.

"Hi," she said as she approached, speaking loudly enough to catch the tall woman's attention. She wheeled around, eyed Digger, and thrust a leaflet at her.

"Can you come to the protest?" she asked.

Digger took the leaflet, read it, then eyed the woman with new curiosity. "So . . . are you involved with this?"

"What do you mean?" the woman asked, a challenge in her black eyes.

"Is this about that new road?" Digger asked.

"Yeah. What do you know about it?"

"I know a little. I work at the *Courier*."

"The *Courier*?" she snorted. "Those developers are going to blast through the cliffs, and no one at your paper seems to care. That road could totally cut off access to a really sacred site that's been here for hundreds of years."

Digger looked down at the leaflet in her hand. Hmm. So she didn't care, huh? That kind of attitude pissed her off. She could put on a little attitude of her own.

"If you knew who I was, I bet you wouldn't say that," she said. The woman looked back defiantly. "So, who are you, then?" Digger countered with her own question. "I got this weird email a couple of nights ago. Sounded like a threat. Was that you?" She had to ask. If this woman was from that group, questioning her might show whether they were serious.

The woman nodded, a smile spreading across her face. "Oh, so you're that reporter?" She took a step back and let her eyes roam over Digger, appraising. "I didn't expect to meet a reporter here."

"You don't have to be straight to be a reporter," Digger said.

The woman raised an eyebrow and laughed. "Well, then, I guess it's lucky we met."

Digger's irritation melted away. She liked the look of this woman: tall and powerful, with almost-black hair swept up behind her head and eyes dark as olives. If she wanted to get to know her better, here was her chance.

"Lucky?" she asked. "How so?"

The woman grinned back at her. "You should definitely come to the protest on Sunday."

"Okayyy," Digger said slowly, meeting the woman's eyes. "I'll be there." The woman cocked an eyebrow. "Yeah, right. We'll see if you make it."

"I will," Digger smiled. "By the way, I'm Digger. What's your name?"

The woman was already moving toward a nest of tables near the wall, but she turned and smiled back, throwing the words over her shoulder.

"Maria Ortiz."

———

Digger rolled over and stuck her feet beneath the spare pillow, fending off the insistent pricking of cat claws. Lady Antonia had decided it was time for breakfast. Lady Antonia got a quarter cup of Iams and a teaspoon of tuna every morning at six thirty, if you please, weekends no exception.

"It's Saturday," Digger groaned. She hadn't gotten home from Frankie's until nearly two in the morning, but she knew that made no difference to the cat. She'd have to give in soon.

Normally she loved getting up on Saturday mornings, when she could look forward to two whole days of freedom. She liked waking up early and just hanging out in her apartment. The complex lay nestled against the foothills. On weekends she had time to sit on the tiny balcony, drink coffee, and take in the sight of the mountains. She'd picked the top floor for the view. Backlit by the rising sun, the crest was slate blue in the mornings, like a steel cutout against the sky.

Today the sky was gunmetal gray and bruised-looking from the storm.

Digger burrowed beneath the covers, stretched, then winced as Lady Antonia's claws struck flesh. She was going at it with a full four-paw attack. It was definitely Tuna Time.

Digger rubbed Lady Antonia's silky black ears. The cat purred. Digger got up, put down cat food, made herself coffee and toast, listened to the news. She took her coffee to the balcony and looked out again at the day. Sun had broken through the clouds and bathed the foothills in shafts of clear light. The clouds might gather again later, but for now the day was so bright it hurt her eyes.

As she sipped her coffee, she thought about Lexi's words at the bar: *What is it you want?* She thought some more, asking herself the same question. What did she want, really?

The old, nagging feeling stirred inside her. She set down the coffee and went to her bedroom. She knew what she was going to do. It was like pulling back a sleeve to look at an old scar, wondering if it would look any different.

She opened the closet door, reached up, pulled down the folder of clippings, and sat on the floor to read them.

The memories flooded back, clear and painful.

She was twelve years old. A call at school. Chubby Mrs. Newman, the school counselor with white flecks of saliva at the corners of her mouth. Mrs. Newman's mouth moving. *Your parents ... a car crash ... fatal.* She could see it again, the front page story: "Frank Doyle, 36, and his wife Lisa Doyle, 35, teachers at Charter Preparatory School, died when a vehicle crossed the median and struck their SUV, causing it to flip."

She'd read every story. Especially that one, the one where the district attorney had said it was impossible to determine whether the driver who had struck her parents' vehicle was impaired. He had attributed the lack of conclusion to the condition of the blood sample taken from the driver. In the end, the driver had only been charged with failure to maintain a lane.

Yeah, right! Failure to maintain a lane!

Seventeen years was a long time. She picked up the clippings one by one, read the headlines, the first few paragraphs. She stared at the pictures of her parents and of the driver who had hit them, Joshua Armando Salazar. He was twenty-two then; he'd be in his late thirties now. He'd claimed there was something wrong with his steering, but the police investigator's report had, been inconclusive.

In her teens Digger would lie awake nights thinking how she could track him down, confront him. The therapist her grandmother took her to had advised her to "let it go." It was like suggesting to someone who'd lost a leg that they should pretend it had never happened.

Where was he now? Was he haunted by dreams of the accident? Did he feel guilty?

Angrily she shoved everything back into the folder and stuffed it under the pile of clothes on the shelf.

She put on her running clothes and went searching for a hat in the wicker basket on the closet floor. Finding one, she clamped it onto her head, strode out the door and made for the trailhead behind the condo complex.

Later, after a long run, brunch, and a shower, Digger fished the leaflet out of the pocket of the jeans she'd been wearing at the bar. "Stop the Road," it said, announcing a protest at the point where the existing road veered by the foot of the escarpment. Digger knew developers wanted a road across the place where the land dropped off because it would provide a direct link from the Los Sueños subdivision to a nearby shopping center. The flyer said the protest would start at two o'clock. Digger glanced at the alarm clock by her bed. It showed nearly one fifteen.

She rummaged through her dresser, rejected a half dozen T-shirts and shorts, working herself into a mild panic. She'd forgotten to do laundry again. She settled on a black V-neck T-shirt and her newest pair of Wranglers. She looked out the window, noticed clouds, and tucked the rain jacket into her backpack again. She might not need it, but it was rainy season; you never knew. Dressed, she jumped into the Subaru and screeched out the gates of the complex.

CHAPTER THREE

THE CLIFFS WERE at the western edge of town, beyond the river valley, where the land rose sharply several hundred feet before leveling off in a mesa that extended westward. Two small, long-extinct volcanoes poked out of the mesa about a half mile south of the city limits.

On the city side of the cliffs was the shopping center. North of the shopping center, the boulevard veered southwest, bypassing Los Sueños. Billboards advertised Los Sueños as an upscale master-planned community with a fitness center, parks, and hiking trails.

The *Courier* had reported that home sales there remained sluggish. She knew Johnny Raposa had been glad-handing folks around city hall, trying to win support for the new road. His spiel was that Los Sueños would bring more high-dollar residents to the city. Digger figured he was desperate to boost sales.

In recent months she'd been to a couple of public meetings where city and state officials had discussed the road plan. There had been no mention of any historic sites, not once. Yet the flyer Maria had handed out at the bar said the road threatened a Spanish Colonial-era chapel revered for hundreds of years. So why hadn't her group surfaced before now? If someone was concerned about the chapel, surely they would have raised objections at the beginning, and knowing Las Vistas, there would have been a stink about it.

Digger parked her car on a side street and walked a hundred yards to the sharp swerve in the road where the protest was supposed to take place. A small group of people was milling in front of some orange-and-white barriers.

She noticed that the crowd was mostly women, including an elderly lady in a wheelchair. There were also a couple of old men and some kids. They held large hand-painted cardboard signs reading "No Road" and "Keep This Site Sacred." She heard a drum and noticed an old Native American man in tribal dress at the back of the group. Maria was there, leaning over a little girl, arm around her shoulder.

A pickup truck sped by, windows down. The driver extended a hand, middle finger raised, and yelled at the protesters, "Outta the way! Assholes!"

Digger watched as the truck disappeared around the corner. Guys like that pissed her off. There were a lot of them in Las Vistas. It made her want to join the protest. She shook her head, putting the thought away, and pulled out her notebook.

Her feet swooshed through deep piles of last year's leaves as she made her way to where the protesters had taken refuge under the shade of an immense cottonwood. Maria, her back to Digger, was now talking to a woman flanked by two young girls.

"Hi!" Digger called.

Maria swung around. "Oh! You came after all."

"I said I would."

"A woman who sticks to her word," Maria said. She gave Digger the appraising look. "I like that."

Digger opened her mouth to respond, but Maria was already in motion, her hands on the shoulders of the two girls. "I have to help them make signs. My friend Alma here will talk to you."

And she was gone, shepherding the girls toward a small folding table where a young man was at work with paper and marking pens. Digger thought about following her, decided against it, then introduced herself to Alma.

Alma looked about thirty-five, with curly dark brown hair that fell just below her shoulders. She wore a faded red T-shirt with the name of some sports team Digger didn't recognize.

"So, what brought you here today?"

Alma took a breath. Her voice came out high-pitched and excited. "I really came because of Maria. She teaches art at my girls' school, San Fermin Elementary. They still have an art program there; it's wonderful. The girls love her . . ."

San Fermin was a Native American pueblo community just north of Las Vistas.

"San Fermin. You live there, not in Las Vistas?" She asked, puzzled.

"Yes. My husband is a member of the tribe, but I grew up in Santa Rita. Do you know it? Hardly anyone lives there anymore, just old people. It's so sad, so many empty houses, everything for sale."

Digger nodded. All those towns around Las Vistas were dying. She'd been through Santa Rita with Rex just a week ago. He'd made some quip about the place needing life support.

Just then she heard a distant rumble. Looking toward the mountains, she saw thunderclouds massing. She needed to get more out of Alma so she could get round to some of the others.

"What do you think about this road, then?"

"It's going to destroy the chapel," Alma said, gesturing into the woods.

"Destroy? Are you sure?"

The skepticism in Digger's voice must have touched a nerve. Alma tossed her head, flinging hair away from her face. "You live in Las Vistas, you know how those people are," she snapped. "My sister works for the city. She says they do anything the developers want."

Digger couldn't argue with that. Wasn't that exactly what had happened with the decision to approve Los Sueños? Three of the councilors had voted against the subdivision, but when it came to a tie, Kimble had sided with those who'd approved it. He was in Raposa's pocket as much as any of the others. Alma's comments fueled Digger's suspicions that someone at city hall must have made sure that information about the chapel, and how it might affect the road, never appeared in official reports. Did Maria know that?

Looking around, she saw her standing beside the road, holding one end of a banner. The woman holding the other end was one of those she'd seen in the bar. A couple of cars went past, drivers slowing, faces puzzled. A man in an SUV stopped, rolled down his window, and shouted.

"I don't know what you guys think you're doing, but you need to get out of the road. You're endangering motorists!"

He sped off. Digger shook her head. Maria waved a fist at the disappearing SUV. "Asshole!" She shouted.

"Hey!" Digger called to her. "Can we talk? Can you tell me what you know about the project. Are you really afraid it will harm the chapel?"

Maria nodded, handed her end of the banner to an elderly man, and led Digger away from the crowd. She stopped a few yards from the cottonwood, where a path led through the trees.

"Thanks for coming today," Maria said. "This is really important to me. I want those people in Las Vistas to know there is history here. They come to live here and they need to respect that this place has meaning. So, yes, I'm afraid this ridiculous road could damage the chapel. There are plenty of other roads those people who buy the big ugly houses up there can drive their SUVs on to go buy groceries."

Digger appreciated the sarcasm but she thought she'd play devil's advocate anyway. "How do you think you're going to fight the city?"

"This is just a beginning," She said, waving a hand at the small crowd. Then she rounded on Digger, her eyes fierce. "This is in my blood. When she was young, my grandmother supported Cesar Chavez and Dolores Huerta in their fight for farmworkers in California."

Listening to her, Digger realized the story was a lot bigger than just the road and the chapel. It was a symptom of a cultural divide that went deep.

She heard thunder again, closer this time. "Look, we don't have much time. Can you show me the chapel?"

Maria indicated a path between the trees, and they began walking. After five minutes, she stopped and pointed. Digger peered ahead. The sky was becoming darker every minute, and it was now hard to see under the gloom of the trees. Digger could just make out a squat caramel-brown building in the distance. Maria started toward it, but a resounding boom stopped her.

They looked at each other. Digger wanted to press ahead, but it wasn't safe to be beneath the trees when thunder cracked overhead.

"Shit! We need to get out of here now!" Maria's voice was tense but firm.

They dashed back to the clearing where the others had already put away the table and gathered the signs.

"I'll call you," Maria shouted. Then she was gone.

Digger gritted her teeth. *Damn.* She needed to see that chapel.

CHAPTER FOUR

JACK KIMBLE STOOD in the anteroom listening to the hum of the crowd gathered in the council chambers. His watch showed two minutes to six. He liked to keep them waiting each week until exactly six o'clock, when the meetings were scheduled to start. These moments gave him an opportunity to contemplate his role the way he used to in his preaching days.

Las Vistas wasn't where Kimble had planned to end his career. Not this vacuous desert city with its population of the disaffected. He'd had his eye on becoming pastor at Baptism Hall, a mega-church with a congregation of thousands. But they'd chosen the other guy, the young, good-looking one. He had to be content with being mayor of Las Vistas.

He was proud of improvements he'd made as mayor. The new city hall building, completed last year, had won awards for design. It had made him realize this new career could be more satisfying than preaching, maybe not in spiritual terms but in the currency of everyday life. If he won a second term, Kimble envisaged more stores, restaurants, office buildings, and businesses. He wanted that, and he needed to win to make it happen.

The elections were just seven months away. He needed to start fundraising, and he needed to get Johnny Raposa on board with that. The developer had deep pockets and could swing a lot of support behind his campaign. Kimble would need all the support he could get, with the drainage work that would have to be done after this flooding problem. Raposa was doing all right with sales in that subdivision. What was it called? Los Sueños, that was it. According to Raposa, things would really take off if they got that road through the cliffs. More sales meant more tax revenue for the city.

The door to the council chambers opened and the city manager's voice broke into Kimble's reverie.

"Jack, the council meeting is starting."

Competent man, thought Kimble; smart and extremely competent, but unsettling. It was the way Adam Fletcher looked at you over his glasses, as if he really had no interest in what you were going to say. He followed Fletcher through the door.

As Kimble surveyed the room, he noted every seat was taken. People were even standing, packed against the back and side walls, their voices edgy and loud. He had expected a big turnout after the flooding incident, but nothing like this.

Still, he was confident he could handle it. The governor had agreed to declare a disaster, and that would release funds for the cleanup. Kimble took his seat behind the dais.

Digger squeezed her way into the chamber. The press seat she normally used was already taken. She recognized some of the people she and Rex had encountered at the house on the flooded street: the woman with the shelflike hips and the angry-looking military veteran. Then there was the usual crowd of folks who appeared regularly at these things, as if public meetings were better than a night at the movies. There was old George, with his gentlemanly smile and his naughty wink. He waved at her, gesturing to the empty seat beside him.

Digger was wondering how Kimble was going to handle the

flooding calamity, but the meeting began as usual with a handful of civic presentations: a fifteen-year plaque for a firefighter, an award for the Boy Scout troop that had gathered the most trash on the annual Restore Las Vistas Day, and a hearty handshake for the high school track star who had aced the state finals. Digger always thought Kimble looked painfully stiff when he had to glad-hand people. He had a habit of brushing off his lapels as he walked back to the dais, as if he were ridding himself of unwanted germs.

She wondered if Maria and her group would show up to speak about the road protest. She'd heard nothing from her yet and had been too busy to follow up. She looked around, hoping to spot her in the crowd. No sign of her.

With the presentations over, Kimble opened the floor to public comment. The New Yorker with the big hips was the first to march up to the podium microphone. She launched into a tirade about how deeply offended she was.

"I'm Sally Jenkins. Me and my husband Al moved here three years ago to buy our dream home. This is our retirement. We pay taxes here! What happened in that rainstorm last Friday was unacceptable! Water just poured into our house. My carpets are soaked, my furniture is ruined. Who's gonna pay for that? The city needs to do something. We shouldn't be living here with dirt roads."

The city clerk's three-minute timer beeped but she kept on ranting.

Kimble endured another minute, then reminded her that time was up.

Al Jenkins was up next. "I served twelve years in the marines and I've been a manager with a major US corporation. I've overseen projects worth millions of dollars, and I can tell you, this is no way to run a city!"

A dozen more people stood up, railing against the incompetence, the weather, the dirt roads, what they expected for their taxes, and how things ought to be like they were in New York, Michigan, or wherever they came from. It was the city's fault, and by golly, they sure as hell weren't going to pay any more taxes!

Digger was used to the tone of personal grievance that characterized public comments, but tonight the attack language reached new heights. As Kimble and the other city councilors listened, their expressions morphed from shock to outright affront. Linda Raccaro, the councilor who represented the area worst hit by the storm, glared daggers at Sally Jenkins.

Councilor Nico Fabrizzi, another New Yorker, knitted his wiry eyebrows together and occasionally moved his lower jaw as though adjusting dentures.

Digger knew Fabrizzi was the only one still on the council who'd been there when construction in the flooded areas had been approved. She figured he must have known about the risks. If so, was he worried about being found out?

Next to Fabrizzi sat Tony Apodaca. Apodaca was the only councilor who looked genuinely pained by the plight of those hit by the flooding. His family had owned a huge ranch on the southern edge of Las Vistas and sold it off piecemeal to feed the demand for new subdivisions. *Wonder if he's regretting it?* Digger thought.

Dave Johnsen, the youngest member of the council, kept fiddling with a pair of glasses Digger had never seen him use before. Johnsen always seemed self-conscious. Whenever he made a comment, he looked around nervously as if seeking approval from the others.

After the last speaker, Kimble straightened his shoulders and stared hard at the people gathered before him. Then he whipped off his glasses and leaned forward.

"I was out there with you in the rain," he boomed. "I saw the flood waters and I vowed that I would bring help—and I have!"

He paused, looking around the room as if to make sure he had everyone's attention.

"I have talked with the governor, and he has agreed to declare a disaster.

That means we will receive state and federal funds to clear up this unprecedented situation. I have also found out there is a process by which the city can make sure this type of flooding will never damage individual homes again. We can start on this as soon as next month."

The room hushed. Digger scribbled notes furiously. What was Kimble talking about? What was this "process"? Did he really have something, or was this just an election ploy? March was still a long way off, but Kimble appeared awfully pleased with himself.

The rest of the councilors looked relieved, especially Linda Raccaro. She rose and held out her hands, nodding to the other councilors and those seated in the chamber.

"I think we're all very appreciative. I hope my constituents know I support this. We are willing to do everything we can to get over this really terrible situation. I mean everything!"

Digger glanced at George. He leaned over and whispered, "Bet she's been getting a lot of nasty phone calls."

Digger suppressed a smile.

As soon as the meeting ended, she rushed to get a comment from Kimble. "Mayor, I'd like to hear more about your plan to address the flooding." Kimble pursed his lips, looking annoyed. "I can't tell you more at this time. Everything is much too preliminary for me to let you put anything in print. I'll get back to you when I can."

He turned abruptly and strode away. Annoyed, Digger looked around.

Maybe Fabrizzi would talk. He knew the history better than any of the others. She hurried after him.

"Councilor! You were on the council when that subdivision was approved. Can you explain why it went ahead? Didn't councilors know about the risks?"

Fabrizzi folded his arms across his chest in a combative stance. "In Las Vistas, the position has always been that owners of land designated for construction have the right to build on it. That's in our city ordinances, as you'd know if you'd ever bothered to read them."

Digger ignored the sarcasm and piled on. "Okayyy. But was the developer required to advise home buyers of the risk? I mean, did you see the damage out there? Whole streets were caved in."

Fabrizzi let out an impatient sigh. "As far as I remember, there was something in the covenants. Yes, I think that was it. Now, if you'll excuse me, I have to get home."

Yeah, right, Digger thought, but she only had forty-five minutes to deadline.

No time for more questions.

CHAPTER FIVE

DIGGER SAT CHEWING her lip in frustration. She'd contacted every one of her city hall sources, and either they didn't know or wouldn't say anything about the plan Kimble had referred to. Judging by the high-octane grumbling of the crowd at the meeting, Kimble would need to pull something dazzling out of a hat to mollify voters if he seriously expected to win a second term.

Even though she had little patience for the chronic complainers at city meetings, Fabrizzi's words bothered her. The storm had done real damage. If there was anything about the flood risk in the covenants, it was probably buried so deep in the small print that a buyer wouldn't even notice. Home builders just wanted to sell houses. Tough luck if you got a lemon.

Right now her heart wasn't in it anyway. She kept thinking about Maria Ortiz. She wanted to see her again soon. Maria blazed with spirit and passion. The way she spoke rang with a truth worlds away from the self-entitled complaints Digger heard at every council meeting.

By itself, the road extension was no big deal. But the location, so close to a historic site, gave it symbolic value. She'd only been able to glimpse the chapel in the distance, but she wanted to go back. The road was emblematic of a conflict that was happening in so many communities: business versus historic interests, newcomers from outside against the culture of an older community. Tie that in with the environmental damage caused by rampant development, and it could be a story that might gain regional, maybe even national, attention. It could be her ticket to a paper higher up in the food chain.

She was still musing on the possibilities when her phone rang. Maria. Excitement hopscotched through her chest.

"I saw your story," Maria said. "Do you really want to write more about this issue or were you just bullshitting me?"

"Of course I meant it. Or were *you* bullshitting me?"

"Okay, so no BS. You want to meet for coffee? No, how about lunch?"

Digger hesitated. Lunch? Something about the tone in Maria's voice made her wonder if the call was professional or maybe personal.

"All right," she said, slowly. "Did you have somewhere in mind?"

"You know Rosario's?"

It was an old café in Los Jardines, a village a few miles north of Las Vistas.

They made a hard-to-beat green chile chicken enchilada.

"Yeah, we could do that."

"*Bueno.* How about noon tomorrow?" Maria suggested.

"See you then." Digger put down the phone. Okay, she could do an interview, but maybe they could also get to know each other a little better. This could be interesting.

➤

Los Jardines sat squeezed between the foothills and the ribbon of green that followed the river plain. On Saturday, Digger drove her Subaru north on the freeway and branched off at the country road that wound through Los Jardines. Along the way she passed several new and imposing custom homes built atop the ridge line. Closer to the village lay small alfalfa fields and rows of grapevines punctuated by clusters of decrepit old adobe dwellings, mobile homes, and an assortment of defunct cars and agricultural machinery.

She pulled into the graveled lot beside the café and parked under the shade of a small cottonwood tree. She was early, so she sat in the stationary car listening to the switched-off engine tick. A tortoiseshell cat studied her from between the stakes of the coyote fence that separated the café parking lot from the property next door. Through the stakes she could see a few droopy-headed stalks of corn and a washing line. Somewhere nearby a rooster crowed. A dog sauntered past the car, and the cat vanished. Even in the shade with the car window open, it was oppressively hot. The smells of frying meat, hot oil, and a hint of chile wafted through the air.

Footsteps crunched on the gravel. Digger turned her head and saw Maria walking toward her, wearing a loose white embroidered top, a skirt that swung around her legs mid-calf, and sandals. *She was stunning.*

"*Hola.* You made it," Maria said.

Digger got out of the car.

"I've been here before. I like their food."

"Let's go inside. It will be cooler than out here," Maria said.

Digger followed Maria through the wood-framed screen door into the low-ceilinged dining room. The building had thick traditional mud-brick adobe walls and small windows that kept out the heat. She had to blink momentarily as her eyes adjusted to the dimmed light.

"Two," Maria said to a stout middle-aged woman inside who

guided them through the half-filled dining room to a booth at the back.

"If you've been here before, you know they make good enchiladas," Maria commented, adding in a whisper, "But not as good as my grandmother's."

They slid into the dark red faux-leather booth seats. The waitress brought them glasses of water, chips and salsa, and dog-eared menus. Once they'd ordered, Digger sat a moment, waiting for Maria to say something. When she didn't, Digger cleared her throat. Polite chit-chat seemed a safe way to get the conversation going.

"That's nice you spend time with your grandmother," she said.

Maria flashed a glance at her, then dipped a chip into the dish of salsa and sucked on it. Digger studied her face. This woman was serious; the intensity in those dark eyes showed she didn't suffer fools gladly.

"So, what do you want to know?" Maria asked.

"You okay with me recording this?" Digger pulled out a lighter-sized voice recorder and laid it on the table between them.

Maria eyed it suspiciously. "Is that how you do things?"

"You want this to be accurate, don't you?"

"Of course I do." She shook her head impatiently. "If that's what it takes—go ahead."

Digger glanced at the brief list of questions she'd prepared.

"The other day you said you'd gotten involved after talking to parents of some of the kids at the school where you teach. You hadn't heard about this road before? Why not?"

"I don't live in Las Vistas, and I don't follow everything that goes on there. When I was talking to some parents one of them said they'd seen people surveying the site and asked questions."

"I'm surprised no one mentioned this chapel at any of the public meetings."

Maria frowned. "Maybe it's because the chapel is deep in the woods. A lot of people prefer it remains kind of private. They don't want people going there who don't appreciate the sacredness of the place. Now they're afraid road construction will ruin the area. When I looked into it, I realized they're right. The road could damage the Spanish chapel. You have to understand how that place is treasured by Hispanic families in this area. It is part of our culture and shouldn't be lost, especially to some stupid development for people who have no understanding, no appreciation for New Mexico. They just want nice weather and a pretty view."

Digger had had similar thoughts so many times about the people who moved to Las Vistas from out of state and made no secret of their contempt for New Mexico. But this was an interview, and she needed to appear objective. She kept her face neutral and stuck to the questions. What did Maria hope to achieve? Who had her group talked to? What was the next step? She got enough details to flesh out another story, but she knew she wanted a lot more. She really needed a good look at the site.

But they could talk about that later. She saw the server approaching with their plates, so she turned off her recorder. As the waitress set the plates on their table, Maria leaned away, swiftly gathering her long hair and twisting it into a coil she pinned at the back of her head. Digger watched her, eyes widening.

"How do you do that? It's like a magic trick."

Maria laughed. "Lots of practice. You'd know too if you had long hair."

"This works for me." Digger rubbed a hand through her blond spikes.

Maria told stories about her sister while they ate. Digger listened. She'd often wondered what it would be like to have a sister, or any sibling at all. To have a family of your own.

Toward the end of the meal, Maria set down her fork and

looked across the table. Digger sensed Maria had more on her mind. Digger put down her own fork, eased back in the booth and looked straight at Maria. They sat there like a cat and a lizard, each biding time until the other made the move.

"So, why did you ask me here?" Digger said at last. "We could have done a phone interview."

Maria studied Digger's face for several seconds. "I looked up some old stories you wrote and reread them—the ones about the environmental reports and those subdivisions." She considered a moment, then nodded. "You and I, I think we're a lot alike," she said, a hint of a smile playing on her lips.

Digger took a breath, leaned away, and crossed her arms. She had to keep this professional.

"How so?"

Maria picked up her fork, took another bite of food, chewed for a few more seconds, then bent over the table. She looked Digger straight in the eye.

"I think you are someone who really cares. When you came to the protest the other day, you said you thought it would be a good story."

Digger nodded.

Maria leaned closer, eyeing her earnestly. "I want your stories to be part of our campaign. You are the right person to do it. I know you get it."

Digger spread her hands on the table and leaned back. She wondered if Maria really knew what she was asking for. "You know there are plenty of people in Las Vistas who really support this road. I take it you've done some research on Johnny Raposa, the developer who's pushing it?"

Maria flicked a hand impatiently. "But you understand! I saw it in your face the day you came to the protest."

"I can write about it," Digger said tersely. "But that doesn't mean I automatically take your side. You know how journalism works. We present the situation and then we give each side of the story. I'll have to talk to the developers as well as your group. Both of you will probably end up pissed at me. That's just the way it is."

Maria exhaled in frustration. "You can't believe in something?" There was anger in her voice.

"You said you read my stories. I thought you got it," Digger snapped. "There's this thing about balance. We're not supposed to take sides when we write stories."

Maria shook her head. "Doesn't that bother you?"

Bother? Digger thought. If Maria only knew! Following a story meant stepping to the edge and keeping it right there where you still had control, you still had perspective.

"Of course it does," she said. "You have to be able to care enough but not lose your emotional balance. Sometimes that is really hard to do."

Maria's eyes flashed again. "When I believe in something, I believe it's important to act, not sit on the fence," she said.

Digger threw up her hands. "I don't think I'm getting through to you," she said. "If you think it's all about sitting on the fence, you're wrong. If I write about this issue, it won't just be about your campaign. It'll be about how the road is a symptom of what Las Vistas is doing to this area. But I will let the developers tell their side of it. I can't be a megaphone for your group, so you'd better be prepared that there'll be things in my reporting that you may not like."

They finished the meal in an awkward silence. Maria signaled the server for the check. Digger took out her wallet, but Maria insisted on paying for her own meal.

When they were outside, Digger started toward her car, but Maria touched her arm. "Come on, don't look so serious. I want you to meet the woman who has inspired me to do this work." She smiled and pointed up the narrow street.

"You live here, in Los Jardines?"

Maria nodded. "This is where my grandmother lives, and me, since I moved in with her. This way."

She led them down a side street that wound and climbed past tiny old homes. Clumps of pink hollyhocks clung to the walls, gardens sprouted rows of chile and squash.

Digger started to think the lunch meeting had been a mistake. If she wanted to keep things on a strictly professional basis, it would be better to keep a distance. She should head home now and forget meeting the grandmother. She was about to make an excuse to leave when they came to a gate in a wooden-slat fence. Maria pulled a latch and ushered Digger in.

If it had been quiet in the street, it was quieter in here. A small apple tree hung with tiny, barely formed fruits shaded part of the small, grassless yard. The house was low, with a tin roof. The window frames and the front door were painted a faded indigo. An old woman was sitting on the brick porch in what had once been a school bus seat. Despite the heat, she was dressed in a checked shirt and corduroy pants. She appeared to be asleep. Maria drew close and stroked the top of her head. "*Hola*, Abuela," she murmured. When the old woman opened her eyes, Maria squeezed her shoulder gently, gesturing toward Digger and introducing her as "*mi amiga*"—my friend.

The old woman took a few moments to become fully awake, her eyes focusing on Digger. They were deep beneath brows still dark despite the hatched lines on her face. Her gaze traveled from Digger's face to her feet. Then she flicked a glance at Maria and back at Digger and gave an approving smile that made Digger flush.

"I like your boots," the old woman said. She grinned at Digger, extending a hand. "Conchita Chavez Ortiz, but you can call me Abuela."

"I'm Elizabeth, Elizabeth Doyle," said Digger, using her full name.

Abuela grasped her hand briefly with a surprisingly strong grip." Maria, can you make us some coffee, *mija*?"

Maria led Digger into the tiny kitchen, where bunches of flowers and herbs hung drying from the ceiling.

"So: Elizabeth?" Maria looked at her, eyebrows raised, grinning.

Digger flushed. "Okay, I know. It just seemed more appropriate if I was meeting your grandmother. My mother was hoping for a girly girl, obviously."

Maria ground beans and primed a drip coffee maker.

"That will take a few minutes. Come see my studio."

The invitation hung in the air. Digger was acutely aware of a fly buzzing against the window, a blade of sunlight that cut across the floor, Maria's eyes, beckoning. Tempting.

The studio was a partially glassed-in shed tacked onto the back of the house.

A few canvases hung around the room, with more leaned against shelves. Every surface in the small space was covered: cloths, photos, stacks of paper, drawing pads, toolboxes. Ivy trailed around the windows. An easel stood to one side, on it a half-finished pastel of a rocky gorge in vibrant blues, reds, and oranges. Digger was no art connoisseur, but she liked what she saw. It had strength and energy.

Maria was bending down, searching through a battered leather portfolio case propped against a small chest. Her hair fell down around her face, exposing the back of her neck, smooth and brown.

Maria turned around and saw Digger looking at her. A frisson of electricity crackled momentarily between them. Digger looked down, embarrassed.

Maria held out a nude drawing of a young woman. "This was the crazy *chica* who brought me out."

Their eyes met again.

Maria faltered a moment, then continued. "When I went to college I got involved with a group that was protesting the war in Iraq. I guess protest groups are my thing. Anyway, that's where I met Isabel—Izzy. She ran the group, and we fell into this crazy affair. It was so crazy I didn't even realize how scary she was until she hid my clothes in the freezer as payback. I must have acted too friendly toward someone—I never knew who. She was insanely jealous all the time. By that time we'd been living together for nearly six months, so I didn't have my own place to go home to, and I couldn't go back to living with my parents. They wouldn't accept that I'd been with a woman. It was Abuela who gave me refuge . . ."

Digger leaned against the wall of the shed. She'd heard versions of the same story from other women. She thought of her own story: Kate, the camp counselor with the blond ponytail and the piercing blue eyes. Kate, who had picked her up when she'd fallen off the horse on the trail ride and lay there struggling for breath. Kate, who invited her for a night walk to hear the owls and then kissed her, changing everything. Kate, who went back to California, wrote twice, and that was all.

She hadn't expected to hear Maria's coming-out story so soon, if at all. Why was she telling it, and what was really going on here?

Maria tossed the drawing toward the table. It missed and fell on the floor.

She gave a bitter laugh, her expression fierce.

"That's why I live here with Abuela. She took me in. Abuela stood up for me against my parents when they totally crushed me. It's for her, and all she stands for, that I fight."

Maria looked at Digger with the same appraising glance she'd given her when they met in the bar. "What about you?"

Digger cleared her throat. "I don't like to talk about my family."

They stood silent for a while. A car passed on the street. Voices murmured in the distance.

"Oh, come on," Maria said, half teasing, half serious. "I don't know why I just told you everything I did, but I wanted to be honest."

Digger turned away. She stared through the dusty window at the fence and the giant sunflowers with their drooping heads. She sighed.

"I lived with my grandmother too," she said, "but for different reasons." "What kind of reasons?" The look in Maria's eyes was uncompromising. Digger hadn't talked about this with anyone in so long. But now—suddenly—the words just started to flow.

"My parents were killed in a car crash when I was twelve. I was their only child. My dad's parents took me in. I left here and moved to Houston, where they lived."

Maria dropped her gaze. Her voice softened. "I'm sorry. That must've been hard."

"It was." Digger had no idea why she was telling the story. Growing up, it had always felt safer to keep that part of herself hidden, but there was just something about the way Maria was looking at her that invited trust. Digger was surprised by how raw she felt. Just when she thought she'd buried everything deep enough that it couldn't break through the surface, something always got through.

Maria eyed her for a minute. Then she asked, "And why did you become a reporter?"

Digger didn't answer immediately. How had it begun? Was it the newspaper stories about the accident, looking for them day after day, reading them obsessively, asking the question, *Why, why?* Wasn't that why she had decided to go to the University of New Mexico instead of a college in Texas, the way Grandma Betty had wanted? She remembered that need to come back to where it had happened, where her life had changed forever.

Maria raised an eyebrow at Digger's silence.

Digger shrugged and looked away. "The accident got me

started. The guy who hit my parents never went to jail. I wanted to know how that could happen. As a reporter, I want to uncover the stuff people try to hide, so they can't get away with it. That's what keeps me going. I hate seeing people get away with shit."

She stopped, thought for a second, then looked at Maria. "I guess I believe in fairness. Isn't that the same for you and this protest thing?"

Maria met her look and slowly nodded. "I was right about you. We are a lot alike."

She gave an enigmatic smile. *Those lips.*

The coffee maker beeped. Maria went to serve her grandmother.

CHAPTER SIX

COUNCILOR DAVE JOHNSEN studied his hair in the mirror. It was getting a tad too long on the sides. He liked it trimmed with a number two blade on the back and sides and a number four on top, like he'd worn it in the navy. He thought it gave him a more professional image, and people remarked that it suited his Scandinavian looks.

Recently he'd had to start wearing glasses, and he'd managed to find frames that made him look serious and manly, and didn't make him look older.

He heard the children shrieking downstairs. His wife, Connie, would be getting them ready for Mass. Dave was an usher at St. Joseph's, and he liked to wear a suit, even though most people were informal these days. When he was growing up, nobody would have dreamed of wearing jeans to church.

He enjoyed Sundays. Back home in Cincinnati, they used to visit his mother after Mass. She was happy to see the children, and they always brought donuts. His mother had been upset when he'd told her he was taking the software job and moving the family to New Mexico. He'd had to point it out on a map to convince her it really was in the US.

"Mom, Las Vistas is a really fine city. The schools are good, it's clean. I read they don't have a lot of crime and the cost of living is low. They have some great-looking subdivisions."

"But I heard they have a big Mexican population."

"Mom, whole chunks of the Southwest were part of Spain at one time, but New Mexico has been a state since 1912."

His mom had been impressed with the neighborhood and the view when she came to visit the grandkids.

The home they'd bought was just perfect. The subdivision was right on the edge of the mesa, and the house had a great view of the mountains from the upstairs windows. Mary was doing well in the elementary school, and they'd found a wonderful preschool for little Jimmy. It had been a busy few months. And now he was on the city council. He'd been so pleased to be appointed when the incumbent councilor had fallen ill. Being involved in local politics made him feel like he was really promoting ideas that would bring in businesses that would make Las Vistas a thriving community.

There was a lot more he wanted to do in the remaining years of his term.

That was why he'd agreed to the meeting with Johnny Raposa, even though it cut into family time. Dave was sure there was a way he could help the developer overcome this problem with the access road. The people who opposed it just needed to see the overall benefit it could bring to that side of Las Vistas and the rural communities nearby. There'd be construction jobs, development, stores, restaurants, more of the things Las Vistas needed.

Dave had agreed to meet Raposa right after Mass, at the Denny's near one of the major intersections in town.

He'd noticed Raposa as soon as he joined the council. The developer was like one of the guys he'd admired in high school: tall and dark-haired, with the looks and build of a quarterback. Johnsen figured Raposa was in his mid-forties. He'd heard that

Raposa came to Las Vistas about twelve years back, and in that time he'd built up an impressive business buying, selling, and developing vacant land.

Dave had been flattered when the developer had asked for the meeting. He was curious to learn why Raposa had contacted him and eager to hear what he had to say. Mass seemed to last forever. Father Heaney's homily was about temptation—one of the priest's favorite topics.

"Beware of rationalization," Heaney said. "We use it to justify our sinful acts."

The priest's stern, angular face reminded him of Mayor Kimble. Dave shifted uncomfortably in the pew. Normally he at least tried to pay attention to the homily, but today he had too many other things on his mind. When Mass was over, he left Connie and the kids at Sunday school and rushed off to the meeting.

—➤—

Johnny Raposa hoped another shot of coffee would get rid of his headache— at least the temporary headache he felt this morning. He'd had a bad conversation with his ex the night before. Every now and then he got sentimental and called her. Sometimes she even answered. He hated how he missed that woman.

Then there was Los Sueños. Every deal, every subdivision had its problems and setbacks, but this business of the access road to Los Sueños was really becoming a pain. He was sure he had support from the mayor, because they'd had a talk recently about the road. But Kimble was focused on drainage in Vale de Oro. Raposa knew the mayor was under pressure from the folks who had been hit by the flooding. He'd even felt a twinge of discomfort when he'd seen the storm damage: great channels gouged right through backyards, sections of road washed away. Sure, there'd been questions raised in the environmental report way back before he and his partners had gotten the go-ahead to develop that land. But they'd been able to convince enough councilors that they had a right to build in the location, and the report had been quietly forgotten. Raposa knew people.

Sure, it was tough for the folks whose homes were flooded. But wasn't that the way it worked? They wanted the views, and that's what they got. Other states had tornados, ice storms, and hurricanes. All things considered, New Mexico's climate was close to perfect, most of the time.

Raposa was pretty sure he and the mayor could come to an understanding that would also help him get Los Sueños moving, but he had to get enough of the councilors on board too. This guy Johnsen was pretty new in town and that could work in his favor. Johnsen was one of those clean-cut guys from the Midwest who talked ideals about business and free enterprise, and that suited Raposa. Anything that would cut the red tape and lower the cost was good as far as he could see.

The Denny's was busy with the after-church crowd ordering pancakes and French toast, and he had to wait a few minutes before the server ushered him to a booth. Johnsen showed up moments later. He came toward Raposa's table grinning as though he were posing for a high school class picture.

"So glad you could make it," Johnsen said, as though he had arranged the meeting.

Raposa proffered a hand and Johnsen shook it enthusiastically.

They ordered coffee. Raposa took his with several creamers and a heaping spoonful of sugar.

"I know you're interested in the Los Sueños project. I thought you'd like to hear more about it," he said, giving Johnsen an opening.

"Sure," Johnsen said with enthusiasm. "I've been doing some research, looking at the plans submitted to the city. I'm really impressed. Back home in Ohio, we had a lot of this type of project—master-planned communities close to commercial development, things of that nature. I see a real need for high-end developments in Las Vistas. I believe it would attract the kind of people we want to see moving here, creating jobs, that kind of thing."

Raposa listened, rubbing a forefinger along his jawbone. The guy was saying exactly what he wanted to hear.

"Glad you're impressed," he said. "I have a lot of experience in Las Vistas. People know me and my work. You've probably heard about it while you've been on the council. In fact, if you have time, I can show you what we envision. I have some of the drawings here."

He didn't give Johnsen time to answer but reached under the table for his briefcase and pulled out a roll of documents. He pushed aside the coffee cups, peeled off the outer sheets, and spread them on the table.

"See here." He stabbed a thick finger on the drawing. "These are the homes we've been building, and this"—he slapped the next drawing down—"this shows the shopping complex we plan. Everything will be so much better than what's available here now. Don't you think this is what Las Vistas needs?"

Raposa leaned in close.

"Oh, sure," Johnsen said, hoping he was making a good impression. "These plans are really impressive. This is exactly what this city needs. You know, while we're talking about innovative projects, I've heard the mayor mention you in connection with plans he has for the city's future."

Raposa didn't reply at once. Instead he gathered his drawings and stuffed them back into the briefcase beneath the table. He shrugged his shoulders and looked at Johnsen intently.

"Hmm. That all depends on whether he's reelected," Raposa said.

The developer studied Johnsen's wide-eyed look for a few seconds, letting his words sink in. Then he gave Johnsen a big smile. "I like you. I think you're gonna be good for this city."

Johnsen nervously returned the smile.

"The city needs a guy like you," Raposa said, tapping the table with a forefinger. "Heck, we need a mayor like you, someone young, with new ideas."

Raposa had just thrown the comment out there, testing the waters, and Johnsen's reaction was better than he'd hoped. The guy's eyes got wider and he flushed slightly. Raposa realized that without intending it, he had hit a nerve. This guy had ambitions. Either that or he was just naive and vain.

"Yeah, think about it," Raposa said in a jocular tone, not wanting to betray what he was beginning to think: He could work on Johnsen. The guy was new and eager to make a name for himself. Kimble was an old ally in the development scene, but that was just it: he was old and cranky. The man had an ego and he could be difficult, really difficult sometimes.

"So, Los Sueños," Raposa continued. "You like the name? It means 'The Dreams' in Spanish. I came up with it after I heard some guy talking in a bar one night. Something about the old days, way back when the Spanish were looking for gold and stuff around here. 'The Dreams' seemed like a good name, something that would really bring people in." He paused, studying Johnsen's reaction. "So, you see, we really need that access road through, and we've had these protesters. I think you agree this development is going to bring real benefits to the city. Think about it: more high-end homes, stores, restaurants, maybe a new school, you know." Raposa paused, took a sip of coffee, then asked flat out, "Is there anything you can do on the council?"

He watched Johnsen stir his untouched coffee and waited. Johnsen seemed to be having some internal dialogue. Eventually, he looked up at Raposa with his bright blue eyes that radiated Boy Scout sincerity.

"Johnny, I believe this project is good for Las Vistas, and I will support it in any way I can." Leaning a little closer, he added,

"I appreciate your confidence in me. I believe supporting free enterprise is the way forward for this city."

After Johnsen had gone, pleading the need to pick up his wife and kids from Sunday school, Raposa called his old ally Fabrizzi. "Hey, Nico, I talked to Johnsen like you said. He's on board with the project. We can count on him."

"See, I steer you right, don't I?"

"Yeah, well, I thought your guy at city hall was going to bury that historic stuff so we wouldn't have any trouble about the road."

"Aw, I'm sorry, Johnny. I thought we were okay on that. I don't know how that protest group got hold of it."

Raposa grunted. "Never mind. I got something better. I think I got Johnsen interested in running for mayor against Kimble. Whaddaya think?"

"No shit?" Fabrizzi said. "If you gave him that idea, it was genius. Kimble is stuck on that drainage thing, and that could be real trouble."

CHAPTER SEVEN

DIGGER PULLED INTO the *Courier* parking lot shortly after nine. She noticed Swenson's aging blue van was already there. That was weird. He didn't usually come in until just before the morning editorial meeting at eleven.

Digger liked to get in ahead of most of the city reporters, browse the headlines, check emails and Twitter, and phone a couple of regular sources. On slow days it was like putting out fishing lines to see what or who would bite. On busy days there was barely time to think; it was just a race to make it through the day to make deadline.

She saw Swenson emerge from Martin Thompson's office. That too was weird. Thompson, the managing editor, normally came in at ten. Digger nodded good morning and went to her desk.

Over the next half hour, reporters trickled in, phones rang, conversations buzzed. Busy, but not quite as busy as it used to be. A few years ago, when she'd started, you could never find an empty desk in the newsroom. Now when someone retired they usually weren't replaced.

Digger was still sorting through the dozens of emails that had come in overnight when she saw one from Swenson. It read, "City desk staff meeting: 10:30 in the conference room." Digger grabbed a notebook. Staff meeting? Alarm gnawed at her gut.

Conference room was a grand-sounding name for the meeting space where the editors hashed out the daily story lineup and grilled political candidates schmoosing for endorsements. A vast mahogany table dominated the room, its surface dulled from elbows and donut grease. Around the walls hung framed copies of awards won by various staffers. A smell of stale coffee hung permanently in the air.

Reporters sidled in one by one and sprawled in the cracked leather chairs or lounged against the walls. Swenson looked around, gauging who was there, then closed the door. His sleeves were rolled up as always, revealing his lean, hairy forearms. He wore no tie, and a tiny blot of red on the left side of his chin showed he had cut himself shaving.

He adjusted his glasses, tugged at his mustache, and began.

"You all know we've been making some changes to reduce costs and improve efficiency."

He paused.

Not good. Digger could almost hear a collective swallowing around the room. Newspapers around the country were seeing big layoffs. Some papers were even reducing the number of days they came out in print or switching to an online-only format. So far she'd felt safe at the *Courier*, but the empty chairs told a story.

Everyone's eyes were on Swenson, waiting for him to continue.

"From next week," he said, "we won't have weekend coverage for a general assignment reporter or the cops beat, and that means each of you will have to take a rotation."

Digger suddenly realized two city staffers were missing. She tried to catch Swenson's eye, but he kept his gaze on the conference table.

So that was the conversation with Thompson she'd witnessed. The two reporters been let go. A chill gripped her insides. She looked around the table; everyone just sat there, dumbstruck. Even reporters she'd seen fiercely grilling state legislators just waited, mouths open. Swenson tugged at his mustache again and looked around at them.

"Manny will give you the contact information for the cops, and someone from photo will be on each day to back you up. Otherwise, it will be whatever comes up on those days." He looked around at them once more, then walked out.

Sampson, the courts reporter finally broke the silence. "Well, that sucks! You work your butt off in this place and there's never any thanks." He toiled somewhere in the basement of the District Court building and rarely came to the main office.

"What are they thinking?" Said the education reporter, "I don't have any experience on the cops beat. What am I supposed to do?"

Dan Halloran, a florid-faced guy from Chicago who did investigative pieces, snorted. "We're supposed to be glad we still have jobs."

Digger shoved her notebook into her pocket and walked out. She didn't feel like hanging around for the postmortem. Outside the conference room, the news day routine quickly resumed as if the bomb had never dropped. Phones rang, people laughed, argued, scribbled notes. It always amazed her that this chaotic environment produced a newspaper every day.

A little while later, Tim Baca appeared at her desk. He waggled a coffee mug at her, their code for "I need to talk."

She and Tim had started on the same day and quickly became friends. They left the building and walked the two blocks to Mojo's coffee shop. Tim fidgeted as they waited for their order. Once they'd sat down with their coffee she threw him a look.

"Well?"

He took his time, blew the froth on his latte, cleared his throat, sighed. "Jesus! Why did we get into this stupid business?"

"Yeah, it sucks," Digger said.

"We do it because we believe in it. You know that. I know that. It's why they call you Digger—you don't give up. But—" He paused, looking at his hands holding the coffee mug. Finally he said, "Digg, I have to get out of here. There's just no upside for me at the *Courier*."

Tim hated his beat as the *Courier's* political reporter. He worked with a cranky editor who'd been around since before Nixon resigned. He'd been hoping for a slot on the sports desk, but none of the old guys showed signs of retiring.

"Have you got a plan? I mean, you can't just walk out, can you?"

Tim stared at his coffee as if embarrassed to look at her.

"I think I've got a job with the *Chronicle* in Houston. I did a phone interview with their city editor last week, and they've made me a tentative offer."

Digger felt as if the floor had just dropped away beneath her. Tim, with his floppy hair and goofy smile, her buddy.

He looked at her apologetically. "I mean, see what's just happened. You've got to look out for yourself, Digg. We could be the next to go."

"Yeah. I hear what you're saying. I was already kinda down before this happened. You feel like you're beating your head against a wall, and the editors never go to bat for you." She paused, took a sip. "But something happened recently, and I think I'm on to what could really be a good story, maybe even a series. I want to see it through."

His eyebrows shot up, disappearing under the mop of hair. "So, you going to tell me about it?"

"It's all about that road project and the protests. It's like this metaphor for Las Vistas. I see it at the city council meetings. The people who come here from Michigan or Ohio—they want the American Dream, the big house, the view of the mountains. But it's like they're insulated inside their own bubbles. They don't want to breathe the air here; they want it to be just like where they came from. They don't want to adapt." She knew she was rambling, her thoughts unfolding as she spoke. "Then there's the people who've been here for generations and are seeing their world being obliterated. It's like those areas that got flooded last summer. Nobody paid any attention to the topography. Developers just got the okay to go ahead and build without regard to the land or what the rain can do. It's all about money."

Tim folded his arms. "Hmm. Have you pitched it to Swenson or anybody else? I hate to say it, but with the way the paper's going, he probably won't be interested in a big piece like that."

Digger sat back, musing. "Yeah. I know. The question is, can the two sides find ways of accommodating each other? Can there be development without destruction?" She frowned. "The really complicated part is that my portal into this other world, the leader of this protest group, is this amazing woman. She's fierce, dedicated, interesting."

She closed her eyes, thinking about Maria at the protest, defiantly waving a banner. When she opened them, Tim was staring at her with a teasing smile. "Oh, Digger, Digger, Digger! What am I hearing?"

"Yup. I keep thinking about her. She's got such strength, such courage." She shook her head. "But if I want to write these stories—and I really do—it's just too complicated."

Tim shook his head, looking serious. "You're right. Crazy as it sounds, if Swenson lets you go ahead with the story, it could be your ticket out of here. You could win awards, get some real recognition. But if you get involved with this woman, it would taint all your reporting. And if it ever came out in public, it would blow your credibility. You know that." He eyed her over his glasses, musing.

She took another sip of coffee. "Yeah. I do. I wish I'd met her some other way. Things are complicated enough." She shook her head.

Tim set down his mug and stood up. "Look, you sound like you're really fired up. So run with it. Keep going for as long as they keep publishing this sorry paper. But be careful, you hear?" He reached out to hug her. "I am so gonna miss you."

Digger set down her coffee. "Shit. I'm going to miss you, too." They hugged.

"If you do go back to Houston," she said, mock-scolding, "don't you dare make New Mexico jokes. I will stalk you on Facebook, you know."

➤

Mondays meant city council meetings. Digger spent a frustrating three hours waiting for something worthwhile to emerge from the lackluster agenda. She kept thinking about what Tim had said. Could she pitch the story to Swenson? After the morning's announcement, she wondered if he would even listen to her. Doing the story would mean going way outside her regular beat.

On her way home, she dropped by the office to pick up notes for the following day. By the exit door, she ran into Rex, who was on night shift and headed for a smoke break. They left the building together. Outside, he paused to light up.

"I heard about the layoffs," he said.

Digger set down her backpack and joined him on the smokers' bench. "Yup," she said. "I didn't really know either of them well, but I read their stories. They did good work. I just can't understand why they let them go."

Rex took a drag off his cigarette and stared out into the

semi-darkness. The freeway was half a mile away, but the traffic sounds seemed almost offensive in the still night.

"I've been here twenty-six years," he said. "Came from a little paper in Gillette, Wyoming. I wanted to get away from that mind-numbing cold. This was my big break." He gave a cynical laugh.

They sat together silently for a bit, looking at the dimly lit parking lot. Rex took a couple more drags, then dropped the cigarette butt and mashed it out with his boot.

"This used to be a great place to work. You know, I actually love my job. It may not sound like it, but I do. How many jobs let you go all kinds of places, meet all kinds of people, and do something you really like doing?" He made a sound like air sighing out of a bicycle tire. "Then it all started to change. It's like we hit the iceberg ten years ago and we've been going down slowly ever since."

Digger said nothing. She liked Rex, and he sounded beaten. He was in his fifties, she guessed, and where did you go when you'd spent half your life in a business that was sinking under your feet?

Digger didn't know where she would go either. Didn't want to think about it for now.

It was time to go home.

"'Night, Rex. We get to have all this fun again tomorrow," she said and walked off into the darkness.

CHAPTER EIGHT

DIGGER WAS MUNCHING a donut from the Krispy Kreme box delivered to the reception desk every Friday. She was keeping an eye out, hoping to catch Swenson before any of the other reporters grabbed his attention. She wanted to pitch the idea she had run by Tim. Shortly before ten, she saw his van pull into the parking lot. She caught him as he came through the door.

"You got a minute?"

He looked glum. "A minute, sure. What gives?"

Digger pitched her story as they walked toward his desk. She painted a picture of a series that would focus on how Las Vistas was growing, the people it attracted, why they wanted to live there, and the impact on the existing culture, the land, and the people who were being displaced by the expanding town.

Swenson eased into his chair, set down his backpack, sighed deeply, and looked up at her.

"Digger, I honestly love the idea. I see how strongly you feel about this, and I know you'd do a great job. You're never going to change hearts and minds in Las Vistas, but I love the way you go after them. The way things are here right now, though, I don't know if we'd have the space to devote to it. Your priority is your city beat, especially with the elections coming up. But if you want to pursue this as an enterprise piece and do your own research and reporting, as long as it doesn't get in the way of what I need you to do, go for it. I'll see what I can do about finding space when you've got something."

This was more than Digger had expected. She beamed at Swenson, thanked him, and sped back to her desk.

She'd just sat down when her desk phone rang.

"Hi," Maria said, as if she expected Digger to recognize her voice immediately.

"Um, hi, what's up?"

"Is the city council going to be discussing the cliffs road tonight?"

"The meeting was last night, and no, they didn't discuss it. I think it might be scheduled for next week. Why?"

"I'm not sure." Maria hesitated. "Our group had a meeting last night, and someone said they saw that new guy on the council at Denny's on Sunday talking with Raposa—you know, the developer guy. It might be nothing, but I don't trust Raposa."

An image from the previous night's meeting flashed into Digger's mind.

Before she'd gone into the council chambers, she had stopped at the bathroom, and when she'd emerged, she'd noticed Dave Johnsen and Johnny Raposa talking together at the end of a hallway, out of sight of the glass doors that led into the council chambers.

"Hmm," she murmured.

"What?" Maria sounded impatient.

"I—uh—thanks for the tip. I'll look into it," she said.

There was silence on the line for a few seconds, then Maria's voice again. "You told me you wanted to see the chapel."

"Yes, absolutely. How soon can we go?"

"If you're free on Saturday, I'll take you there."

"Saturday I have to work."

"Sunday, then. I know a shortcut so we don't have to park on the road where we held the protest. Meet me at my grandmother's and we can go in my car. Noon. Okay?"

The Spanish chapel was key to the story. *Damn!* She wished she and Maria could just go out for a beer and forget about the story.

"Okay, see you there."

Digger set down the phone carefully. She sat, mulling over the information Maria had passed on, trying to recall anything she knew about Raposa. She closed her eyes and thought about the times she had seen him at council meetings. He always sat in the front row. Any time the city planned to bring in a new regulation, he had something to say. He didn't like rules. The cameras that filmed the proceedings showed his face, with those dark eyebrows designer stubble, always so angry.

She remembered seeing him talking with Fabrizzi sometimes before or after meetings. Right. Fabrizzi usually voted with whatever Raposa seemed to want.

Fabrizzi had already announced he was stepping down at the end of this term, giving the old excuse that he wanted to spend more time with his family. Digger was skeptical. She'd heard a rumor that his wife wanted to move back to New York to be with their grandchildren or something like that. It made sense Raposa might be trying to schmooze his way into favor with someone new.

Johnsen came across as a guy full of fuzzy, well-meaning ideas. Sometimes he really didn't sound very smart.

Time to do some digging into Raposa's business, maybe find out more about Johnsen too. She pulled up the courts website. Nothing much there: Raposa had a couple of traffic violations and a divorce after a brief marriage. She switched to the secretary of state's site where they listed campaign contributions. Maybe that would be more fruitful.

Digger thought of the dramas at the last municipal election. There was always drama. Breathy phone calls, people leaving nasty messages they thought would be anonymous. Printed flyers full of distortions and lies. Sometimes they just called her outright and made accusations. Sometimes it was so bad she wanted to take a shower as soon as she hung up.

A little digging showed Raposa had contributed the maximum allowed under state law to both Fabrizzi's council race and Kimble's mayoral run. Nothing unusual in that. She thought hard. What else would reveal Raposa's dealings?

Tax liens, a bankruptcy filing? Maybe someone who'd worked with him in the past?

On a hunch, she went looking for Halloran. The old guy knew plenty of stuff people wanted forgotten.

Halloran was eating a burger at his desk. She explained the research she was doing as his finished it, tossed the wrapper into a nearby wastebasket and wiped his hands on his pants. "So-ooo, you're looking into Raposa."

"Yeah, you got anything?"

"Now that's a coincidence!" Halloran said. "One of my old contacts from the county called me yesterday. This guy retired a few years ago, but he keeps his eye on things. He's kind of a conspiracy nut. Anyway, he called to remind me about a lawsuit I'd written about, must be six or seven years ago. It had to do with a company that got approval for a master-planned subdivision called Rancho Milagro, just beyond the city limits. The county agreed to put in roads, water, sewer, that kind of thing. The developer was supposed to pay it back from the sales of the homes. But what nobody said was that the ground needed to be compacted. It was on some kind of dried-up pond or something. They only built a few houses, and even before anything sold, the houses developed huge cracks. They were so bad the gas company wouldn't even provide service."

Digger was intrigued. "Was Raposa involved in the development company?"

"I'm getting to that," Halloran said. "The county sued the developer to get back the money it had spent. The whole thing dragged on for a couple of years, and finally there was a settlement. The developer was supposed to pay back the county within a few years. I can't remember the details. Anyway—yeah, Raposa was in on the deal."

"No shit?"

"The reason the guy called me yesterday was to let me know that nobody seems to know whether the money—and we're talking taxpayer money—was ever paid back. All the people who were in charge back then are gone. We have new county commissioners, a new county treasurer. You know how those elected guys put in all their own people. There's even a new county manager. The whole thing seems to have been forgotten. Anyway, I've got files on it somewhere here, and you can always read the court documents."

He pushed down the glasses perched on top of his head and began rummaging through the barricade of files. Digger waited. It amazed her that someone who could write with such precision could craft his work from this chaos.

"Ah, here it is." He handed her a dog-eared file about an inch thick. "Read through it. You might find something useful. You might not."

"Thanks. I really appreciate it."

"I wouldn't help just anyone." He glanced around the newsroom. "Some of these people bend the rules too much for my liking. But you? I like the way you work."

CHAPTER NINE

IT HAD BEEN several weeks since the storm. Patches of yellow were appearing among the aspen groves on the north-facing flanks of the mountains. The rains had stopped and the days were now still, warm, and sunny. But today there was a chill in the morning air, and the damage the storm had inflicted on the streets and neighborhoods of Las Vistas was still a sore point among the residents.

Kimble thrummed his long fingers on the desk. The mayor's office was on the third floor of the city hall building, with a window that had a panoramic view over the city and out toward the mountains. He could see the new subdivisions that had sprung up just west of the freeway and the dark reddish-brown ribbons where the recent rains had gouged new pathways through the soft, sandy soil.

Scars on the landscape. Guilt pricked at him like a goat-head thorn stuck to the bottom of his shoe. The story in the *Courier* said there'd been a report that had warned about the flood risk, yet the council had ignored it. The realization that city leaders before him had done that gnawed at him. They'd let the land be paved over with acres of asphalt, where rainwater became a destructive force.

Well, he would do something to stop that happening again. He needed to win reelection, because this was his mission. He was sure of it.

Still, the past few council meetings had been brutal. That fat woman—what was her name?—and that husband of hers! And Linda Raccaro! How did that woman ever get elected? Had she ever walked on the streets of her district? Didn't she have any idea that they were all unpaved and faced all the problems that went with dirt roads? This was not Brooklyn, or wherever she came from.

The reports from the city engineer and the firm they'd hired to study the flooding problem showed it was going to be an expensive fix. Building drainage ponds, gutters, swales, all those things to channel stormwater safely away from houses—it was going to cost millions. The federal disaster money would cover some of it, but it could take months, years before they saw a penny of that. In the meantime they had to find a way to pay for the work, or people would be howling again next summer. He'd wanted to get things rolling long before now, but everything had to go through meetings, revisions, and more revisions. It was tedious, so tedious!

He looked out again at the landscape, the areas savaged by the storm's vicious claws. People never should have been allowed to build in those areas. He'd done his own research and found that paving areas actually increased the risk of flooding. This was new to him, but he knew about sin and retribution, moral rectitude and moral turpitude. He was outraged. The decision-makers who had let this happen were irresponsible, sinful even. He was a different kind of mayor.

Kimble picked up his phone, called Adam Fletcher, and asked him to come through to his office. The city manager appeared moments later, carrying a sheaf of papers. He looked faintly irritated, as though he found the interruption unnecessary.

"What can I help you with, Jack?" he asked, managing to make it sound just civil enough.

Kimble knew Fletcher really ran the city. His job as mayor was to chair city council meetings and cast tie-breaking votes. He was also supposed to represent the city, glad-handing business groups and state legislators, congratulating the winning high school team and the top cookie sellers in the local Girl Scouts.

That was what Kimble's role was meant to be, but he'd carved his own niche. He might be seventy-three years old and have high blood pressure, but he'd been a preacher, and that really gave him an edge. Kimble knew how to get a crowd going. He could smell righteous indignation a mile away and knew exactly how to stoke the fire.

Right now he smelled something. Fletcher was a smoker, and Kimble usually caught a faint odor of tobacco off his clothing. Kimble abhorred smoking. This was something different, something very faint but somehow familiar.

He peered at Fletcher the way he had once stared down the teenage boys whose parents dragged them to church on Sundays. Fletcher glared back at him.

"Yes, what is it? You know I have meetings."

Kimble pulled out hard copies of his latest emails from the engineering company about the drainage work.

"Do we have all the information we need about how we're going to pay for this and how it's going to be put before the city council?" he asked.

"Yes, I had my assistant prepare all that this week. I can call her in and she can show you. May I?"

Fletcher used Kimble's desk phone to make the internal call, and moments later his assistant, Carol, came in with a manila folder. As she bent to lay it on the table between the two men, Kimble caught the scent again, noticed where Fletcher's eyes lingered. Aha!

Kimble filed away the information. It might prove useful at a moment when Fletcher's support was unforthcoming.

He and the city manager spent the next half hour going over the details of the drainage plan and working out schedules. At the end of their meeting, Kimble leaned back and rubbed his hands through his beard.

"I know it's going to be expensive to fix this flooding problem, and I know people aren't going to like what we have to do. We've been promised state and federal money, but I won't hold my breath on how soon that'll materialize. We've talked about creating a special levy to raise money from residents. I know everyone wants something for nothing, but they're going to have to see that this will be for the best in the long run." He let that sink in for a few seconds, then leaned over, spreading his large hands on the desk.

"I'm planning to run again," he said.

Fletcher showed no reaction. Disappointed, Kimble pressed on.

"I'm going to be working a lot with those I've worked with before," he said. "I know I can count on them."

He paused. Still no reaction from Fletcher. The man could be so irritating. "We've got a very serious situation here," he went on. "It seems as though there was a distinct lack of foresight. The city should never have allowed some of those developments. I want to put that right." He jabbed a finger at the desk.

When Kimble finished, Fletcher pursed his lips and loudly expelled air from his nostrils. He'd been around a long time, seen mayors come and go. As far as he was concerned, elections were a waste of time. He took in a breath and—this time—exhaled patiently. "Jack, I understand your concerns. You see this as a 'very serious situation,' but telling the residents of Las Vistas that they're going to have to pay higher taxes for their own good is not going to get you reelected—and if you're counting on developers for support in this campaign, you might want to keep that in mind too."

Kimble stood abruptly and turned toward the window, his back to Fletcher.

"You said you had meetings."

Fletcher took the cue and left.

The email about the neighborhood meeting hit Digger's inbox at five fifteen. Damn! It was supposed to start at six, and traffic would be backed up over the river. She grabbed her notepad.

"There's some kind of meeting in the neighborhood that flooded in south Las Vistas," she told Swenson. "I think it might be something. I'm headed out there now. I'll let you know."

Thompson, the editor, was hovering over Swenson's desk, and Swenson barely acknowledged what she'd said.

Digger pulled her car into the senior center parking lot and hurried to the entrance. She had to stop abruptly at the doorway to make way for an elderly couple. The husband edged forward with a walker, his wife hovering protectively at his side. Digger waited impatiently as they inched through. Inside, the mingled smells of disinfectant, institutional food, old flesh, and old clothing hit her like a wet washcloth across the face.

She made her way to the meeting room, where people were seated on folding metal chairs facing the far wall. An middle-aged man in a golf shirt with smooth-coiffed white hair was speaking. Digger slid into an empty chair near the front and perched her notebook on her knees.

"The city's got a plan to pave the dirt roads and put in gutters," the white-haired man was saying. "I've got a friend at city hall, and he passed on an email to me. Apparently they're going to bring in some kind of tax to pay for it, like adding another ten percent on top of what we already pay in property taxes."

"That's not fair!" a woman behind Digger shouted.

"We don't need paved roads. We moved here because we want to be in the country," shouted another.

Digger recognized the first woman as one of the people huddled beside the cratered street during the rainstorm. The area had custom homes priced at half a million or more and production homes built by a company that had gone bankrupt. Digger wanted to get her hands on the email White Hair was referring to. She'd been reporting on the plan the mayor and city staffers were working on, and she already had the sense it was going to be about as popular as dog shit on a putting green.

She looked around the room to gauge the reaction to White Hair's comments. Raposa was leaning against a wall in the corner watching him, grinning. She wondered if they were buddies.

Just then, Linda Raccaro pushed through the entry door and strode breathlessly to the front of the room, where White Hair was still talking to the crowd.

"Hi everybody! Sorry I'm late." Her voice pierced the air like the sound of an angry seabird. Raccaro wore a brightly colored, gauzy top that disguised her immense breasts, black stretch-fabric pants, and sandals with glittery ornaments.

"I wanted to be here tonight to talk to you as your city councilor," she squawked.

The crowd wasn't having it. Shouting erupted all over the room. Digger saw the old man she'd waited for at the entrance standing and pounding the floor with his walker.

Sally Jenkins, the heavyset woman with the big hips whom Digger had seen at the flood scene and numerous council meetings, suddenly stood and shouted, "Me and my husband moved here to retire. This was our dream! We bought our house because it was on a dirt road with no streetlights, so we could see the stars at night. We don't want the city coming in telling us we gotta pay for paved roads and gutters."

Linda Raccaro looked panic-stricken as she scanned the room as though desperate to find an ally.

"Please, please," she cried, flapping her hands as if that would make everyone pay attention. "I understand your concerns, really I do. My house was damaged too, and I'm sure it's not something any of us wants to happen again. That's why we're trying to find a solution."

"Yeah, but nobody at city hall consulted us," snapped a man in the front row. "Would you go for a plan when you don't know how much it's gonna cost you?" he sneered.

Digger listened to the arguing, feeling almost sorry for the councilor, who seemed so clearly out of her depth.

As the meeting wrapped up, Digger looked around for White Hair. Where did he get his information? She spotted him heading toward the exit, but before she reached the door, Sally Jenkins stopped her.

"You're with the *Courier*, aren't you? I hope you're paying attention to this, because I think them folks at the city is trying to get away with something here."

The interview with White Hair would have to wait.

"How so?" Digger asked.

"Like I said earlier, we like living on a dirt road. We always wanted to be in the country."

"Las Vistas isn't exactly the country."

Sally gave her a withering look. "Believe me, honey, compared to Long Island, it's rural."

Digger tried a different tack. "How long have you lived in Las Vistas?"

"Four years and we love our house. The developer made sure there was covenants so nobody could block the views."

Her words gave Digger an idea. "When you were buying the house, did the Realtor, or whoever sold it to you, ever mention anything about the land itself?

Drainage, summer storms, anything like that?"

Sally shook her head. "No. Nothing like that. We was mostly interested in the views, that and air-conditioning. It was June when we looked at the house, and it was so hot! I know it's dry heat here, but hot is hot, and I need air-conditioning! I heard about them swamp coolers they have here—evaporative coolers that take forever. No way!" She looked meaningfully at Digger. "Honey, believe me, when you get to my age, you want to be able to flip a switch and get cool right away."

Digger hoped she would never look like Sally Jenkins when she got to whatever age that was.

"So, if you oppose the solution the city is proposing, how do you plan to protect your home from future flooding?"

Sally frowned. Digger waited. Finally Sally shook her head irritably. "Me and my husband can look after our own place. We shouldn't have to pay for the whole street. We pay too much tax as it is. Now I gotta go."

Digger headed outside, still hoping to find White Hair, but there was no sign of him in the hallway or in the parking lot outside. *Shit! Shit! Shit!* She needed to find out who he was and how he'd gotten that email. And Raposa, where was he? And where was Linda Raccaro?

She rushed back into the hall and found the councilor in heated discussion with an elderly couple. Raccaro's face showed relief as she spotted Digger, giving her a chance to escape.

"Councilor," Digger began, "the man who was speaking just before you arrived said he'd gotten some information from city hall about how drainage improvements could be paid for . . ."

Raccaro's large bosom heaved as though she were out of breath.

"I don't know where he got that. He certainly upset people here tonight. We don't need that. I am trying as hard as I can to help. I mean, what more can I do?" She looked helpless.

Digger checked the time on her phone. Just over an hour to deadline.

"I need to find out who that guy is. Can you get me a name? I'll call you tomorrow. Right now I have to run."

Digger headed for the door, found an empty office, banged out a ten-inch story on her laptop. She called Swenson but got the night editor.

"Gimme what you got. Can you file it from there?"

"There's no Wi-Fi here. Can you wait till I find somewhere with a connection?"

"Sure, but hurry."

Digger drove to the nearest Starbucks and sent the story. She waited twenty minutes; no call from the night editor. Thank God. She was too tired for more shit.

When she got to her apartment, she grabbed a beer from the fridge and sat for a long while in the darkness, holding Lady Antonia on her lap. She thought about Sally Jenkins, who had gotten no information about flood risks. She'd said they'd bought their house for the views. Of course: Las Vistas.

CHAPTER TEN

DIGGER PARKED ON the narrow side street by Abuela's house. Maria was standing by a faded blue RAV4 in front of the gate. Digger waited while Maria cleared a jumble of folders, papers, and coffee mugs from the passenger seat.

Maria drove fast, grinding jerkily through the manual transmission, braking abruptly as they came to the main road. About a mile before the river, she slowed and made a sharp turn down a side street. They traveled through a neighborhood of shabby mobile homes and broken-down cars before the street narrowed and became a dirt track into the bosque, the wooded area by the river. They bounced along another half mile and then pulled into a clearing.

Maria killed the engine, and for a few seconds there was only the sound of a breeze rustling through the yellow leaves. Digger waited. Maria looked at her, then cocked her head to signal they should get out of the car. "We go this way," she said, pointing to a faint path through the trees.

Digger followed Maria, and they walked for several minutes without speaking. From a distance came the rumble of traffic on the freeway. Close by, Digger could distinguish the sound of suburban traffic on the road that abruptly ended at the edge of the subdivision just beyond the cliffs. Ahead of her, Maria paused and signaled toward something in the distance.

On their left, about a hundred yards away, Digger could see the road and a barrier where the project was supposed to start. Beyond the barrier, the land rose steeply in an escarpment of dark rock. She pulled out her phone and took a couple of pictures.

"That's where the road is supposed to go," Maria said, pointing across a dry streambed. Digger wondered if water ever flowed there. After summer rains, perhaps? The land on the far side was thick with willows. Maria led them across the sand through a break in the underbrush, where they followed a narrow trail to the rock face.

"If the road goes through, they will bulldoze this area. They'll tear up the land and all these trees," Maria said.

Digger took more pictures. "How can you be so sure it'll be right here?" "Someone saw some documents and contacted a friend of mine. I trust them, but you can confirm it yourself. You do research, right?" "Sure."

Maria waved her onward. Digger shoved the phone into her back pocket and hurried on. The path wound ahead through cottonwood trees. Leaves crunched beneath their feet. The sun shone brightly and the canopy of leaves glowed like beaten gold against a deep blue sky. After several minutes Digger spotted a low adobe building ahead. Long and rectangular, it rose at one end to an arch that held a wooden frame and a bell. Beyond the building she could see three wooden crosses planted in the earth.

Maria stopped. "Do you know what this is?"

"This is the chapel, right?"

"Yes. It was a Spanish mission chapel. It's hundreds of years old. This is something unique to this land."

Digger approached the building, noting the ragged cracks in the mud plaster, an earth-and-straw mixture used to cover the traditional adobe bricks. She admired the ancient technique and the labor that had gone into building these walls.

She ran her hands over the surface of the adobe, feeling its roughness, the weight of centuries. Her heartbeat quickened.

Maria's voice broke the silence. "Abuela used to bring me here when I was little. I came back again when things got really bad at home after I came out to my parents. As soon as I went through that door, I felt this sense of peace flow down over me. It was so still, so safe." Maria looked around at the cracked walls. "You can see it hasn't been used for years. It became the chapel of a family that lived in this area, but they died off and there was no priest here anymore."

"Does the chapel have a name?"

"Nuestra Señora de los Sueños. Our Lady of the Dreams."

Digger swung around. "Dreams? What dreams?"

Maria smiled. "There's a legend about this place. You'll have to ask Abuela. She can tell you."

Was the name Raposa had chosen for his subdivision just a co-incidence, Digger wondered, or did he know about the so-called legend? She pushed the thought away. Right now she wanted to soak in the atmosphere of the place.

"Can we go inside?" Digger asked. It came out as a whisper.

The wooden door was a sun-bleached gray, deeply grained and dry. Digger clasped the rusty iron handle and gently pushed. It yielded. Inside, the chapel smelled of old wood, earth, and stale, closed-in air. One of the roof beams had fallen, leaving a scattering of whitish plaster crumbs on the floorboards. There were no pews, but a couple of low wooden benches leaned against the walls on each side. A wooden statue of St. Francis stood on a spindly table just in front of the altar rails. On it was a small glass vase filled with fresh marigolds. Someone still came here.

They stepped forward carefully, feeling the floorboards sag

beneath them. Water stains colored the walls around one window. A spattering of droppings and twigs were evidence that birds had made themselves at home in the rafters. Behind the altar was a *retablo*, a wooden panel covered with images of the Virgin Mary and the saints.

Digger pointed to one of the images, a young man with a ring of hair around his shaved crown. The paint was faded and peeling, but the artist had captured his expression of melancholy concern.

"Who is that?"

"I think it's San Lorenzo. He was revered here in the 1700s. Still is, in Los Jardines; he's the patron saint of the poor and of cooks. We have a festival every summer to honor him."

Digger took a step closer to study the painting and the young man's face. Why so sad? It was as if he foresaw the impending fate of the chapel.

Birds fluttered above them; then there was silence, stillness. "I think you get why I'm fighting for this place," Maria said.

Digger turned to face Maria. They eyed each other, one breath, two. Digger wanted something to happen and yet she didn't. What did she want? Companionship, love, a family? That was a lot to put on someone.

Maria dropped her gaze, turned away, and gestured toward the SUV. "Since your car is back at my grandmother's, do you want to stay for lunch?"

Digger wondered if Maria really wanted her company or if it was just about the stories she could write. "Are you sure?"

Maria raised an eyebrow, inviting. "It's lunch! Don't you eat?"

Digger couldn't argue with the gnawing in her stomach.

→

Warm aromas of green chile and freshly made tortillas filled Abuela's tiny kitchen. Digger sat back in the decrepit armchair by the window, where a tortoiseshell cat lay curled in a puddle of sunlight. She wanted to ask Abuela about the legend of the chapel, but she was distracted watching Maria prepare the food.

The more Digger watched her, the more she wished they'd met some other way. It had been a long time since she'd felt such an attraction. *Stop.*

Thinking of Tim's warning, she wondered if even being here was okay. Maybe she shouldn't have agreed to lunch. Was accepting a home-cooked meal getting too close?

They ate at the dark wooden table. Hungry, Digger finished her plate before the others. Abuela noticed and chided Maria.

"Give her more, *mija*. She needs good food, this one," she said, patting Digger's hand.

Maria rolled her eyes at Digger and passed the dish of enchiladas. Abuela nodded at her granddaughter with a mischievous grin.

"She was always a rebel, this one. That's why I like her. She's like me when I was that age. Cesar Chavez and Dolores Huerta were my idols," Abuela said. She leaned over to Digger as though they were conspirators. "When I was sixteen, my family made me marry this old man. He was nearly thirty. It was all because he had land and that little store down the street. Aie! I had four children with him and then he went to California. I never heard from him no more. I ran the store and people paid me rent for the land. I did okay. She'll do okay too." Abuela beamed at her granddaughter.

Digger looked over at Maria. Again that enigmatic smile, the same smile from the studio, their eyes meeting.

After lunch, Digger helped clean up and wash the dishes. As she stood over the sink, she felt Maria close behind her, felt Maria's arms rest on her hips, Maria's lips brush her neck. Yes.

Digger sucked in a breath. She wanted that kiss—she so wanted that kiss.

Instead she took another breath, a long one, then turned around to face Maria. "Look," she said, exhaling slowly. "I know you said you trust me. But I can't . . . not now. We have to work together. This could go so wrong." *And I have a lot of baggage.*

Maria tilted her head back and eyed Digger through half-closed lids. It was hard to read her face, but Digger thought she detected a hint of a smile. Then Maria touched a forefinger to Digger's left breast, letting it rest there.

"Don't underestimate me," she said. "I don't bruise that easy."

Then she wheeled around and walked off toward her studio.

CHAPTER ELEVEN

"Who is this guy and what is he talking about? Digg, can you explain this to me?"

Swenson was reading an email on his screen and shaking his head, a combination that meant *watch out*. Digger stood beside his desk feeling awkward. The email was about the story she'd written after the neighborhood meeting.

"This guy is mad because your story"—Swenson glared at her accusingly—"says virtually nothing about the city's plan to ask residents to pay for the drainage improvements. How come?'

Digger ran a hand through her hair and shifted her weight from foot to foot. "There was a guy speaking to the people at the meeting. I'd never seen him before. He made a lot of claims; said he had a source inside city hall. Then this woman, someone from the neighborhood association, gets up and starts venting. I had to interview her. By the time she finished, I couldn't find the other guy, and nobody else knew enough to comment on the plan."

Swenson shook his head irritably. "Well, find out who the hell that mysterious guy was and how he got that information. I need something daily."

He turned impatiently to answer the phone. "Swenson. Yeah, we just talked about it. She's on it."

Digger slumped back to her own desk. She was rattled. The encounter with Maria had thrown her off balance. The touch of Maria's lips, so brief, unexpected, yet not. *Do not get involved with sources.* Following that rule had never been an issue; she'd never even been tempted, until now. She wanted that kiss, oh yeah, but yielding to temptation would set off an avalanche of complications. And right now she was not ready for complications.

After the uncomfortable moment at Abuela's house, Digger had hastily thanked the old woman for her hospitality, nodded at Maria, and left.

Maybe one day . . .

"Excuse me."

Deb the cleaner was standing by her desk. She pointed at Digger's boots resting on the wastepaper basket.

"Oh, sorry." Digger swung her feet to the floor and threw Deb an ingratiating smile.

Deb scowled at her. Today Deb's wiry gray hair was braided in pigtails and a pink plastic "Birthday Princess" pin sparkled on her chest.

"Hi, Deb—uh, happy birthday! How ya doing?" *Whoops!* Digger realized her mistake too late. Asking Deb a question like that meant listening to a torrent of complaints.

"The birthday was last week and not so good. I hadda take my husband to the ER yesterday. He's got high blood pressure, ya know. We hadda wait. It was hours. He was so mad! I can tell you."

"That's too bad. Um, Deb, I've got some phone calls I've got to make, I—"

"Yeah, yeah." Deb turned and trundled her cart away.

Digger picked up the phone on her desk and dialed Linda Raccaro's number.

"Hello, Linda, this is Elizabeth Doyle with the *Courier*—" she began. "You've got some nerve, calling me after that story!"

Digger gritted her teeth. "So, Linda, who was that man who spoke at the meeting, telling everyone about the city plan? Was he right?"

There was a long pause on the other end of the phone, punctuated by unidentifiable noises. Digger waited.

"Well, I'm not sure," Raccaro said. Her accent made it sound like *shuu-err.* "I seen him before at golf club dinners—you know, my husband loves golf, that's why we moved out here. I think he's a friend of the club manager."

Digger typed notes as she listened. Linda Raccaro clearly didn't know squat. Too bad. She thanked the councilor, hung up, and went back to her contact list.

She called George of the naughty smile. The phone rang for a long time. It was a landline, of course; George wouldn't have a cell phone. Finally a recorded message said, "This phone does not accept solicitors. If you are a solicitor, hangup and—"

Suddenly a voice broke in. "Hello? *Hello?*"

"George, this is Elizabeth Doyle with the *Courier.* Do you have a minute?"

"Oh yes, Ms. Doyle, of course. Of course I have time for you. How can I help you?"

"I thought I saw you at the neighborhood meeting. Do you know who the speaker was? The one who was talking about the city plan for drainage?"

"Oh, him. I think he works for the golf club. You know, they're close with people in public works. They have that big contract to buy water from the city."

Digger's hands were busy typing; otherwise, she would have pounded her forehead. Of course, the public works guys. Who there would talk? She thanked George, put down the phone, and thought for a moment. She flipped through the stacks of business cards on her desk. There must be somebody with the city, somebody she could call instead of having to go through that pompous communications director Fletcher had hired. The guy was an information sadist.

There was Jill Anderson, she was a budget analyst in the public works department and the representative for AFSCME, the city employees' union. Digger used to be able talk freely to her until Fletcher clamped down on everything. She knew the union was due to start negotiations for a new contract in a few weeks and she'd heard rumors that city hall was not exactly a happy ship. Maybe Jill would talk.

Digger dialed.

Jill Anderson sounded nervous, but she agreed to speak with Digger away from the office. They met at a hole-in-the-wall diner on the outskirts of town near a truck stop. Digger slid into a booth and ordered coffee while she waited. Jill was late, and when she showed up she looked tired and irritable.

"This is what I can tell you," she began. "Fletcher and the mayor have been working with the company that has the city contract for engineering work. They've drawn up a tentative plan to prevent streets flooding the way they did this summer. I can show you some documents that outline the details. The big thing is that they plan to pay for it by adding a special charge to the property of everyone who lives in the area. It would be like an extra item on their property tax bill. State law allows this. Here's a map showing the areas."

Jill pulled some folded papers from her oversized purse and spread them on the table.

Digger took pictures of the maps, then studied them, trying to identify the streets.

"Wait a minute. Why are they including the area beyond the cliffs? That's Los Sueños, isn't it?"

"That's because of the new buildings that are supposed to go in next to the subdivision: the stores and parking lots. Every bit of paved surface creates more runoff. Because Los Sueños is on high ground, it poses a risk for everything below, you get it?"

"Okay. This confirms what that guy was saying the other night. But based on the reactions I saw, nobody wants the tax, even if it will fix the problem."

"True," Jill said. "That's why Kimble and Fletcher are cozying up to all the councilors and developers, Raposa in particular. They want them on board with this."

Digger shifted focus. "You've worked for the city for a long time. Do you remember when the council approved plans for the areas that got flooded last summer?"

Jill nodded slowly and frowned.

Digger prodded. "You saw my story. I based it on an old study that referred to the risk of flooding if the developers built in that area. Nobody at city hall would give me any explanation. Do you have any idea why they didn't act on the information in that study?"

"Oh yes, I remember that study," Jill said slowly. "One of the engineers in our planning department was really upset. He talked to people on the planning and zoning commission, but they treated him like a crank. They went ahead and approved everything, so it was just a formality when it came before the city council. Everyone was gung-ho on expanding and bringing in new business—just like now," she added sourly. "Listen, I've got to go. You can't quote anything I've said. If you need to, just say 'documents obtained by the *Courier*.' Are we clear?"

Digger nodded. "Of course, and thanks."

Jill left and Digger headed out. She had more phone calls to make.

Back at the office, she reached the golf course guy. His name was Danny Murphy, and he'd only been in New Mexico a few months. The golf course manager had hired him in from Phoenix. He hadn't even been there during the flooding. He just said "people" had asked him to speak at the meeting; he wouldn't say who. Frustrated, Digger tried asking questions from half a dozen different angles, but he was slick enough to keep spouting the same happy crap without saying anything. He must have had corporate training, Digger thought. There was a secret to public relations babble: the more benign the words, the more insidious the real story.

Never mind; she had what Jill Anderson had given her. Digger ran with it and wrote her story. Swenson read it and was satisfied she'd confirmed a city source. Time to go home.

Next morning, shortly after she sat down at her desk, an email from Martin Thompson popped up in her inbox. Before she'd even finished it, she heard outrage erupt around the newsroom. The email reminded her of the conversation she'd had with Murphy. It had the nauseating language of corporate press releases written to sound well-meaning when in fact the recipients were all being shafted.

The memo informed *Courier* staff that, "after careful consideration, certain changes were being made to ensure the ongoing financial stability of the newspaper. These changes included reducing the geographic reach of the paper's circulation, eliminating some areas where subscription rates were minimal, reducing staffing in some departments, and changing retirement benefits."

She heard Dan Halloran's irate voice. "What is this crap?"

Digger knew the changes would hit people like Rex and Halloran the hardest. They had spent decades at the *Courier*. She went to the photo department, but Rex wasn't there. Halloran was cursing behind the jumble of papers and stacks of files that formed a defensive wall around his desk. His face had the worn, reddish cast of a man who had lived hard.

"I guess I don't need to ask what you think about this, Dan."

He looked at her sideways. "You're right. For people like me, it's a knife in the back. People your age, you've got options."

Digger had to admit he was right. She looked around the newsroom. She'd only been there five years, but even in that time, familiar faces had gone, people had taken on extra duties, and pay raises had become a thing of the past.

―

That evening Digger found the council chamber packed. She'd had to fight heavy traffic and was late. Ever since the floods in the summer, more and more people had been showing up at meetings, and they were mad. She was so tired of hearing the same complaints: my garage flooded, my carpets were ruined, the city ought to do something. Now there was a new level outrage because of the rumors that residents were going to have to pay more to get anything done.

Linda Raccaro was still making sympathetic noises, but the rest of the councilors had clearly lost patience. Fabrizzi rolled his eyes as the ranting went on and on. He'd scowl and ask the mayor to limit comments or sigh loudly when people kept talking beyond their allotted time.

Digger had just squeezed into her press seat when Kimble strode in. He had a habit of pausing beside the dais to survey the room, like an actor making a stage entrance. Every meeting started with the same performance.

Tonight, as usual, Kimble began the meeting with bland announcements about community events, wonderful citizens, blah, blah, blah. Digger usually spent the first part of the meetings watching the people around her. Sometimes she thought the councilors looked like a row of bobbleheads. Tonight, though, Johnsen seemed on edge. A couple of times he interrupted Kimble, questioning him on a point of order. Digger remembered what Maria had told her a few weeks back about Johnsen and Raposa. Since then, she'd heard rumors that Johnsen might even be thinking about running against Kimble in the mayoral election.

While the mayor was still rambling through the accolades, the public entrance door opened and a group of people hustled in. Maria was with them. Digger shot a glance her way but couldn't make eye contact.

Minutes later, when the mayor opened the public forum part of the meeting, it was clear why the group had come. Maria and a Native American man marched up to the lectern in front of the dais. Maria wore a red sweatshirt with "No Road!" printed in white on the back. The man held a banner that read, "Listen to We the People!"

Maria began her speech by saying, "We are here because we have rights, and we demand you listen to us!"

Kimble looked annoyed. Linda Raccaro shook her head like an elementary school teacher discouraging bad behavior in the lunch line. Fabrizzi appeared to be concentrating on his lap. The other three male councilors exchanged embarrassed glances.

"This road the city wants to build is a desecration!" Maria continued.

Watching her, Digger admired how tall and proud she looked, her head held high, her hair gleaming. How fearless.

"You have no right to tear up that piece of earth where our ancestors built a chapel to their faith!" Maria continued, her voice high-pitched and fraught.

Kimble frowned. "Your time is up, Miss Ortiz."

Someone in the crowd shouted, "Get 'em out of here!"

Las Vistas Police Chief Joe Armitage, who attended every council meeting, swiftly made his way to the front of the room and gestured for Maria and her companion to leave. Maria looked around, furious. "Freedom of speech! We have rights!"

Another officer, standing by the door, helped Armitage escort the group out.

Digger jumped up to follow them, but the officer at the door barred her way. She sat down. A woman behind her whispered, "Who are those people? How dare they disrupt a meeting!"

Kimble pounded his gavel. "Next item!" His voice was almost a snarl.

As soon as the meeting ended, Digger hurried to her car. Outside the building, the night sky was full of stars, and a silver sliver of moon was peeking over the crest of the mountains. She pulled out her phone and punched in Maria's number. She wanted to get a comment, but more than that, she wanted to hear Maria's voice.

"It's me," Digger began when Maria answered.

"I can't talk to you now." Maria's voice was angry.

"But, Maria—"

"Please just leave me alone!" She hung up.

Breathe, breathe.

Digger put the phone away, started the engine, and headed back to the office. In her story she wrote, "Maria Ortiz declined to comment." Sometimes that was all you could do.

CHAPTER TWELVE

THE SOUND OF Lady Antonia retching up a hairball woke Digger. It was still dark—and cold. Twice in the past week she'd had to scrape frost off the windshield of the Subaru. She got up and peered through the blinds. The crest was barely perceptible, but there was a glow in the sky, and it grew brighter as she watched. By the time she had coffee and breakfast, she thought, it should be light enough to get in a short run.

Afterward she decided to go to the county assessor's office to find out more about the subdivision Halloran had mentioned. She wanted to find out exactly where it was, maybe learn more about who was paying the taxes, and see if she could unearth something about the lawsuit settlement.

The assessor's office was tucked away down a long corridor on the second floor of the county administration building. Digger asked for Nick Lopez, a guy she'd worked with on a couple of stories in the past. He was in a tiny cubicle office dominated by twin monitors the size of coffee tables.

"Hey, what can I do for you, Digg?"

Nick had a bushy black beard and thinning hair cropped so short he almost looked bald.

"Hi, Nick, glad you had time to see me."

She pulled out the file Halloran had given her. She'd spent time reading over the court case and had the name and the map coordinates of the subdivision. She knew Nick would have the software to pinpoint it on the map. Maybe he could fill her in on a little more history too.

He took note of the coordinates and started a computer search. Seconds later he zoomed in on the location.

"Okay, that's about where I thought it was," Digger said. "Do you have any details about who owns it or who pays taxes on that land?"

"Hmm." Nick frowned and twirled a spindle of beard hairs in his fingers. "There's some basic stuff in our data." His fingers flickered over the keyboard and new information popped up on the screens. He peered at them a moment.

"Okay, so it looks like it's owned by a company called Milagro Millennium; I'm guessing that's the developer. And the taxes— well, it looks like they're three years in default, which means the county could soon be telling them that the land will be sold unless they pay up."

"How much?" Digger asked.

Nick's fingers flew over the keys again. He frowned. "This is weird. I can't seem to find a figure for that. Anyway, this was from before my time here. Maybe my co-worker Jim Archuleta can help out. He's been here a long time, and he knows . . . well, let's say he knows where a lot of bodies are buried."

Nick shot her a glance. She knew exactly what he meant. Just like at the *Courier*, it was the old guys who remembered stuff a lot of people hoped would be forgotten.

Nick disappeared into the warren of cubicles and reappeared a minute later, followed by a plump middle-aged man with a ring of curly gray hair and thick glasses.

"Jim, this is Digg—uh, Elizabeth Doyle from the *Courier*. She's interested in some history about the Rancho Milagro subdivision.

There was a master plan the county approved years ago and some kind of legal issues. You were here back then."

Jim brightened, clearly delighted to be consulted. He stretched out a hand and gave Digger a genial smile. She had the feeling he was one of those guys who loved to talk, sharing every minute detail. She glanced at Nick and raised an eyebrow. Nick nodded, so she switched her full attention to Jim and followed him back to his dingy cubicle. She was prepared for a long conversation.

Jim gestured toward a hard plastic seat in the corner of the cramped space, then settled his ample frame on the worn upholstery of his own office chair. He opened a drawer, pulled out a package of Oreos, and offered her one.

"These are my secret weakness. My wife won't let me have them in the house, so I always keep a package or two here. "Course, it's not good for my waistline." He chuckled.

Digger smiled. "Thanks, but I have to get back to my office by noon. Can we talk about the subdivision?"

Jim munched on his cookie with a guilty smile, then slipped the Oreos back into the drawer. "So, you want to know a little about Rancho Milagro. Hmm, let's see." He paused, rubbing his pudgy fingers together. "I remember—must be about ten years ago now—they came to the county with this proposal for that land out southwest of Las Vistas. They were asking for help from the county to put in infrastructure. You know: roads, sewers, that kind of thing. Discussions went on for a few months."

"Who is 'they'?" Digger asked.

Jim blinked, thought for a second as if trying to recall. "Well, the development company was called Milagro Millennium."

Digger pursed her lips, in an effort to be patient. "Yes, I know that much. Who actually talked to the county people?"

"Oh, um, yes. I remember Joe Raposa was one of them."
"Don't you mean Johnny Raposa?"

"Oh yes, I'm sorry. Yes, him and another guy. He had red hair. Let me see. Some kind of Irish name."

Red hair? Digger thought. It was ten years ago. Murphy's hair could have turned white in the meantime.

"I've read some of the background," she prompted. "As I understand it, the county was going to float some bonds to pay for the infrastructure, and the company would pay it back through some kind of assessment on the properties when they sold."

Jim nodded. "Right, right. You're exactly right. That's how it worked.

Milagro was going to build high-end homes priced at half a million or more. There was a lot of excitement about it. But they'd only sold a few when the subsidence problems emerged and the market crashed, so the whole development was in limbo."

At that point he stopped talking as if that were the end of the story.

"What about the lawsuit?" Digger asked.

Jim's genial smile suddenly faded and he looked uncomfortable. He shuffled in his chair, looked at his watch, and said he had to go to a meeting.

Digger realized she'd hit a nerve. She was on to something bigger than she'd thought.

—◂——

She left the county building and headed for the outskirts of town to look at the planned subdivision. About fifteen minutes' drive west, she came to the turnoff on the road to the airport. A quarter mile down the side road, she spotted a fire hydrant. She stopped, got out of the car, and stood looking out across the mesa.

She could make out a grid of paved streets, fire hydrants, and faded green cable units.

In the distance she spotted three partially built homes. She drove toward them, noting the weeds poking through cracks in the street paving. The window of the first house was boarded over with plywood, but it looked as though vandals had broken in. A peek through one of the smashed pieces of plywood revealed scattered piles of clothing and trash on the floor of the empty room. Someone had obviously been squatting there at some point. Not exactly the high-end neighborhood the developers had planned.

Next she drove to find Halloran's contact, Alex Simpkin. She found herself on a run-down street on the western edge of town. It was the kind of neighborhood Digger knew well from the cops beat: chain-link fences, pit bulls in the front yards, derelict cars in the driveway. Simpkin's house had no dog or defunct car, but it fit in with the others on the street, a one-story box with peeling paint and a graveled front yard polka-dotted with dead weeds. She pulled into the driveway and hoped her old Subaru would still be there when she returned.

She pressed the bell and followed with a rap on the door in case it didn't work. Somewhere inside a dog barked, and she heard the sound of footsteps approaching slowly. The door opened, revealing an elderly man in shabby gray sweats with oxygen tubes sprouting from his nose. He looked puzzled and apprehensive.

"Hi, I'm Elizabeth, I work with Dan Halloran. You called him this week to—"

Simpkin's face lit up.

"Oh, come in, come in. I'm so glad you're here. I knew Dan was the man to call."

He pulled the door open wide and ushered her into a dark hallway. The smell of stale cigarettes and dog hit her like a wave. Simpkin shuffled ahead of her, his oxygen machine making a *piff-piff* sound. He opened a door and an overweight black Labrador burst out, its whole body wiggling with delight at the sight of a new person.

"That's Geraldine. She's very friendly, as you can tell. She's been my companion since my wife passed."

Digger gave the dog's graying muzzle a little scratch, then looked around for somewhere to sit amongst the jumble of boxes and stacks of magazines that covered the floor and most of the furniture.

"Here, you can sit here. Make yourself comfortable," Simpkin said, brushing a pile of magazines onto the floor. He settled himself into an armchair and Geraldine flopped at his feet.

"So glad you came," Simpkin said again. He rubbed his hands together as if he were cold, even though the heat in the room was stifling. Simpkin then pulled a pack of cigarettes out of his pocket and reached for a lighter that lay on a side table next to him.

Digger swallowed in alarm. Lighters and oxygen tubes—she wanted to hear what he had to say before he blew the place sky high.

"Um, you know, Mr. Simpkin, would you mind not smoking? I'm really allergic."

"Oh, very well, then." He set down the lighter and stuck the cigarette behind one ear. He leaned toward her. "I have so much to tell you."

Geraldine groaned and let out a soft fart that seeped across the room, enriching the already pungent stew of smells. Digger felt like gagging, but she managed a tight smile.

"Dan told me you called about the subdivision," she began. "He said there'd been a lawsuit and that you think the county is still owed a lot of money."

"Yes," Simpkin said, rubbing his gnarled hands on his knees. "I retired from the county five years ago. I was there thirty-seven years altogether, worked in different departments, saw a lot of people come and go, especially the elected officials. Some of them were wonderful to work with, some were not. Some of them were outright crooks. By the way, that's not for publication—but I think you know that, don't you, being in the newspaper business?"

He gave her a meaningful look.

"Anyway, as I told Dan, the county planning and zoning commission approved the master plan for Rancho Milagro. Then somehow those developers . . . the name will come to me in a minute . . ."

"Milagro Millennium. I read the court filings."

"Oh yes, you've done your homework. Good girl." Then he frowned. "Those people, Mr. Raposa and his partners, they presented this great story to the county commissioners. This new subdivision would boost property tax revenues, give Las Vistas an exclusive area where people from out of state would want to come live. I'm sure you've heard that kind of glory-story plenty of times."

Digger nodded.

"They persuaded the commissioners to approve an agreement whereby the county would pay for all the infrastructure through a county economic development program. You know from your homework how it was supposed to be paid back."

Simpkin leaned forward earnestly, as if trying to make sure she understood.

"From what I read," Digger said, "the county sold about $5 million in bonds to put in all those streets and stuff. I drove out there this morning and saw it."

"Precisely, and those bonds were backed by taxpayer money. If the developer's plans didn't work out, the county was on the hook to pay them off in seven years." Simpkin shrugged. "Well, you know what happened, of course.

There was the problem with the houses cracking, and then the economy crashed and the whole thing evaporated like a rainstorm that never hit the ground."

"What about the lawsuit?" Digger prompted.

"Oh, that." Simpkin gave a dry laugh followed by a fit of coughing. "The county sued. It dragged on for a couple of years, and finally there was a settlement. Halloran wrote about it. And then nothing more happened. The county commission got rid of the county manager over some other issue. There was an election, and we had a new treasurer and assessor and three new commissioners. By the time I retired, there was no record of any of that money being paid back."

He looked at her, his eyes bright with indignation. Behind him a wall clock bonged. Digger counted twelve strokes in the silence that hung between them.

Surreptitiously she glanced at her watch; it was only eleven o'clock. Simpkin had forgotten or hadn't bothered to change the time when everybody else did.

Digger shifted in her chair. "If you knew about this, what made you suddenly call Dan Halloran?"

Simpkin reached for the cigarette behind his ear, twirled it a moment between his fingers, replaced it, then looked at her directly.

"I don't know how long you've been around this business. Halloran and I go way back. As I said, I worked in county government for nearly forty years, and I saw things that made my stomach turn. A lot of times we just had to keep our heads down and say nothing because we needed our jobs. I don't have to worry about that anymore, but I guess those who are still there do. Anyway, an old colleague called me recently—I'm not going to name names. They knew it bothered me, so they suggested I go to the newspaper. It's bothered me for a long while, and I think people should get what they deserve. People should keep the promises they make."

He fell silent, breathing heavily, as though speaking that much had exhausted him. Geraldine made tiny whimpering sounds and rustled her feet in a doggy dream.

"How do you think I should proceed with this?" Digger asked.

Simpkin shrugged. A mischievous smile spread across his face, shifting the oxygen tubes.

"Just keep after them. Stick it to them any way you can." He cackled and began coughing again.

Digger thanked him, said her goodbyes, and made a beeline for the front door. Once outside, she gratefully gulped in the fresh, cold air.

CHAPTER THIRTEEN

BIG FLAKES OF snow were falling, obscuring the mountains, dappling the juniper bushes, and turning the earth from brown to beige. The sky, normally so deeply blue and endless, was close and gray and softly cocooning.

Digger peered out of her bedroom window, contemplating a run. Behind her the cell phone on the bedside table pinged an incoming text. Reluctantly, she dragged herself away from the window.

The text was from Maria. It read, "Do you have plans for Christmas?"

Christmas?

Did she have plans? Some years she went back to Houston to spend the holiday with her grandparents. But last year, when Grandma and Grandpa had treated themselves to a cruise, Tim had come by and they'd had a few beers together and given each other silly gag gifts. This Christmas Tim would be in Houston with his own family, ready to start his new job. And she hadn't heard from her grandparents yet.

"No. No plans," she typed. "What's up?"

A minute later the message came back. "Abuela wants to invite you for Christmas Eve."

"Me? You sure?"

"Yes. She invites lots of people. We make tamales. It will be fun."

Digger rubbed a hand through her hair and looked around the room. Should she give in to temptation? All those complications? Screw it. She didn't want to spend Christmas on her own. She tapped an answer.

"Okay. Tell her thanks."

Digger put down the phone. *What have I got myself into now?* She hadn't seen Maria since the council meeting and, before that, their expedition to the road project site.

Christmas was just a week away.

➤

As she drove into the *Courier* parking lot, she spotted Halloran and Rex smoking outside the employee entrance. She parked and headed toward them.

"Hey, Halloran, I went by and talked with that guy Simpkin, the one who called you."

"Yeah? Bet that was interesting."

"Simpkin backed up everything he'd told you—and the stuff I found in the court filings."

Halloran rubbed his jaw thoughtfully. "You talked to the county people yet?"

"A couple of them. It's like Simpkin said. The county manager's only been there a year, and she's from out of state. She was all smiles but said she wasn't aware of the settlement, would definitely look into it—that kind of thing."

Digger paused a moment to make sure Halloran was following her, then continued. "The assessor hasn't been there much longer. He's got a heart condition, and he's hardly ever around. I talked to the deputy, who confirmed that the property owner was behind on taxes but wouldn't say whether they've started any kind of proceedings. And I found out Milagro Millennium no longer exists. Looks like the company dissolved right after the crash."

"You talk to Raposa?"

Digger rolled her eyes, recalling the conversation she'd had with the developer shortly after she got back from talking to Simpkin.

He'd sounded genial when she'd asked if he had a minute to talk. "Oh, sure. You got lucky today. I've got at least half an hour; I can give you all my attention. How can I help you?"

"I wanted to ask you some questions about Milagro Millennium. That's the company you were involved with for the Rancho Milagro subdivision, right?"

At that point Raposa had cleared his throat, sounding irritated. "That was a long time ago. What do you want to know?"

"Why did you dissolve the company?"

He was silent for a moment, then continued in a softly cajoling voice. "I really don't know why you're interested in this. Right now I'm working on Los Sueños. I'm sure you'd like to know more about that."

"No, really," Digger said. "I've been reading some background about Rancho Milagro and the lawsuit. I'd like to get your comments."

"Well, that's exactly why I can't comment. There are still ongoing lawsuits, and I'm working with my lawyers. I'm sorry, I'd love to talk with you, but I really can't say anything at this time. Thank you." He hung up.

After she'd put down the phone, Digger had poked around and found the cases Raposa was referring to. The lawsuits had been filed by a couple of the people who'd put money down to buy homes in Rancho Milagro.

Halloran sat smoking while Digger talked. When she finished, he tossed the butt of his cigarette into the dirt and ground it with a heel. His face split in a grin, showing his yellowed teeth.

"You got the start of a good story. Go pitch it to Swenson, and if he gives you a hard time, let me know and I'll kick his ass. I've been around here a lot longer than he has."

Digger laughed, thanked him, and headed into the office. Halloran watched her go. "You know Rex, I grew up Catholic and the nuns drummed it into us that her kind—you know what I mean—were an abomination and guaranteed to go to hell. I think those nuns were just jealous because they weren't getting any. Thank God I'm not Catholic any more." He paused, "She's a smart girl, that Digger, but I wouldn't want to be starting out in this business now."

Rex took another drag on his cigarette and blew smoke out of the side of his mouth. "She'll be all right. She's young enough to find something else. In a year or so I bet she'll be gone like that other kid—what was his name—Tim?"

The light was fading, throwing the canyon shadows into sharp relief, as Digger drove toward Los Jardines. A red flush seeped down the flanks of the mountain, and for a few minutes the whole range glowed pinkish-gold before it deepened into purple and deep blue. By the time she drove up the narrow side street to Abuela's, it was full darkness.

Cars clustered around the fence and lights blazed from inside the low building. The sound of laughter and many voices spilled out into the courtyard. Digger had to knock several times before a young boy finally opened the door and waved her in.

The small living room was full of people, mostly men, but she saw Maria in the doorway to the kitchen. She was wearing a burgundy-colored silky top cinched at the waist with a silver concho belt and a pleated broomstick skirt that grazed the top of her boots. She looked stunning.

Digger had wondered what to wear and decided on black jeans, boots, and a striped shirt she'd bought at the Western store.

She waved at Maria, who caught sight of her and made her way through the crowded room.

"You're looking very 'Santa Fe' tonight," Digger said. "And you are very 'cowgirl,'" Maria shot back.

The small boy who had let Digger in grabbed Maria's arm.

"Is she your girlfriend?" he asked Maria, flashing a cheeky smile at Digger. Maria shot him a withering look and swatted him away.

"Come on." She nodded to Digger. "Come and say hello to Abuela."

Maria led her into the kitchen, where half a dozen women were seated around the table working on the tamales. Abuela turned around from the stove, caught sight of Digger, and beamed.

"Hola, I'm so glad you could come. I thought you would be here earlier. We are nearly finished. We will do *posadas* at seven; it is the last night, and they will end up here. That's why we need a lot of tamales. You can help us. Maria will show you how."

Digger was familiar with the old tradition of posadas, how neighbors reenacted the Christmas journey of Mary and Joseph seeking a room in Bethlehem, going to a different house each night.

A rich sauce of aromas permeated the kitchen: the heavy scent of slow-cooked pork mixed with the sweetness of corn and the tangy sharpness of chile. The women had been busy all afternoon, and beer bottles and glasses cluttered the spaces on the table between platters of corn husks, masa corn filling, and shredded pork. They made space for Digger next to the seat where Maria had been sitting.

"Who's your friend?" asked a woman on the other side of the table.

"She came to one of the meetings to protest the road," Maria said, pulling up a chair so Digger could join the group. Digger sat down to smiles all around.

Someone handed her a bottle of Corona and an apron.

"Maria, show her how we do tamales," Abuela said again. She was standing by the stove attending a pot where wrapped tamales were steaming.

Digger breathed in the smells of pork and chile, her heart warmed by the jolly bantering of the women. Maria leaned in close beside her, demonstrating how to spread the yellow masa paste on the dried corn husk that had been boiled to softness, then how to add the red meat filling in a line down the middle.

A woman to her left butted in to show how to fold the husk in from each sid, overlapping slightly, then how to turn the bottom of the husk toward the middle. "Just like putting a diaper on a baby," she said, to peals of laughter.

At first Digger felt embarrassed as the only Anglo in the room, but the warmth and closeness of the little group—and the Corona—lulled her into a sense of contentment. They spoke a mixture of Spanish and English and she didn't understand everything that was being said, but somehow it didn't matter. Christmas Eve with her grandparents had always been a stiff, uncomfortable time, with a formal meal and a strict ritual of unwrapping presents, Grandma Betty noting each gift-giver's name to refer to when writing thank-you letters. Here, though, Digger could let go, laugh, and be part of this different world.

Suddenly there was a commotion in the other room. A man's voice rose above the hubbub. "*Hola a todos.*"

Digger saw Maria stiffen, and their eyes met. *My parents,* Maria mouthed.

A tall, burly man appeared in the doorway, followed by a slight woman with gray hair scraped back in a tight bun.

"Mama!" The big man cried, engulfing Abuela in a hug.

"Aie! *mijo,* you're late," Abuela said, kissing him on each cheek. Then she turned to his wife, Maria's mother.

"Ah, Consuela." She took her hands and they brushed cheeks.

Digger couldn't hear what they said after that, but she felt eyes on her. She shot a glance up at them and saw Maria's mother saying something in Abuela's ear. She saw Abuela's features harden, and she sensed trouble brewing. She had a feeling it revolved around her.

Maria's mother elbowed Abuela out of the way, barging around the women at the table until she halted between Digger and Maria. Digger caught the whiff of hard alcohol from her despite the pungent cooking smells. Her eyes were shiny with rage, reminding Digger of a bipolar girlfriend she'd briefly dated. The next moment, Consuela lashed out at Maria with a torrent of words in Spanish. Then she rounded on Digger furiously.

"This is a family gathering! Maria has disgraced us again. She has no shame, bringing your kind here. We are decent people."

The rest of the women at the table eyed Maria's mother nervously, as if Consuela Ortiz might attack one of them next.

Abuela's voice rang out, shrill and angry. "This is my house. I invited her, and I welcome who I will."

Maria jumped up, knocking over her chair as she rose. "We're leaving!" She screamed at her mother.

"Maria, no!" Abuela pleaded.

Maria hesitated, her eyes darting around. Then she grabbed a plate, scooped a dozen tamales onto it and covered them with a napkin. "I'm taking these tamales over to your neighbor José like you promised, Abuela."

She shot Digger a glance. "Help me with these?" she said, handing Digger a bowl of chile sauce.

Digger followed Maria out of the kitchen, carefully carrying the bowl of sauce. They cut through the living room, ignoring Maria's father, who stood chatting by the fire, ignoring the scene next door.

At the door they paused to put on jackets. Even so, the icy air outside nearly took Digger's breath away. Maria hurried across the narrow street to the nearest house, where she pounded on the door. They waited in silence. Finally the door opened and a wizened old man peered at them with a mixture of puzzlement and apprehension.

"*Hola,* Señor José," Maria said. "I brought you tamales from my abuela. She wishes you and your wife a blessed Christmas."

The old man's face split in a smile, and he looked as if he were about to burst into tears.

"We made them this afternoon," Maria said. "Tell your wife she'll have to steam them for a while before they will be ready, but you know my grandmother always makes the best."

Maria pushed the plate into José's hands and repeated the Christmas wishes while Digger set the bowl of chile sauce on a small, worn table just inside the doorway. After José shut the door, Maria turned abruptly and walked the few steps back across the street.

Outside Abuela's gate, she stopped and her body sagged against the fence. The air was cold and sharp, and above them the stars were like stabs of light in the vast, dark sky. Digger stood very still. It took her a few seconds to realize that the muffled sound she heard was Maria sobbing.

Digger put her arms around Maria and held her close. The internal voice that told her to be careful stayed quiet. At this moment, in this darkness, under this sky, this closeness felt right.

CHAPTER FOURTEEN

JACK KIMBLE DROVE into the country club parking lot and squeezed his Buick into a slot close to the entrance. He looked at his watch. It showed a couple of minutes to noon. He decided to wait. He'd agreed to meet Raposa at noon, and he didn't want to show up early. He wanted Raposa to be the one waiting. At five minutes past the hour, he climbed out of his car and strode purposefully through the front door.

The Las Vistas country club had been built in the early 1970s, and although it had been renovated at least once since then, the lobby retained the aura of bell-bottom pants, mullet hairstyles, and droopy mustaches. Kimble approached the reception desk, where a young woman was engrossed in conversation on her cell phone. Kimble had to clear his throat a couple of times before she acknowledged him.

"Oh, hi, may I help you?"

"I'm Jack Kimble." He waited for her to react, but she merely smiled, looking a little puzzled. This irritated him.

"I'm the mayor of Las Vistas. I'm here to meet Mr. John Raposa."

"Oh," she said with another perfunctory smile. "Yes, of course. He's inside in the restaurant."

Kimble restrained his urge to say something sarcastic and headed in the direction she indicated.

The restaurant's outer wall was lined with floor-to-ceiling windows that looked out over the ninth-hole putting green. Kimble stopped for a moment, stunned by the view. He'd always thought golf was a frustrating and ridiculous game: pursuing a small ball across acres of grass for hours in the heat of the summer when allergies and insects were at their peak. Especially here in the semi-desert it made no sense, and he resented the enormous volume of municipal water needed to sustain those lush carpets of green.

He spotted Raposa's broad shoulders across the room and made his way between the tables to meet him.

"Ah, Jack, Jack, good to see you," Raposa said, half rising from his seat and extending a hand.

Kimble relaxed his face, trying for a friendly expression. He took the seat opposite Raposa, his bones sinking into the deep cushioning. The country club restaurant boasted well-padded captain's chairs designed for generous behinds.

"Good to see you, Johnny."

They exchanged pleasantries for a couple of minutes until a young waitress with vivid red hair came by to take their drink orders. Raposa grinned, commented on her hair, and ordered a Bloody Mary; Kimble asked for iced tea. Shortly after, when she returned with their drinks, Raposa decided on the rib eye, Kimble the rainbow trout.

Raposa chuckled. "You trust the fish here? I guess you still got California tastes. Me, I'm a steak guy."

Kimble pursed his lips. He didn't want to waste time talking about fish. He mustered a smile.

"Johnny, you know I'm going to run for reelection in March, and you and I have worked well together these past few years." He paused, leaving Raposa an opening in the conversation.

The waitress returned, bringing them plates of salad. Raposa flirted with the waitress again, angling for a phone number. Kimble fumed inwardly at the interruption. He wanted Raposa's full attention. He cleared his throat.

"As I was saying, you and I have worked well together these past few years—"

"Yeah, yeah, great years, Jack, you've done a great job. I mean, take my business—we had some hiccups when the economy crashed a few years back—but things have picked up. There's some really bright spots on the horizon."

"Well, I'd like to think I can count on you for support in my upcoming campaign," Kimble said, fixing Raposa with a piercing look.

Raposa dumped copious globs of ranch dressing onto his salad and chuckled.

"My doctor says I should take it easy with this stuff, but I love it." Then he grabbed a bread roll from the basket in the middle of the table, smeared a gob of butter on it, and took a bite.

"I really appreciate you, Jack. I mean, you get it. You get what this city really needs."

Raposa said all this while chewing on his bread roll, and moist, half-masticated white morsels of food glistened around his tongue as he spoke. Kimble felt a twinge of distaste and switched his gaze to his plate. He pushed a few wispy arugula leaves around, waiting for Raposa to finish his mouthful. He needed to stay focused on the purpose of this meeting. When he looked up, the waitress reappeared with their main courses. Raposa took a slug of his drink and gave Kimble a disarming smile.

"Jaaaaack," he said, dragging the word out, "you know me. We've worked together a few years now. My Los Sueños project is set to really take off. All I need is for that road to go through, and think how much new business revenue it will bring. That's tax revenue for Las Vistas. Then you've got the money to make that drainage project happen, don't you?"

Kimble poked at a fragment of fish. He didn't want to talk about the road project. The protests each weekend were a distraction he didn't need. He was pretty sure the city was going to have to use whatever funding he could muster to put toward the drainage project. But he wanted to appear attentive to the developer's needs.

"You're right. Los Sueños is a good plan for Las Vistas. We need that kind of business, and we need to take care of our infrastructure too. That's why I feel I can count on your support for—"

The sound of laughter interrupted him as a couple made their way across the room, and Raposa's head swerved in their direction.

"Danny!" he called. "Over here."

Kimble put down his knife and fork to watch the progress of a white-haired man and his deeply tanned blond companion as they approached the table. He needed to continue the conversation with Raposa. He needed reassurance that he could count on him for a hefty campaign contribution. But it was too late. The couple were almost at the table, still laughing.

Raposa rose and clapped the man on the back, then gave the woman a generous hug.

"Danny, Melinda." He turned toward Kimble. "This is Jack Kimble, our illustrious mayor."

"Danny Murphy," the white-haired man said. "And this is my girlfriend, Melinda. She's visiting from Phoenix."

Kimble rose stiffly and held out a hand. If this man was a chum of Raposa's, he needed to make a good impression.

Raposa waved his hand, inviting them to sit down.

"I met Danny a few years ago and we clicked right away. When I heard the country club needed a new manager, I persuaded him to come over here, and he landed the job. He's got a lot of experience in the Phoenix area. Isn't that right, Danny?"

Murphy grinned at Raposa, patting his shoulder. "Yeah, Johnny's right. Besides golf, I was involved in a lot of great development deals in Scottsdale. I think Las Vistas has got great potential. I'm really excited about being here. And I'm trying to convince *somebody* to join me." He grinned at Melinda.

Kimble decided it was worth making an effort with the man. He forced a smile and launched into the campaign speech he'd been preparing.

"Nice you decided to choose Las Vistas. We have a lot to offer. I was just telling Johnny here how much his input is valued at city hall. I'm running for reelection in March, so I'm counting on outstanding members of the business community like Johnny—and you—to support me to keep making Las Vistas a great place to live."

Murphy smiled, shot a glance at Raposa, and gave Kimble a thumbs-up.

"You've got my vote," he said. Murphy, Raposa, and Melinda shared a laugh, and then the couple headed back toward the bar.

As soon as they were out of earshot, Kimble rounded on Raposa.

"Johnny, I hope I've made myself clear. I've appreciated your support in the past, and I think you recognize that I helped steer some things in the right direction so you could get some of the approvals you needed for Los Sueños. But we're in a different situation now." Here he looked at Raposa pointedly. "I'm sure you wouldn't want to see flooding in Los Sueños like in those other subdivisions— where, I believe, you were involved."

Raposa gave him a condescending smile. "Not going to happen, Jack. Sueños is at the top of the hill. As you know, water runs downhill."

Kimble found the rest of the lunch meeting equally frustrating, and he left the restaurant feeling deeply uneasy. He wasn't at

all sure that he could count on Raposa's financial support or the
newcomer's. He wasn't sure if the meeting had even been worth
enduring the vile-tasting trout.

Raposa waited till the mayor's tall frame disappeared into the
lobby, then went to find Murphy. He found him and Melinda
sitting at a corner table. Raposa signaled to Murphy, who excused
himself from his companion. The two men walked toward the bar.

"You wanted to see me?"

"Yeah, Johnny. I need to tell you, the guys in Arizona are worried about their investment. They've got a lot of money riding
on Los Sueños, and things haven't been looking good. I've tried
my best to reassure them that we know what we're doing here.
But some of them remember the Milagro thing." Murphy leaned
in, speaking more softly. "Speaking of that, what are the lawyers
saying about the lawsuit? You know, those buyers bitching about
their down payments?"

Raposa laid a hand on Murphy's shoulder. "I got it under control, Danny. I've got a plan. Kimble hopes I'm going to support
him, but I'm going to back this new guy, and he'll get the road approved. We just need to make sure Kimble's drainage plan doesn't
get any traction. If that goes through and people have to pay more
taxes, you can bet it will kill sales."

Murphy eyed him for a few seconds, then grinned "Okay. I'm
with you."

CHAPTER FIFTEEN

DIGGER STOOD LOOKING out her window on Christmas morning, wondering if she would hear from Maria. She had no plans. Nothing. Last night was still with her—Abuela's face, the women and laughter at the table, the moment when she'd held Maria. She stood looking out at the snow-dusted mountainside and ached.

What would it be like to be part of that world? Maria's world? To belong, instead of being an observer who was always writing what other people said and thought, hiding herself? Last night, as she'd lain in bed, she'd thought about holding Maria outside under the icy stars outside Abuela's home. She wanted to do so much more: breathe in the scent of her, run her lips over the back of her neck, cup her breasts in her hands, feel their bodies together.

She thought now about texting Maria. *How long can I hold back? Is it really worth it?* The image of Maria at the chapel came to mind, the silence between them in that old, sacred space. She'd opened up, telling Maria about her parents, the accident. It had felt okay at the time, but now there was so much at stake.

Maria's story needed to be told now, and people needed to know what Raposa had done. If she was going to write those stories, she could not cross that line. She groaned. Someday, maybe, but not now.

A storm swept in just before New Year's Eve, dumping almost a foot of snow on Las Vistas. Whole sections of the freeways near the Colorado and Texas borders were closed. Digger worked on the Milagro Millennium story from home and filed it two days into the New Year.

Five days later it still hadn't appeared in print. On the morning of the fifth day, she checked the status of the article and again saw it was stuck in the holding folder. She was furious.

She marched over to Swenson's desk and interrupted him in the middle of a conversation with one of the photographers.

"What's the delay? It's been days! You know that's a good story."

Swenson rolled his eyes, turned away from the photographer, and glared at her. The fingers of his left hand clenched. Digger backed away a couple of inches. Lately Swenson's legendary temper had been getting the better of him.

"Sorry, sorry," she said. "I just wondered why it hasn't run yet."

Swenson compressed his lips as if he were inwardly fighting to keep calm. He took a deep breath, shuffled some papers on his desk, and said, "We'll run it sometime in the next few days. We've just had breaking news and other stuff that's taken priority. You got it?"

Digger nodded. She knew that was the end of the conversation. She turned and headed for the photo department. She needed to talk to someone. Rex was there, staring intently at a screenful of high school football images. She plopped down on a stool beside him.

"Which one of these guys would you take for an opioid addict?" he asked, pointing at the colorful tangle of bodies on the screen.

When she didn't answer, he looked around. "Uh-oh, who rained on your parade?"

Digger balled her hands into fists. She felt like pounding them on the desk.

"Swenson! I can't understand it. He was all for that story I wrote about the developers who still owe the county millions, but it's been sitting there for days, waiting to run. I just asked him about it, and he gave me some BS about other priorities. I mean, what the hell? We blow out the front page with a story about a fundraising event for some university women's group, and that's news?"

Rex looked at her with a mixture of sympathy and world-weariness.

"My dear Digger," he said in a fake English accent. "Because you are a good reporter and you are dedicated to your craft, out there, diligently uncovering the tawdry misdeeds of our elected officials, you are insensitive to the odor of scandal that wafts around this newsroom."

"Rex, what the hell are you talking about?"

"I mean," Rex said, nodding at her like a teacher explaining the birds and bees to a fifth grader, "rumors have been floating around for months that someone high up in our organization—and I'm not mentioning any names—and the executive director of that charitable organization are taking tango lessons together." He held up his hand with the forefinger and middle finger entwined.

Digger felt like a deflating bicycle tire. "Tango!" She looked at him, shaking her head. "Guess everybody has their weak spot."

"Uh-huh," Rex said. "Don't worry, your story will run. It's a good story.

And with the municipal election coming up, maybe it's better if it's delayed. The closer to the election it's published, the more impact it could have."

On her way out, Digger passed the features department. Vicky Sandberg was hunched over her desk, earbuds in and deep in conversation. She sounded pissed off. A flyer about the mayor's charity ball lay in her in-tray. The photo caught Digger's eye as she passed. There was something about the man's face. She stopped and studied it while Vicky, turned her back and continued arguing.

Beneath the picture of the dark-haired man the caption read, "Celebrity Chef Armando will host the auction for the fundraising event." There were a couple of paragraphs about the chef. Born and trained in New Mexico, he had made it big in California, where he'd had his own radio show and a restaurant that specialized in locally sourced dishes based on authentic recipes from his homeland.

Digger stared at the photo. Seventeen years older, his face a tad rounder than the pictures in the clippings she had kept, but it was him. She was sure of it.

➤

Digger sat in the passenger seat waiting for Rex while he loaded his camera gear into the back of the Cherokee. He had on the grungy yellow barn coat that he wore all winter, and the smell of old cigarettes filled the car when he climbed in.

"How come you're going to this gig, anyway? I thought it was one of Vicky's features things," he asked.

"Oh, you know, the mayor's involved and the *Courier* has a table there.

Swenson was glad to have another warm body to fill the places."

"Warm bodies!" Rex snorted. "That's something we're about to have fewer of."

She stared at him. "What have you been hearing?"

Rex was her source for company gossip. He worked different

shifts, got around. Somehow he heard things long before anyone else did.

"We're probably going to have more layoffs. Just a couple here and there, where they can find ways to cut fat—maybe circulation, accounting. No one in the newsroom."

"Where'd you get that?"

"The maintenance guy. You know, the tall one with the big beard. He and I sometimes smoke out there at the back of the building. He hears stuff."

"Not good."

"Nope," Rex said grimly. He turned the key in the ignition. "Nope, it's not good. I wish I had options, but I've got a son with two more years of college. My wife's a nurse, I keep telling her she should have married a doctor. She doesn't appreciate my sense of humor."

The hotel lobby was bustling, and it took Digger a few minutes before she spotted the sign directing guests to the "Acoma Room" for the mayor's ball. She wondered if there would be any actual dancing or if there would be the usual rubber chicken and speeches.

People were milling around inside the vast room. Digger scanned the space, counting the tables to estimate the size of the crowd. She spotted Raposa standing near the podium, chatting with Danny Murphy. She headed toward them, weaving her way through the tables.

Raposa greeted her with enthusiasm. "Miss Doyle, so good to see you. My, how nice you look tonight."

Digger was wearing her dark suit and a striped blouse. In an effort to look festive, she'd put on a pair of dangly earrings an old girlfriend had given her.

"This is Danny Murphy," Raposa continued. "He's recently come here from Phoenix to manage the clubhouse at the golf course."

"Oh yes," Murphy said, flashing a bleach-white smile. "We've spoken on the phone. Miss Doyle. I guess we're both Irish, then."

"My grandparents—well, my grandmother, at least, was born there. My grandfather, where the 'Doyle' comes from, was second generation," she said. She shook his outstretched hand. "And you? Ireland via Chicago?"

Murphy raised his eyebrows. "Yeah, just outside. How'd you know?"

"I have a thing for accents," Digger said. "So what brings you here to New Mexico? I thought most people went the other way, looking for brighter lights."

Murphy looked around the room, glanced at Raposa, and looked pleased with himself.

"I met Johnny when he was in Scottsdale. He persuaded me to come have a look at Las Vistas, and I liked what I saw. I think there's a lot of potential here."

"That's right. A lot of exciting things are gonna happen here in the next few years," Raposa said, nudging Murphy's shoulder.

Just then, there was a hubbub from the other side of the room. The mayor had just arrived. He stood in the entryway with his mousy little wife beside him like a faithful retainer. He was wearing a tuxedo that looked out of place among the business suits. Las Vistas wasn't much for dressing up.

Digger plowed her way through the meal and looked attentive when they began the speeches. She felt nervous, wondering when the chef would appear. How many years had she wanted to confront this man? And would it really be him? The photo looked like the young man in the clips she had kept, but people did change, and the name could just be a coincidence. If she did get the chance to talk to him, what would she say?

She took notes while Kimble spoke about his plans for the city and his intention to run for a second term. No surprises there.

Afterward, the mayor introduced the celebrity chef Armando as a local boy who had made it big in Los Angeles. Armando walked up to the podium and beamed at the audience.

Digger's heart lurched. Sure, he was pudgier, but the features were unmistakable. It was the face from the newspaper stories she'd looked at countless times as she'd grown up.

Was anyone else in the room thinking what she was thinking? Did anybody else recognize him, remember his story?

Armando gave a short speech about his loyalty to his roots and his family and how all that support had helped him find success in LA. After his speech, Kimble asked him to pull raffle tickets from a bowl and announce the winners for the evening's fundraising effort.

Once the formalities were over, a band struck up. Vicky made a beeline to collar Armando for an interview. Digger circulated, keeping an eye on them as they talked for several minutes: nodding, smiling, hands gesticulating. Finally, Digger saw Vicky stuff her notebook into her purse and shake Armando's hand. They parted and he headed for the door.

Good. She could catch him in the hallway outside. They could talk there with less chance of being overheard by the other guests.

"Mr. Armando!" She caught up to him in the hallway. "Hi, I'm Elizabeth Doyle with the *Courier*."

He stopped, turned around, frowned.

"I've already given an interview."

"Yes, I know. My colleague, she does feature stories. I'm here on the mayor's behalf. Since you grew up here, can you comment at all on how Las Vistas has changed since you've been gone?"

Armando waved a hand dismissively. "I didn't really grow up in Las Vistas. I'm from a community just north of here."

"Oh? Which one? There are so many little places with such colorful histories."

"San Lorenzo—ever been there? My family there goes back three hundred years." He spoke with pride. "My father was the local sheriff, and he had a big reputation."

So that was it. Digger's heart banged inside her chest. Last night she had gone through the clippings again, trying to memorize the details: the time, the road, the car. She took a deep breath, swallowed, and asked the question.

"Did you ever drive a white 1990 Honda Civic?"

Armando looked puzzled at the non sequitur. Then his body stiffened. His eyes opened wide, his mouth fell open.

"Who the hell are you?"

"I'm Elizabeth Doyle. And I'm guessing you are Joshua Armando Salazar. My parents . . ." She trailed off.

He swallowed a couple of times, and he seemed to be having trouble breathing. His face went pale, so pale it looked almost green under the hallway lights. His eyes darted right, left, as if he hoped to escape. Digger blocked his way.

"How did it happen?" She hissed.

He looked away, exhaled. "I was young," he said, his voice shaky. "I was late to work. I had this shitty old car—"

She stepped in closer. "Yeah. But you got to be a celebrity chef in LA, and I had to live with my grandparents because I didn't have parents anymore."

All the confidence he'd shown on stage disappeared, and his body seemed to crumple in on itself.

"I have to sit down," he said.

Digger wondered if, throughout the seventeen years since those life-changing few seconds on the freeway, somewhere deep inside he had been afraid this moment would come.

"I'm so sorry, I'm so sorry." He whispered the words over and over again.

Digger stood there watching him. Ever since the accident and the judge's verdict, she'd thought about what it would be like to confront this man. Yet here she was, carrying years of anger and resentment, years of being the girl with no parents—angry, so angry. All those years asking: *Why? Why my parents? Why them?*

She gritted her teeth. How many times had she imagined this moment? How she wanted to focus all that anger on him. Yell, scream, punch him. Now here he was, this man who had grown up in a tiny community and somehow escaped the consequences of what had happened that morning. He had gone on to make it big in California, yet all the while he'd known that he'd escaped because somebody knew somebody who had put in a good word for him.

Here he was now, standing in front of her, pale and weak.

Digger looked around. Where could she find a place for him to sit? She noticed a door a few yards away. Grabbing Armando's arm, she guided him toward it, hoping it would lead to an empty room.

It did. Inside, she steered him toward a bench where he sat, head down. Through the thinning hair on top of his head she noticed tiny beads of sweat glistening on his scalp.

As she watched and waited for him to compose himself enough to talk, it sank in that she wasn't the only one who'd been suffering. He had lived with his guilt all these years. Maybe it was just a different kind of suffering, not like the pain that crouched inside her, pouncing with unexpected ferocity at moments of weakness—his, she imagined, was more of a nagging pain, like a decaying tooth.

After what seemed a long time, he asked, "What do you want?"

Digger's shoulders sagged. All this time she had expected him to be defensive and angry. Seeing him broken and weak disarmed her. *What do I want? What do I really want?*

Nothing he says or does will bring my parents back.

She closed her eyes a minute, trying to get back to that place, those moments when she'd ached for them and felt that helpless rage. Finally she spoke.

"You know the one thing that's been eating me most all these years? It's *how*. How come you didn't go to jail?"

Armando rocked back and forth on the bench, moaning.

"This could ruin me," he said.

Anger surged inside her. "You expect me to care?" She spat the words at him.

He looked up at her. "Okay I get it." He gasped. "But can we— is there some way—I've tried to put that behind me and make a new life. That's why I left here and changed my name."

"You get to put this behind you! And me, what about me? Didn't you ever think, just once in all these years, about the people you killed and the family they left behind?"

Digger closed her eyes, compressed her lips, and then took several long, slow breaths, the way the therapist had taught her. She couldn't undo the past. She just wanted to know, to put that question to rest.

"Just tell me how," she said at last, in a low voice, emphasizing each word.

He took in a deep breath and let it out slowly. "It was my father. He had connections from when he was a sheriff. And he had people who owed him. One of them was the DA. Whatever they agreed, it delayed things so that some of the evidence wasn't okay to use in court. I don't know how it worked. The police investigated my car. It was in bad shape, before the accident, I mean: I couldn't afford to get things fixed, and the tires were shit. I don't really know how they did it. I was just so relieved I didn't have to go to jail. I'm so sorry."

He looked up at her, his eyes frightened, pleading. "I have nightmares where I still see the car," he said. "Not my car—theirs."

"Do you see them? My parents?"

He looked down, shook his head. "I couldn't look at them."

Digger dropped her head. There was nothing more to say. It wasn't justice, but it was all she was going to get.

She left him slumped on the bench, called Rex and told him she'd take an Uber home, then walked down the empty hotel hallway. She could still hear voices and music from the ballroom as she passed, heading for the exit. A walkway bordered by trellises covered with climbing roses led to a circular flower bed that surrounded a small fountain. She noticed a bench and sat down.

The turmoil she'd felt just minutes before had solidified into a deep, dull ache. She was tired, so tired. It felt as if she had been slogging through the years since the accident, burdened by an invisible weight. At times like this, she wanted so much to lay that weight down, to have someone else hold it while she rested, just for a little while. But who? Her grandparents were never there, not really. She thought of Tim. He'd been the one she could trust on those days when the shit rained down. But Tim was gone.

She thought of Maria. In spite of the professional wall she'd erected, she felt they trusted each other. Could she turn to Maria? She could imagine Maria's reaction to Armando, all fury and passion. But the more she sat thinking, she knew that for her, the time for fury was past. Maybe that was what the therapist had meant when she'd talked about letting go—that you could finally get to a place where you understood that nurturing anger was futile.

Digger realized she had tears running down her cheeks. Armando lived with his guilt, she with her loss.

CHAPTER SIXTEEN

DIGGER AWOKE WITH the warm weight of Lady Antonia on her chest, the vibration of the cat's purring, and the green glow of her eyes in the darkness. She kept seeing Armando's chalk-pale face. She tried to remember the faces of her mother and father. At twelve years old you should be able to remember your parents, shouldn't you? *The sound of their voices, their laughs, their smiles? What was it Mom used to say when they parted ways at school?* Mom was at the elementary school, Dad taught at the middle school. Summers, when they were free, they went on walks, camped, visited national parks. Then all that ended and it was Grandma and Grandpa in the big old house in Houston. Hot, lonely days.

She got up, put on her running clothes, and went out on the foothills trail. Running in the cold morning air helped clear her head. She pushed herself till her legs and lungs hurt and sweat dripped into her eyes.

All along she'd wondered how Armando had gotten off. How could someone kill two people in a car crash and not be found guilty of some serious crime? From what he'd said last night, she knew she had guessed right: somebody had pulled strings for him. Her experience as a cops reporter had taught her how hard it is to assign blame. Crash investigators just look at the scene, the distances, the angles, the damage. They tell you what happened. They don't point the accusing finger. And Armando's father and the DA he'd mentioned—they were both dead now. She had followed their careers too and read the obituaries. Now there was nobody left to tell the real story.

She stopped in the middle of the path, hung her head, and let out a howl. Then she stood. Sometimes shit just happens for no reason, she told herself. *Not to make you suffer, not to make you stronger. It just happens, and you just live from sunup to sundown and repeat what works.*

She ran back to her apartment, got into the shower, let the hot water ease her body, and let her thoughts turn to the workday. She couldn't do anything about Armando, but there were plenty of other ugly secrets to find and expose—oh yeah!

Digger decided it was a night for Frankie's. The place was quiet midweek; only a handful of people were there, a couple of women bent over the pool table and some couples at the tables on the far side of the tiny dance floor. The dim lighting barely illuminated the Frida Kahlo posters on the wall.

She sat at the bar and chatted with Lexi, whose eyes were riveted on the TV screen showing a college basketball game. Digger had no idea who was playing, but she was glad of the company; anything to lift her spirits. The roar of the onscreen crowd competed with the background country music track. Digger had finished a beer and was about to order another when she felt a hand on her shoulder. She swung around.

"Hey, you." It was Maria.

"Oh, hey."

"Why the long face?"

Digger shrugged. "Just one of those days."

Maria slid onto the barstool beside her and waved to catch Lexi's attention. Lexi tore her gaze away from the screen and shot the two of them a knowing look.

"Two beers?" she asked.

Digger nodded and turned to face Maria. "What brought you here?"

Maria pointed at the shoulder bag beside her. "I was going to hand out flyers for the next protest meeting. We need to keep pushing it because of the election."

"Of course." Digger let out a sigh. "They're going to vote on the road soon; probably right after the election. I'll have to write about it—and about your involvement."

There was so much more she wanted to say. Ever since Christmas Eve at Abuela's, she'd felt a shift inside herself. She wondered whether she could write the story in the way she'd planned. It wasn't just Maria; it was what she'd felt that night, like she belonged—even for that brief moment—to that other world. It was getting harder to stay objective.

Maria leaned close. "It's okay. I'm sorry I crossed the line with you that day in Abuela's kitchen. Do you trust me?"

Digger nodded but said nothing.

"What else is going on with you?" Maria asked, concerned.

Digger waited until Lexi had slid the drinks over the counter toward them. "Today would have been my mom's birthday," she said.

Thinking about her mother's birthday had brought back the memory of the encounter with Armando and the aching need to talk, something that was always so hard to do. She took a sip of beer.

"A couple of nights ago, I actually met the guy who crashed into my parents."

"What? He's in town? How did you find out?"

"He was the celeb at the mayor's dinner. Turns out he's a big-time chef now. I recognized his face from a publicity photo."

Maria laid a hand on Digger's arm. "If you need to talk about it, I'm a good listener."

"Thanks." Digger expelled a sigh. But how to begin?

After the accident, a lot of people had asked her questions, even kids at school. She didn't know how they'd found out. She didn't want to be known as the kid with no parents, she didn't want to be different. She didn't want to talk.

"Let's go sit over there." Maria gestured toward a table in the corner. When they were seated, Maria leaned close. "So, you really met this guy?

What did he say about the accident? Did he say how he got away with it?"

Digger recapped the way she'd met Armando at the hotel, how he'd reacted when she'd revealed who she was, and his story about his father's influence with the justice system.

"Couldn't you go to the police with that?" Maria asked.

Digger shook her head. "It's too late now. The police were a waste of time then, the guys who did the cover-up are dead, and there's probably no one else who really cares except me and my grandma." She let out a long breath. "I'm not even sure why I told you about my parents that day in your studio."

"You trusted me." Maria reached across the table and took Digger's hand.

Digger hung her head. "Yeah, I did. There's not that many people I would trust that way. I'm not used to talking about it. When I was growing up, my grandma took me to this therapist, and she used to quiz me about it, about how I felt—but she was just someone paid to listen, not like a friend. I didn't want to talk to. I'd just sit there and wish she'd leave me alone."

Maria sat for a moment, studying Digger's face. "How did you feel when you found out how he got away with it? Me, I think I'd have wanted to tear him apart."

Digger went on staring at the table, as if she hadn't heard. Finally she said, "It was weird. When I was a teenager, I thought about ways I could make him pay, make him hurt the way I did. Then there he was right in front of me, looking so scared, so pathetic. He hurt too. I couldn't be mad at him anymore."

"Did that make you feel any better?"

Did she feel any better? Maybe, but knowing his father pulled strings to help him get away with it still rankled. Meeting him hadn't erased how the accident had shaped everything since.

"I'm not sure," Digger said finally. "I'm still mad I can't do anything about it. Nobody should get away with something the way he did."

Maria's eyes searched Digger's face. "Maybe you can't change what happened to that guy, but you can make a difference with what you write about the road."

Maria's words resonated. All the stories Digger had written about the flood risks had gone unheeded. Maybe this could make a difference.

"Yeah, you could be right," Digger said, nodding slowly.

Maria picked up Digger's hands and held them to her lips. "Look, I admit, I followed up with you because I wanted you to write about the campaign and I wanted you to be on our side. But now—I care about you. You were there for me when my mother ruined Christmas Eve. There's something going on between us. You can't deny that."

Digger shrugged. "You're not upset with me because I'm focused on my work?"

Maria shook her head. "No. I like your calmness, your stillness. I'm glad you have good memories of your mother. Me, I grew up with people shouting all around me. My mother feeds on drama. You saw her. She hates me for what I am and I can't forgive her for it. But you were able to forgive the man who did such damage to you. That's like my abuela, she is stronger than any of us."

Maria had been staring down at her hands as she spoke, turning the salt shaker in her fingers. Now she looked up.

"Abuela. She likes you, you know."

Digger hung her head, thinking of the warmth and camaraderie she'd felt while sitting among the women of Maria's family, making tamales. She remembered the awkwardness and tension of Christmas gatherings at her grandparents' house, the cousins from Dallas sniggering at the clothes she wore.

They sat for a while sipping their drinks while the TV game noise washed around them. When Maria had finished her beer, she pulled a handful of flyers out of her bag and went over to the women at the pool table.

Digger walked back to the counter and asked for the check. Lexi cocked a glance over at Maria on the other side of the bar, then back at Digger. She put her hands on her hips.

"So, what's going on with you and her?"

Digger eyed Lexi, looked back at Maria, and hesitated. "She's somebody . . . very special," she said. "Trouble is, I just can't go there."

"Wanna tell me about it?"

"It's a work thing." She shrugged.

Lexi raised her eyebrows, shook her head. "Maybe. I think you're scared."

Their glasses empty, Digger and Maria walked outside and stood for a moment in the parking lot. Maria put her arms around Digger and held her.

"Thanks for listening to me," Digger said, enjoying the warmth of Maria's body against her for a moment. Then she gently pried Maria's arms loose.

Maria looked at her, hurt. "I thought you trusted me."

"I do—I just can't go there right now. You understand? It's the same way you can't stop fighting for what you believe in."

Maria opened her mouth as if she were going to say something, then decided against it, sighed, and walked away.

"Wait!" Digger called.

She watched Maria get into her car and drive off. Standing there in the glare of the parking lot lights, Digger wished she could follow her right now.

CHAPTER SEVENTEEN

DAVE JOHNSEN EYED himself in the mirror, rubbing a hand over his broad jawline to feel the smoothness after he'd finished shaving. He patted his hair, adjusted his tie, and tried on the serious but benign look he'd been practicing for his campaign speeches. Ever since Raposa had intimated he should run for mayor, he'd been obsessed by the thought. Tomorrow was the date for candidate filing. He was up for it, already thinking of the projects he could champion for Las Vistas.

He thought about what he could say to his mom. She called each Sunday to talk to the children, and he still sensed her skepticism about his move to New Mexico. As mayor of Las Vistas, he could make his mark on what went on in this state, maybe even run for state office someday. His thoughts ran on while he stood in front of the bathroom mirror.

"Honey, are you done in there?"

His wife's voice broke into his reverie. He opened the door and she came in, stood behind him, and clasped her arms around his waist.

"Dave, are you really sure about this? What about me and the kids? You're always busy: if it isn't your work, it's the council. If you get elected mayor, we'd never see you."

Johnsen turned around and patted his wife's head. He felt protective, but the thought of having a chance to make a difference in this town was an urge he couldn't ignore.

"Connie, it'll be fine. You'll see. I'd make time for you and the kids, and we could make a great team," he said soothingly. Meanwhile he was thinking about his upcoming meeting with Raposa. He'd agreed to meet the developer again at the Denny's where they'd talked before. He glanced at his watch.

"Sweetie, I gotta go. I'm meeting Johnny Raposa. He's an important guy in this town. His support could mean a lot for my campaign."

➤

Johnsen pulled into the Denny's parking lot shortly before the agreed meeting time. He walked into the restaurant and paused, scanning the tables for Raposa. Not seeing him, he smiled at the woman behind the cash register and decided to find a good spot. He made his way through the crowded dining room where the air was thick with the mingled aroma of stewed coffee, frying bacon, and pancake syrup.

He spotted an empty booth that overlooked the parking lot and slid into the seat so he could keep an eye on the entrance. He looked at his watch. It was still a couple of minutes before the time they'd agreed to meet. A waitress appeared, and he ordered coffee and water while keeping his eyes fixed on the parking lot.

Moments later he noticed a big silver BMW pulling in to park beside his Ford Escape. The door opened and Raposa emerged. Johnsen felt a pang of envy. He wondered if Raposa had a wife and kids.

He watched the developer as he came through the entrance. Evidently Raposa knew the waitstaff, because he paused to chat briefly with the girl behind the cash register. They both laughed. She gestured toward the window where Johnsen was seated.

"Dave, so good to see you," Raposa said, greeting him effusively.

He sat down opposite and thumped his forearms on the table. He was dressed in a white turtleneck and dark blazer. Johnsen glanced surreptitiously at Raposa's hands—no ring—but that watch, it looked like a Rolex.

Raposa leaned across the table. "Okay, so I'm guessing you wanted to meet today to talk about the election."

Johnsen cleared his throat, squared his shoulders, and made a conscious effort to arrange his face in the look he'd practiced in front of the mirror.

"That's right. Tomorrow is the date for candidates to declare, and I've decided to run. I give a lot of credit to you for encouraging me."

Raposa grinned broadly. "Like I said before, I think I'm a good judge of character, and I think you could be good for Las Vistas."

Johnsen flushed slightly and waited for the waitress to take their orders before he launched into one of the speeches he'd been mentally rehearsing. He talked about his experience growing up in Ohio and all the great advantages they had there that he thought he could bring to Las Vistas. Johnsen recalled how shocked he'd been when he found out that many parts of the city had dirt streets. He couldn't understand how the people who lived in the homes there—and they were fancy, custom-built homes, a lot of them—put up with that.

"As mayor, I'd like to focus on infrastructure. We could get the streets paved and extend the water and sewer system to all those neighborhoods. And drainage, so people wouldn't have to go through what happened last summer with the rains."

He went on in this vein for a while, pausing when the waitress returned with their plates.

Raposa dug in, listening to Johnsen, occasionally making mm-hmm sounds as he loaded forkfuls of hash browns into his mouth.

Johnsen finally stopped talking, looked down at his own untouched plate, and took a gulp of coffee.

Raposa put down his fork and leaned over the table. "Listen, Dave, I think you're spot-on. But all that is going to take a lot of money, and Las Vistas is hurting right now. Before the crash, money was pouring in from all the construction that was going on here. But that pretty much dried up. If you want to get all that stuff done, you're going to have to beef up the economic base, get some new business here."

Johnsen felt as if he'd fumbled the ball on a critical play.

Raposa looked at him sympathetically, like a middle-school teacher explaining a tough math problem. "Dave, I know you want to do right by those folks who had problems in the floods last summer, but what Jack Kimble is proposing is going to hit Las Vistas residents with higher taxes, right?"

Johnsen felt conflicted. He believed in free enterprise, and he'd heard folks grumbling about the solutions Kimble was proposing. But he'd seen the storm damage, and he thought fixing that problem was a good goal.

"Like I said before," Raposa continued, "that Los Sueños project will bring in more revenue for the city. There'll be new construction and commercial space for new businesses. Here, I'll show you again."

Raposa grabbed the container of crayons the restaurant provided for fidgety kids and began drawing on the place mat. He sketched out the streets and plazas of the development.

"See, the master plan's been approved, and we've got more investors interested in expanding the project. But we've gotta get better access, and that means getting the green light for that road project."

Johnsen frowned. "But a lot of the voters I've talked to really want something done about drainage."

"Yeah, sure they do, but they're not willing to pay for it. You go ahead with what Kimble was talking about and everybody ends up with higher taxes. You go with the road project and it'll bring you revenue that'll pay for whatever you need. Trust me, I know what I'm doing."

Johnsen stared at Raposa's big hands and the glint of his watch. This wasn't quite the direction he'd anticipated the meeting going in. From their previous conversation, he'd thought Raposa was ready to back him to bring change to Las Vistas. But Raposa was right: change had to happen one step at a time, and waiting a couple of years to get the drainage project started wasn't likely to cause any more damage than this year's storm already had. Backing something that meant higher taxes wouldn't get him elected.

If Raposa's development could bring in the kind of money he talked about, people wouldn't have to worry about higher taxes. What was the point of denying the road project, anyway? The people who were protesting it didn't even live in Las Vistas, as far as he knew.

Johnsen looked up and gave Raposa a thumbs-up sign.

A waitress came to clear the table and slipped the check between them.

Johnsen reached for it, but Raposa waved him away and grabbed it.

"It's on me. You're a good guy. I believe in you," he said, and rose to leave.

The phone in Johnsen's pocket jingled. He fumbled for it as Raposa waved and walked toward the door.

"Connie, what is it?"

"Honey, are you going to be much longer at your meeting? I think Jimmy's running a fever."

Johnsen reassured her he'd be home in a few minutes, then sat looking out at the parking lot. He watched as Raposa got into his big silver car and headed out toward the street. The sunlight glinted on the BMW as he left.

CHAPTER EIGHTEEN

DIGGER PULLED UP outside city hall with twenty minutes to spare before the city clerk's office was due to open. Today was the official date for candidates to declare their intentions to run in the upcoming election. She had a pretty good idea of who would show up: maybe two or three people vying for Fabrizzi's seat. She knew that Kimble wanted to hold on to his job as mayor and that Dave Johnsen would be challenging him, so that would leave another empty seat.

She decided to wait in the car. Outside, the wind made a moaning sound, churning up wisps of fine brown dust around city hall. Its walls of steel, glass and concrete rose stark and angular out of the landscape, as though it had been teleported there from a different dimension.

Odd to think that just a few miles away, Abuela might be drinking coffee in her little adobe house, with all the homes clustered around hers made of the same soft mud bricks. The people in those houses were aging, the young ones leaving, the empty homes gradually melting back into the earth. She thought of Maria, picturing her walking away in the darkness, and felt a lump in her throat.

A car swung into the other side of the parking lot. Dave

Johnsen and his wife got out. Digger followed them into the building, hoping to get a few comments before they reached the city clerk's office.

"Councilor!"

Johnsen looked, in his somber black suit, as if he were going to a funeral.

His wife, a little on the plump side, was in a floral-patterned dress.

They waited for Digger.

"I just wanted to ask a few questions about your plan to run for mayor. Was this a recent decision?"

Johnsen flinched slightly when she held her tiny recorder up to his face.

"Oh, no. I've been thinking about it for a while. In fact, some very influential people here in Las Vistas encouraged me to run. You know, back home in Ohio we did things a lot differently, and I think I could bring a lot of that here to the city. I—"

"You still think of Ohio as home?"

Johnsen obviously realized his mistake and quickly back-tracked. "Oh, no, what I meant was—"

The door of the clerk's office opened and a woman waved him inside.

———

On the fourth floor of city hall, Kimble looked at his watch and waited until it showed one minute past eleven. Then he got up and walked the two floors down to the city clerk's office. The room was hot and crowded, and the windows were fogged with condensation.

He'd worn his pale gray double-breasted suit for the occasion, hoping to make an impression. He elbowed his way through, nodding at faces he recognized from council meetings.

The city clerk, Jody Dunlop, was already handing out

paperwork for the candidates to fill out. This must be old hat to her, Kimble thought; she'd seen mayors and councilors come and go. Fletcher had told him she'd held the job longer than anyone could remember. No wonder she was looking at the roomful of would-be candidates with about as much enthusiasm as a theater critic watching the same show for the fifteenth time.

He heard Dunlop call out Johnsen's name. The young councilor stepped forward and bent over her desk. The clerk walked him through the forms while the others in the room chafed at the wait.

When he was finished, Johnsen turned to rejoin his wife, who was waiting near the door. He came face to face with Kimble.

"So it's true," Kimble said. "You're running against me."

Johnsen flushed. The old man, with his wiry hair and beard, reminded him of characters in his childhood Sunday school books.

"Yes, that's right. I've had a lot of supporters urging me to run. I think I've got a lot to offer Las Vistas."

Kimble, half a head taller, looked down at Johnsen.

"This is a tough game, you know. I've got my supporters too, and voters in this town know me."

Johnsen swallowed. Was Kimble threatening him? He thought they had worked well together on the council. Instinctively he reached a hand behind his back, searching for his wife's arm. She caught his hand and held it.

Digger was backed into a corner, squashed between a TV reporter and a hulking cameraman. She caught the movement of Johnsen's hand and noticed the way Kimble appeared to tower over him. The next moment, Johnsen thrust his head forward and spoke again. The words were inaudible to the others in the room, but whatever Johnsen said made Kimble frown and back away.

"Those are the two guys who are running for mayor, aren't they?" the TV reporter asked Digger.

Digger hadn't seen her at any previous events and figured

she was new. She looked about twenty-five and was wearing a form-fitting red dress, dark tailored jacket, and heels.

"Yeah," Digger said. "The tall guy is Jack Kimble, the current mayor. The other one is Dave Johnsen, a city councilor."

"Is that woman his wife?" the TV reporter asked, looking Digger over as if she were sizing up the competition. "You're from the *Courier*, aren't you?"

The big cameraman hovered behind the TV reporter like a bodyguard. He had a shaved head and a beard that splayed out over his chest like an invasive plant. Digger had encountered him a few times in the past at SWAT scenes, and he'd made it clear he had no time for print reporters.

"We should go talk to those guys," the cameraman said, cocking his head toward the door through which Johnsen and his wife were just leaving.

Digger watched them go. She'd come to watch the candidates make their formal declarations in case of something unexpected, and she'd gotten something: the way Kimble had backed away from Johnsen. She'd followed Kimble since he was elected four years ago. He was wily and astute, but—if rumors were correct—Johnsen had already attracted backers with deep pockets. That could make all the difference.

CHAPTER NINETEEN

SPRING ARRIVED IN New Mexico with a blast of wind. Day after day, gusts filled the sky with brown dust and tumbleweeds bounced across the streets. As always, spring also meant the start of election season. Within days of the candidates announcing their intentions, campaign signs began sprouting. Like wildflowers, they popped up along roadsides, splashes of color in neighborhood yards.

This morning the wind was still and the sky a soft, billowy gray. A layer of cloud nestled like a baby blanket on the crest of the mountains, slipping gently into the canyon hollows. Despite winter snowfalls, the land was dry, dry, dry. The desert grasses carpeting the foothills were dull blond and gray, with here and there a spiky green tuft of yucca, and brown and twisted fingers of cholla.

Digger sat at her desk, pondering a story examining the rivalry between Kimble and Johnsen. But before she could tackle it, she wanted another jolt of coffee. She was just standing up when her desk phone rang, caller ID unknown.

"Is that Elizabeth Doyle?" a woman's voice asked.

"Yes."

"They call you Digger, don't they?" Digger grabbed a notepad. "Who is this?"

The caller ignored the question. "Raposa. You need to do more digging there."

Digger's heart was racing. That voice—had she heard it before? She tried to pick up a clue, any accent. What did the woman mean about Raposa? She tried to remember what she'd seen in the court records.

The woman's voice broke in again, as if she were reading Digger's thoughts. "You're not looking in the right place."

"What do you mean?" Digger asked.

"There are other court records. Raposa isn't from here. Start with the divorce."

The line went dead. Silence. Who was the woman? An ex-wife? A jealous former lover?

Digger didn't know how long Raposa had been in Las Vistas. Halloran would know; he'd been around forever. She headed for Halloran's desk. He was hidden behind a towering stack of files, his head resting on his hands.

"I thought you didn't take a nap till after lunch."

He stirred, looked at her, and made a face. "I'm thinking," he said gruffly. "I'm trying to find the lede on my story. What's up?"

"I thought I'd do a little poking around in Raposa's background. Know anybody who's been in real estate going way back?"

She didn't want to mention the phone call just yet.

"You still plugging away on that guy?"

"Yup. The story about the settlement and the money owed to the county, I'm kinda stalled on that one. Trying to find another way to get at it."

Halloran rubbed his chin. "So, you want somebody who's been around long enough to remember when Raposa came to town."

He put on his glasses and grabbed a grimy-looking Rolodex

from a corner of his desk. He thumbed through it, mumbling, and finally found the card he was looking for.

"Here you go. Mel Brewster. He's an old drinking buddy of mine from back in the days before I got sober." He hesitated, shot her an embarrassed look, then carried on. "Anyway, Mel goes way back. He knows everyone."

———➤

Digger called the number Halloran had given her, letting it ring and ring.

She was about to hang up when a gravelly voice answered. She introduced herself, saying she was a colleague of Dan Halloran.

"Hey, how the hell is he? Staying out of trouble?"

The man's East Texas twang reminded Digger of her grandfather.

"He's still the life of the newspaper. Anyway, he suggested you might be able to help me with a story I'm doing. It's about people who have been involved with the development of Las Vistas over the years. He said you'd probably know some of the background and the people."

"Oh, sure, sure. I think I know just about everybody who's been around here for the past thirty years. And if I don't know 'em, they probably aren't worth knowing." He chuckled at his own humor. "Tell you what, why don't we get together over a beer? I got plenty of stories I can tell you. Does six thirty work for you?"

Digger considered. Was this a come-on? Did he think she was like one of the TV reporters, all makeup and manicured nails?

"Where do you want to meet?" she said after a moment.

"Well, now, I don't live in Las Vistas anymore. Moved out years ago when it started to get too big. I'm out toward Los Jardines. There's a little place called Silvio's. You know it?"

"No, but I can find it easy enough. Okay. See you later."

———➤

Twilight was approaching as Digger drove to the meeting with Mel Brewster. For a few moments the sun touched the mountains, turning them pinky-orange, fading to purple, then blue. When she spotted Silvio's on the side of the road, she wondered how she hadn't noticed it before. It was a low stucco building with a porch along the front side and a faded Schlitz beer sign protruding from the wall above the front door. It looked deserted, but she parked anyway.

She pushed open the door and stood for a moment peering into the gloom. The ceiling was low, with thick wooden beams—vigas—and wood-paneled walls. Lights glowed faintly above a pool table to her right. The few tables at the edge of the room were empty.

The only customer she could see was sitting at the bar with his back to the door, deep in conversation with the man behind the counter. Digger nearly stumbled on the uneven brick floor as she walked toward the bar.

"Mel?"

The man swung around and looked her up and down.

"You the reporter gal? Dan Halloran's friend?" "That's me."

He looked faintly disappointed. "Well, come on up here and we'll get you fixed up. What are you havin'?"

"Corona, if they have it."

Mel turned to the barman. "Pedro, you got one of them Mexican beers for the lady?"

Pedro gave him a long-suffering look. "*Si, por que no?*"

Under the fluorescent glare of the light behind the bar, Digger noticed Mel's flushed, leathery complexion. No wonder he'd wanted to meet in a bar. He probably spent most of his days here. She remembered Halloran's comment about the two of them being drinking buddies.

She guessed Mel was about seventy. He wore a cowboy hat, turquoise shirt and black jeans, with a fist-sized belt buckle emblazoned with cow horns. Digger figured it was probably a long time since Mel had seen a cow.

When Pedro brought the beer, Digger asked if they could sit at one of the tables. In the corner there was just enough light to take notes.

She eased into the conversation, asking generally about Mel's background, how he had come to Las Vistas, what projects he'd worked on. True to his word, he rattled off one anecdote after another. Digger had never heard of some of the characters, and she mentally filed away the details as grist for future stories.

Eventually she slipped in a question about Raposa, wondering when he had come on the scene.

"Oh, Mr. Big Shot—at least that's who he thinks he is. That guy just popped up and suddenly he was into everything."

"Where did he come from?"

Mel leaned forward over the table, so close she could smell his beery breath.

"Seems to me like I heard he was from Michigan. Yeah, that's it, one of them towns that's like the name of a car." He paused, thinking for a minute, rubbing his chin. "Pontiac. That's it. But I believe he went to Arizona 'fore he came here. Think he was into real estate deals over there. Then he showed up here 'bout twelve years ago.

"I remember one time we were both at some kinda convention in Dallas. There was a social event in the evening, and Raposa walked in with this woman just hangin' on him. Real looker, ya know, blond, tight dress, mm-hmm." He paused as though he were mentally licking his lips at the memory. "Anyway, 'bout halfway through the evening they start yellin' at each other right there in the bar.

Man, I thought one of 'em was about to haul off and punch

the other. Then she just hauls ass outta the place. I could hear her heels just clickin' away on that floor."

Mel took another swallow of his beer, emptying the bottle. His breath gave her the creeps. She shuddered inwardly, then focused on her notepad.

"Do you know anything about Rancho Milagro? I heard Raposa was involved with that somehow."

Mel guffawed.

"Yeah! That mess. He and some friend of his—a guy from Arizona—came to me asking if I'd be willing to come in with them. I wasn't interested. But they gave me the spiel anyway, showing me drawings and a fancy-looking proposal they were going to take to the county. They had it all worked out—or thought they did." He laughed again. "Later they suckered the county folks into approving money to pay for sewers and suchlike. What they didn't do was make sure the land was sound. That and not expecting the financial crash. 'Course, a lot of people were stupid about that. But not me! I got out of everything in time."

He gave a sloppy grin, shoved aside the beer bottles, leaned closer, laid a hand on her arm, and looked at her with a hungry leer. Digger wondered just how many beers he'd had before she arrived.

"Now, how about you and me?" he said. "You stick around and we could have us a real good time. You ready for another beer?"

Digger pulled her arm away and shoved the notebook into her backpack. "Thanks, but I've got to get back to town."

She fled out the door, ran to her car, jumped in, and locked the doors. She felt like ripping off the jacket where he'd touched her sleeve.

It was fully dark now, with a sliver of a moon hanging just above the crest.

She looked to her right and saw the glimmer of lights from Los Jardines. Instinctively she drove toward them, following the narrow road into the village to Abuela's house. No sign of Maria's car, but she parked anyway, walked up to the front door, and knocked.

It took a while before the door finally opened and Abuela peered out cautiously. Recognizing Digger, she opened the door wider.

"Come in, come in. Why haven't I seen you since Christmas?"

"Oh, I've been busy with work. I just happened to have a meeting near here and thought I'd drop by."

Abuela led Digger into the small living room and gestured for her to sit by the fireplace.

"You'll have some hot chocolate? I always have some before I go to bed. I'm old, so I go to bed early."

"That sounds wonderful," Digger said, touched by her kindness. "I haven't had hot chocolate since my mom made it when I was a kid."

Abuela disappeared into the kitchen. Digger hunched close to the fire, soaking in the warmth, even though the night wasn't yet cold. Abuela returned with a tray bearing two mugs of hot chocolate and a plate of *bizcochitos*, crisp cookies flavored with anise and cinnamon.

Digger took a sip of chocolate. The thick, sweet, milky smell of it brought back a flood of memories. "I remember my mom used to make this on Sunday nights in the winter."

Abuela eyed her over the rim of the mug, nodding thoughtfully. "Maria is at one of her meetings tonight. She told me about your family. I am sorry about your parents."

Digger set down her hot chocolate. She knew now why she'd come here instead of heading back to Las Vistas.

"I know Maria is upset with me. I was kind of hoping to see her here." She released a sigh. "Last time we talked, I told her about meeting the guy who caused the accident. It was weird, after all these years. Maria asked me so many questions. I know she wanted to help, but I had a hard time talking about it."

Abuela sat perfectly still in her armchair, her dark eyes focused on Digger, waiting for her to continue.

Digger stared at the fire, the flames now subsiding to a red glow over the logs. It seemed easier to start at the beginning. Once she started, the words came flooding out. She talked about growing up in Albuquerque, going camping with her parents, the day of the accident, Grandma and Grandpa arriving late at night, the whispered words, the wailing and tears. The funeral.

She recalled the distinctive smell of her grandparents' house in Houston, so gray and gloomy after the bright skies of New Mexico. So silent. Grandma Betty's grim, grief-stricken face as she mourned her eldest son. Grandma Betty didn't believe much in talking. She'd grown up on a farm in Ireland where hard work was the only choice. No warmth in her family; you just got on with life.

Digger sat thinking for a minute, looking at the fire. "I care about Maria," she said, finally. "I do. It's just hard in so many ways. Part of it is me and part of it's the way we met—over this road business. Right now I can't be close to her in the way she wants. I want it too, but I don't know how to handle it."

Abuela sipped from her mug and let the silence hang between them. The fire crackled. Somewhere nearby, a neighbor's dog barked. After a while she said, "It's okay, you know. We survive. We find new ways of living, don't we?"

Abuela's voice was the voice of an old woman, like a wooden tool worn smooth by years of handling.

"Maria, she's had her own struggles," Abuela continued. "But she found a home here. You can find a home here too, if you want. My door is always open."

Digger felt the shift inside her happening again. Abuela's

house, her world: it was claiming her heart. Something that had been torn asunder was knitting itself together. She finished her cocoa and set down the mug. She had started to rise out of her chair when there was the sound of a car outside. Moments later the front door opened and Maria walked in. She spotted Digger and stopped.

"I thought that was your car."

Maria was wearing a long, loose top over an ankle-length skirt, with a silver choker around her neck. Her dark eyes glittered in the reflected light from the fire.

"I happened to be nearby and thought I'd say hello," Digger said.

She was aware of Abuela's glance darting back and forth between them.

Maria just stood in the doorway looking at her. Digger stood up.

"I should be going." She looked at Abuela. "Thank you for the hot chocolate." Then she picked up her bag and moved toward the door.

"I'll walk you to your car," Maria said.

They left Abuela sitting by the fire and stepped out into the darkness.

Outside, Digger took hold of Maria's hand and turned to her. She laid her face on Maria's neck, breathing in the scent of her skin, listening to the night sounds, aware of the glow of light from Abuela's living room.

"I'm sorry it has to be this way," she said.

Maria gently took Digger's face in her hands. "This won't last forever. We'll get past this. I have to keep fighting, and you have to keep being who you are." She wrapped her arms around Digger, gripped her tightly, then released her.

"Soon, okay?"

"Soon."

CHAPTER TWENTY

WHEN SHE GOT to the newsroom the following morning, Digger went straight to Halloran's desk and found him eating a bagel.

"Yes?" he mumbled, brushing at his mustache. Digger grabbed an empty chair and pulled it close.

"Okay. So, what's the deal here? You send me off to meet that old lech without any warning?"

Halloran burst out laughing, nearly choking on a mouthful. "Oh, God. Mel never changes. Don't tell me he put the moves on you?" Halloran continued to laugh, tears seeping from behind his glasses.

"Yup. Old beer-breath thought we'd make a great couple. I had to skip out of there before he got me in his clutches. But he did give me some useful background on Raposa. Can you still do one of those LexisNexis searches for information on people?"

"Mmmh." Halloran swallowed the last bite of bagel and wiped his mouth. "It depends. I still have access, but Thompson made it clear that there has to be a pretty good reason. Another cost-saving measure. That's the way things are going around here."

Back at her own desk, Digger opened the court records website and typed in Raposa's name. When she'd looked at his records before, she'd noticed a divorce but at the time it hadn't struck her as important. The marriage had lasted only a few months, and there was little information about the settlement. Yet the voice on the phone had said to start with the divorce.

She found it again and began poring over the details. There was something familiar about the wife's name, Phyllis Lynton Raposa, but she couldn't place it. Reading on, she noted a reference to Dallas. Maybe Phyllis was the woman Mel had seen Raposa argue with so publicly. The time frame seemed plausible, and it didn't sound as though Mel knew Raposa well enough to have met his wife before the conference. She wondered if Phyllis was the voice on the phone.

Digger kept reading. She'd worked her way through several more entries when something about the wording of a sentence, a reference to "previous assets," struck her as odd. Then it hit home. Raposa had obviously been married before Phyllis. The caller must have meant a different divorce, probably when Raposa lived in Michigan. Digger practically ran across the newsroom to find Halloran.

"Have you got anything for me yet?"

Halloran grimaced. "You young people. No patience."

"Ha, ha! Like you haven't worked on deadline for forty years."

"Yeah, but in the old days we could still smoke at our desks. Come on, I'll print it and we can pick it up on the way out. I need a cigarette."

Digger was itching with excitement as she followed Halloran to the printers. She waited impatiently while they watched a couple of proofs for the Friday magazine to come out and then nearly snatched the report from Halloran when he picked it up.

"Uh-uh!" He swatted her away and gestured. "We need to take this outside. I wasn't really supposed to do this for you, and I don't want Swenson or Thompson to get wind of it."

Finally, when they were seated on the smokers' bench, well

away from the newsroom door, Halloran handed over the sheaf of papers.

Digger rapidly scanned the pages. There was a lot of general stuff about cars, insurance, a mortgage in Las Vistas, one in Arizona. She was hoping to find a connection to Pontiac, whether it was the name of a person, a company, or even a phone number.

On the fourth page she found it: Henderson & Raposa, commercial real estate. A few lines below, she saw the partners' names, John F. Raposa and Joan A. Henderson. There was an address and a phone number. Digger guessed it was probably defunct, but it was worth a try.

"This is great stuff. Thanks, Dan, I owe you one."

Halloran exhaled a cloud of smoke. "Naw, I owed you one. I shoulda warned you about Mel. He always had a reputation. Glad I could help."

Digger tried the Pontiac phone number and, as expected, heard a recorded message saying it was no longer working. A quick search of state records showed that the company's license had lapsed years before. She tried the Michigan court records site, wondering if it would show a divorce. It did. Turned out Raposa and Joan Henderson were partners in life as well as business. By the number of filings in the case, it looked as if the proceedings had been long and contentious. It could take a while to wade through them. On a hunch, she looked up the Pontiac newspaper, the *Oakland Press*, and called the editorial number, hoping there might be a reporter who had come across Henderson & Raposa.

She first had to explain to the receptionist that New Mexico was indeed in the United States. She was put on hold, then passed to several different people, each time having to repeat her request. Finally a man's voice snapped, "Business desk, Matthews here."

Digger gave her brief speech about Raposa and looking into his past because of his prominence in Las Vistas.

There was a long pause, so long that Digger thought he'd hung up. The man on the other end of the line finally cleared his throat.

"I'm assuming you've done your homework about Joan Henderson," he said.

Digger cursed herself for trying to take a shortcut instead of reading the divorce documents. She decided to wing it as best she could. "I know she was married to Raposa as well as being his business partner and that they divorced in 2003."

Matthews gave an impatient sigh. "So, basically, you don't know very much."

Digger gritted her teeth. Every now and then she came across guys like this. They got off on being condescending with women reporters.

"I just thought you might be able to fill me in with some local knowledge that might not show up in the court filings. If that's too much . . ."

"No. Wait." Matthews's tone softened. "I've covered commercial real estate longer than anybody should have to in this lifetime. I always thought Johnny Raposa was involved in some shady stuff, but I could never get what I needed to do the story."

He sighed again. "Anyway, Joan Henderson came from big money out of Detroit. I mean big money. Johnny Raposa was doing remodeling jobs and office build-outs. I'm not sure how they got together, but suddenly, in the late nineties, they were this power couple doing all kinds of projects. Joan had political connections through her family, and rumors swirled about the way they'd landed a couple of no-bid contracts. We looked into them. So did the state attorney general, but they could never come up with any solid evidence that Henderson or Raposa had bribed anyone. You know how it goes.

"Anyway, a couple of years after Bush came into office, the

local rumor mill went crazy. Apparently Joan was having an affair with some woman they'd hired to do interior design. Well, you can imagine how that went down. Raposa was a macho kind of guy. They had a very high-profile divorce, lots of headlines. You can probably still find the stories online, and a lot of it will be in the court records. The upshot of it all was, Raposa landed a big fat settlement and lit out of town. I think he went to Arizona first, but you say he's been in New Mexico for a few years?"

"Yup. He's been here a while. He's quite the mover and shaker around town.

Sounds like the divorce was what got him the seed money to take off. Thanks for your time. I really appreciate it."

"Always glad to help out a young reporter." Matthews actually made it sound genuine.

———➤———

Digger was puzzled. The mysterious caller had indicated Raposa had something pretty serious in his past. Based on what Matthews had said, maybe it was worth finding out more about Joan Henderson.

From the documents in the divorce case, Joan Henderson came across as one of those highly accomplished, driven women who climb corporate ladders swiftly. Only, in Henderson's case, she had inherited business and political connections from her family. She never denied Raposa's accusations about her affair; she just claimed they were irrelevant. Raposa actually sounded like he got the worst of it, except financially.

Records Digger was able to find showed Raposa started an LLC in Mesa, Arizona, which operated in the greater Phoenix area for five years and then closed. That corresponded with the dates she'd heard mentioned regarding when he'd come to Las Vistas. That was back when the economy was booming and building permits were practically flowing out of city hall.

So, who was Phyllis Lynton? Digger reread the brief documents in the New Mexico divorce. She stared at the name, grasping for the connection. Why was it familiar? Then it came to her: the gym. Digger remembered a yoga class she'd taken once with a three-day membership offer. The instructor's name had been Phyllis, and she'd been tall and blond like a magazine model. What was it Mel had said? He'd called her "a real looker."

Maybe it was time to try out a few sun salutations.

The online gym schedule showed Phyllis taught at six. Figuring she might be able to catch her right after the class, Digger managed to reach Southwest Fitness shortly before seven. She chatted with the girl at the reception desk for a few minutes, asking about membership deals, while keeping an eye on the door to the yoga studio. Soon after seven the door opened and people emerged carrying yoga mats. Digger ambled over to peer inside and spotted Phyllis packing a gym bag. She kicked off her shoes and walked in.

"Hi," she said. "Phyllis? Phyllis Lynton?"

Phyllis, bent over struggling to zip up the bag, didn't respond.

"I'm Elizabeth Doyle with the *Courier*. I'm covering the city elections, and I wondered if you could help me with a couple of questions about Johnny Raposa. He's been very influential in the past couple of mayoral elections, and—"

Phyllis Lynton dropped the bag and swung around to face Digger.

"I was wondering when you'd show up."

There was no mistaking the voice.

CHAPTER TWENTY-ONE

"Bitter, bitter woman," Digger said, shaking her head.

She was sitting on the smokers' bench next to Halloran and Rex, watching a tumbleweed blow across the parking lot. After the bizarre conversation she'd had with Phyllis Lynton the night before, she needed to talk to someone.

"Sounds like she was either jealous of Raposa getting so much money out of the first wife or just mad at him for dumping her," Rex said.

Digger let out an exasperated sigh. "You should have heard her. She went on a rant that must have lasted fifteen minutes. I mean, yoga teachers talk all about being in the breath and calmness, but this was none of that. She was full-on rage.

Apparently Raposa charmed her away from her life in Arizona, then ran after other women. Then, in the divorce, he screwed her out of getting any of the money he'd made. I think she's just one of those crazies who thinks we can put a story in the paper about how they were done wrong. God, I hope I never have to deal with her again." She shuddered.

Halloran took another puff of his cigarette and made a face as he burst into a fit of coughing. When he'd recovered, he looked at her and said, "Don't be hard on yourself. It's always worth checking out a tip. What you did learn is that Raposa is ambitious and doesn't let things stand in his way. Keep an eye on him during the election campaign."

Digger shrugged, glad of the support, and headed inside. About two hours later the bombshell hit. A memo from Thompson announced a meeting in the conference room. The nervousness around the room was palpable as they waited for the editor to show up. Thompson strode in, his face even grimmer than usual. Rex, standing next to Digger, muttered under his breath, "This doesn't look good."

Thompson began with a painfully awkward speech about how great the staff was, how hardworking, all their achievements, the innovations they'd made to keep up with changing times. Blah, blah, blah. Finally, he cleared his throat and cast a glance around the room.

"I asked you here today because the publisher informed me yesterday that he has decided to put the paper up for sale." He paused, looking uncomfortable. "Now, that won't mean any immediate changes, but I wanted you all to be prepared in case you face questions out in the community."

"Oh, that's rich," Rex muttered. "We care so much about the community. What about us? The people who actually work here? You dick."

Digger felt as if she'd been hit with a giant hammer. Everybody had talked about something like this; it was happening all over the country, and there'd been all kinds of warning signs. But like Rex and Halloran and the others, she'd kept putting it to the back of her mind. Each time the floor sank a little more beneath her feet, it steadied again and life went on. The new, shrunken world became the norm—until the next time.

This time was worse. It was as if the floor itself had fallen away.

Much as they all grumbled about the *Courier* and its dysfunctional management, it was their world. Digger looked around at the stunned faces of her colleagues.

"Have they got a prospective buyer in mind?" someone asked.

"Not as far as I know. This is all very preliminary," Thompson said. He dispensed a few "keep your chin up" platitudes and left.

"Well, I guess we'd better start polishing up our resumés," Vicky, the features writer, said sarcastically as she marched out.

Digger glanced over at Halloran. His craggy face looked like a deflated football. While the rest of the room erupted in a hubbub of mingled anguish and outrage, Halloran just got to his feet and made his way slowly to his desk as if he were sleepwalking. Digger followed him.

"Are you going to be all right? Should I call someone?"

He seemed not to hear. He was staring at his Rolodex, mumbling under his breath. Worried, Digger repeated the question.

"Call who?" he said. "I'm fifty-seven years old, divorced, no kids. I've been here thirty-four years, and I'm waiting for the results of a biopsy of this thing on my leg they think is cancerous." He pulled up one pant leg to reveal a bulging lump. Digger was shocked.

"If one of those big corporations buys this place," he said, "you can bet they'll get rid of people like me. I've seen it before. And that's if they find a buyer at all."

He stood up, brushed past her, and walked toward the door to the parking lot. "I'll see you tomorrow," he said, without looking back.

Digger made her way to her desk and sat there in a daze. The old feeling of being adrift, which had been so familiar as she was growing up, washed over her. This odd place, with its unique daily rhythms and its quirky characters, was a home of sorts.

She looked around, marveling that there was some semblance

of normalcy. Swenson was arguing with the photo editor, and phones were ringing. Like a well-oiled machine, they came in every day, did their jobs, and somehow put a paper out.

Today Digger had no daily story and no deadline to meet, so she followed Halloran's example and walked out. She drove to her apartment, put on her running clothes, and hit the trail. Pounding along in the warm spring air, she thought about Halloran, the ugly lump on his leg. All this time he'd said nothing. How did you deal with something like that? And if he had no job, no health insurance, what would that mean?

She kept running, sweat seeping down her face. What if the paper closed? What then? She thought about Tim. He'd seen it coming and bailed at the right time. He'd emailed that he'd gotten the job in Houston, but she'd heard nothing more. This might be a good time to call him. Maybe he could put in a word for her at the *Chronicle*.

But Houston—she'd left to make a new life here in New Mexico, where she felt a connection with the family she'd once had—before the accident.

Digger stopped and sat on a rock, looking out at the mesa and the distant mountains. It was one of those days when you could see for seventy miles into the bright, clear, high desert emptiness.

She thought about Maria. Recalling the last moment they'd had together, she ached for the feel of Maria's arms embracing her in the darkness. *If only.* She thought about Abuela and yearned for the warmth she felt in that tiny house.

CHAPTER TWENTY-TWO

KIMBLE WRINKLED HIS nose at the smell of gasoline. He was filling the Buick when he saw the panel truck bearing his rival's youthful image and the slogan, "Vote for Johnsen and be part of the future."

He watched the truck drive up and down the busy street and scowled. How was the man raising money for publicity like that? Last night Kimble had gone over his finances with Dillon, his campaign manager, and thought there had to be some mistake. So far, Raposa and a couple of the other developers he'd relied on before hadn't come through, not a dime. After the frustrating meeting with Raposa at the golf club, he'd still hoped they had an understanding. With difficulty, he'd resisted the urge to pick up the phone and call the developer. No, he would not beg, but he had to do something, and quick.

Later, as Kimble stared at his plate of meatloaf, canned green beans, and mashed potatoes and gravy, he was still thinking about Johnsen. It was Tuesday night. His wife, Imelda, had been making the same meatloaf dinner every Tuesday for thirty-three years. He blamed himself for this. The week before their wedding, she had shyly confided that she didn't know how to cook, and he'd casually mentioned it to his mother. *Oh, irreversible, thoughtless error!* His mother had proudly bequeathed to his new bride her cherished copy of the Betty Crocker cookbook. Oh, how he hated that book, with its red-and-white floral-patterned cover and its loose-leaf pages filled with 1950s recipes. Monday nights it was macaroni and cheese, Thursday nights ham loaf, Fridays tuna casserole. And then there were the inevitable bilious green Jell-O salads.

"Dear?" Imelda said. "Dear, you're not listening."

Of course he wasn't listening. She'd held forth on the same topic almost as many times as she'd served meatloaf.

"Since your term as mayor here is ending, have you thought any more about what we talked about?" She looked at him brightly over her plate. "I mean, have you thought any more about how we could go back to California? I know the kids would love to have us closer. You know how the weather here is bad for my allergies—and the drivers here in New Mexico! I'm afraid every time I have to get on the freeway—half the time they don't signal when they're going to change lanes—and they overtake you on the right. I'm sure we could find a little place that would suit us, you know, something outside San Diego—El Cajon, maybe?" She paused while she loaded a forkful of mashed potatoes into her mouth.

Kimble said nothing. They'd had the same conversation—if you could call it a conversation when Imelda did most of the talking—a hundred times. That made no difference. Imelda continued, her eyes focusing dreamily through the window at the distant mountains as if she could see California.

"You remember Angela," Imelda went on, "one of my friends from the fellowship group? She said there's new homes going up all the time. Of course, we could maybe go into an apartment, I don't mind. Dear, are you listening? I mean, coming to New

Mexico was your idea. I said I'd try it for a while, but really, this place is not what I expected."

"Imelda," he said firmly, "You know as well as I do that we moved here because of the cost of living. We could afford a house here. I'm retired now, dear, and we simply cannot afford to go back to California. I know it's disappointing. We can go back to visit the boys, but we have to make the best of it here." He'd made the same reply a hundred times. It made no difference.

Imelda set down her knife and fork and gave him that look, the one that reminded him of a defecating baby. Not that he'd had that much to do with babies and diapers—he'd left that to Imelda—but he remembered that expression of pained concentration on their infant sons' faces.

As he looked at her, he tried to remember the young woman he'd met at the church picnic. She had been so shy, so eager to please. How had she become so— he struggled for a word—so desiccated? That was it: she was like an apple left out in the sun. He wondered if Imelda could ever be truly happy. She hadn't really liked California either; she'd complained the neighbors were unfriendly, there was too much traffic, they could barely make ends meet.

He said nothing, waiting for her to recompose her face. Long ago they'd worked out a way of being together, like cogs in a machine, the teeth fitting snugly as they went round and round, propelling the days forward.

"Jack," she said finally, "you're thinking about the election, aren't you?"

She paused, waiting for him to respond. When he didn't, she rearranged her expression and said brightly, "Whatever happened to your plans for the drainage project? You were all about that just a few months ago. Did anything ever get done?"

Bless her, Kimble thought. The drainage project was just the thing to talk about at the candidate forum! In his anguish over seeing the panel truck, Kimble had put the chamber of commerce event out of his mind. It was still two days away, time enough to get Dillon on to it.

Already his mind was buzzing. Johnsen didn't understand the drainage project or why it was critical, and Kimble knew just how he could use that to skewer the simpering pup. That would be his card: he would show voters that Johnsen didn't care, that he wasn't prepared to help them avoid disaster when the next rainstorm hit. Kimble had plenty of pictures from last summer. They'd make great photos for campaign flyers.

Excited, Kimble made a show of finishing his dinner and went to call Dillon.

They met later that evening at Dillon's studio apartment. Kimble loathed having to meet there; the place was messy and smelled of unwashed clothes. The computer paraphernalia crammed into the tiny space blasted out heat, making the smell worse. Kimble put up with these discomforts because he valued the young man's enthusiasm for politics and his graphic design skills.

Kimble stood awkwardly, waiting for Dillon to indicate where he could sit, but the young man didn't notice. He was already seated and bent over his keyboard, gazing intently at his computer screen. The only other chair in the room was piled high with rumpled clothing. Kimble lowered himself gingerly onto the edge of the unmade bed.

"I think you understand where I'm coming from on this," he said. "Some of the people who backed me in my previous campaign, people I counted on to be loyal because I've looked out for their interests—some of those people are now supporting my opponent. I need to hit back. I need flyers or posters or something that will show that this man Johnsen is just not right for Las Vistas."

Dillon swung around, head cocked to one side, eyes bright behind his thick-lensed glasses.

"Are we talking negative stuff here?"

Kimble closed his eyes. The almost gleeful expression on Dillon's face disturbed him. He wished Johnsen no harm. The man was young, inexperienced, and, frankly, ignorant. But there was an earnestness about him. He meant well. Still—Kimble thrust out his jaw—he had to win this election. He had to make sure Las Vistas was safe. And that man Raposa! He thought about the developer's breezy manner during their recent lunch. The man had no integrity!

"Yes," he said gruffly, "I want something that will really get people's attention. Is that clear?"

Dillon nodded, smiling.

Within a couple of hours, he had produced a mock-up of a flyer that accused Johnsen of being an outsider in bed with developers who cared nothing about the plight of those Las Vistas citizens at risk of being flooded out of their homes. He even added a dramatic photo showing Kimble holding his arms out to a small crowd as water gushed down a residential street.

"That ought to do it," Dillon smirked.

———▶———

Johnsen spotted something on the lawn when he drove the family back from Mass. He wasn't sure what it was, but he resented anything disfiguring the small plot of grass that he so carefully nurtured against the harsh elements. While his wife and kids clambered out of the car, he walked over to inspect. As soon as he picked it up, he realized it was a flyer with a picture of the mayor looking his most Biblical, hands outstretched to a crowd of bedraggled people standing in a flooded street in the pouring rain. The slogan beneath it shouted, "Kimble cares, Johnsen doesn't."

Waves of humiliation, hurt, and righteous anger surged inside him. How could anyone accuse him of not caring? He had plans for Las Vistas, plans he believed would make it an even better place for families like his own.

"Honey! Honey! What's keeping you?"

The sound of his wife's voice fueled his indignation. He crumpled the flyer into a ball and threw it toward the street. But as he watched it fly, he caught sight of the neighbor's yard and the telltale rectangle of colored paper lying on the lawn. They were everywhere; no escaping. How would he explain it to Connie? And the kids? He imagined how they'd be teased at school. Tears pricked his eyes.

As if on cue, his six-year-old daughter Mary appeared, no doubt sent to summon him to breakfast.

"Daddy, what's this?" She picked up the ball of paper, spread it open and studied it. Mary was learning to read.

"That's our name, isn't it, Daddy? What does this mean?" Johnsen grabbed the crumpled flyer and stuffed it into his pocket.

"It's just nonsense, sweetie. Just nonsense. Come inside and we'll have pancakes."

After breakfast Johnsen stole away on the pretext of getting the car washed.

Once away from the house, he pulled out his phone and looked up Raposa's number. He stared at it for a moment, a sick feeling in his stomach. Calling Raposa played right into what the flyer accused him of. But who could he talk to? It was Johnny Raposa who had encouraged him to run, and it was mostly Raposa's donations that were funding the campaign. He took a deep breath and punched in the number. The developer picked up right away.

"Johnny, have you seen these flyers?" Johnsen realized his voice sounded shaky.

"Dave, don't worry about it," Raposa answered matter-of-factly.

"But I do worry. This could really hurt my wife and kids. I'm not sure I signed up for this."

"Dave, don't let this get you rattled. This kind of thing happens all the time. Kimble's afraid, and he's gonna do anything he can to fight back. Looks like he's focused on that whole drainage scheme thing he was pushing."

"Well, he's got a point there, we do have a problem. I—"

"Don't even go there. You gotta stand your ground. The fix he's proposing would end up costing taxpayers plenty. That's what you gotta keep telling people. Voting for Kimble means higher taxes. That's how you hit back. You got it?"

Johnsen wasn't sure he liked Raposa's tone, and he hesitated to answer. Raposa let the silence hang for a moment, then went on. This time his voice was soft and coaxing. "Look, there's a lot of people out there counting on you, Dave. Believe me, I've heard them talking. They like that you're young and you've got a family, and they can identify with all that."

"Okay. I got it."

CHAPTER TWENTY-THREE

The Las Vistas Chamber of Commerce always held mayoral candidate forums in a former elementary school. Digger hated the smell of cleaning fluid that clung to everything.

She'd arrived half an hour before the forum was scheduled to begin so that she could keep track of who showed up. As people trickled in, she recognized several city council meeting regulars. Old George winked at her and made his way through the crowd to sit beside her. There was Sally Jenkins, who had taken to speaking at every meeting. She was still upset about the storm last summer. People who didn't clean up after their dogs in local parks was another of her pet gripes.

Her husband Al was there too, still wearing his Vietnam veteran ball cap. Digger recognized several more faces from the day she and Rex had gone out to cover Kimble's response to the storm. An anonymous source had thoughtfully sent her Kimble's campaign flyer, refreshing her memory.

She found a seat near the front, where she could be sure not to miss anything. Where was Rex? He was supposed to be taking photos of the event. She spotted him slipping through the door at the back of the room. Maria came in right behind him. Digger's pulse quickened. Just then a voice boomed out over the microphone, triggering a feedback screech.

Jimmy Jordan, the chamber chair, was a burly man with a florid face and ingratiating smile. Some people called him Jolly Jim. Right now he looked embarrassed and flustered as he wrestled with the mic.

"Sorry about that, ladies and gentlemen. I'm so glad to see you all here tonight to listen to our mayoral candidates. Jack Kimble, to my right, is seeking reelection to a second term as mayor. On my left is Dave Johnsen, who has served as a city councilor for the past two years.

"I want to remind you that the chamber does not make any endorsements. Tonight's forum will be conducted the way we've always done. Each candidate will have two minutes to introduce himself and talk briefly about his vision for Las Vistas and his plans if elected. Then we have a list of ten questions submitted by members of the public. Each candidate will have a minute to give his answer to each question. After that we will allow a few questions from the floor, as time allows. I will flip a coin to decide who begins."

Jordan pulled a coin from his pocket and tossed it into the air. Kimble called heads, Johnsen tails. Kimble won.

The mayor unfolded his tall, lean frame from the chair and stood up to the mic. His hair and beard were freshly trimmed, and he wore a brown tweed sport coat and a bolo tie. He gazed out at the crowd like a pastor preparing to deliver a sermon.

"Good evening, everybody," he began. "It has been my honor to serve the citizens as mayor of Las Vistas for the past four years. To me, the position of mayor is not just a job, it is a calling. When you, the people of this city, elected me as your mayor, I believe you entrusted me with your safety and welfare. Before I came to New Mexico, I was for many years the pastor of a house of worship in California. I cared deeply about the members of that community, as I now care about residents of Las Vistas. I believe in doing what is right for this city and for every man, woman, and child who lives here. My opponent is new to the city, and he's untested. But, as you saw in the storm last summer, I've been there for you in times of crisis."

As he paused for a breath, Jolly Jim interrupted. "Thank you, Mayor Kimble. Now we'll hear from our other candidate, Councilor Johnsen."

Johnsen stood up, squared his shoulders, and beamed a class-president, homecoming-king smile. In his navy blazer and tan slacks, he looked fit and youthful. Digger heard Old George give an approving murmur from his seat beside her.

"Hi, everybody! If you don't know me already, I'm Dave Johnsen. I'm the city councilor for District 2, and I want to give a shout-out to all my constituents out there."

He waved at the audience.

"I'm the guy who helped get you the speed bumps on Spring Avenue and the crosswalk signals by the elementary school. So you know I'm the kind of guy who listens and cares. Sure, I grew up in Ohio, but a lot of us here are from out of state. That doesn't mean we don't understand what matters in Las Vistas."

Johnsen went on to talk briefly about schools and jobs and how growth would benefit everyone. When he finished, Jolly Jim leaned in to his microphone, smiling at the audience.

"Now it's time for questions. Each candidate will have a minute to respond. My assistant here will keep time." He gestured toward a woman in the front row. "We want everything to proceed as smoothly as possible, so please, no interruptions, no heckling. We will have time for some questions from the floor at the end."

He began by reading a question about the city's animal control ordinance. Digger was sure Sally Jenkins had submitted that question. She settled in for an hour of tedium as they debated the nitty-gritty grievances of suburban life.

When it was Kimble's turn to respond to the questions, he used every opportunity to remind people about his record as mayor: street cleanup initiatives, a program for the homeless, a drop in property crime rates, and on and on.

Johnsen, by contrast, kept talking about schools and kids and families. He outlined his vision for Las Vistas as a city of growth, new jobs, exciting events. On the last question, some obscure detail about zoning requirements, he went off topic to hammer Kimble on the drainage project, accusing him of wanting to drive up taxes.

Kimble looked like a dog straining at the leash, glaring at Johnsen as Jolly Jim wrapped up question time so he could invite the candidates to make closing remarks.

At that point, Kimble leapt to his feet. "Make no mistake," he boomed. "When a storm brought rivers of mud flowing down your streets and floodwaters pouring into your homes, damaging your property, ruining your cherished possessions, and threatening the lives of your pets"—he stretched out his arms as if embracing the crowd—"I was there for you!" He paused, letting his words sink in. Then he leaned forward, his voice soft and coaxing. "Past city leaders let you down. They approved home permits in areas prone to flooding." Then he boomed, "I will not betray you with false promises! I have been working with contacts in state and local government on a plan that will make Las Vistas safe! It's not a Band-Aid solution. It's a comprehensive plan that will prevent this kind of thing from ever happening again."

Kimble rose to his full height again. Like a speaker at a revivalist rally, shaking with emotion, he intoned, "With my plan, the sounds of thunder and rain on a summer night will no longer strike fear into the hearts of Las Vistas citizens!"

Kimble's voice had been rising as he spoke. Now he pointed a finger accusingly at Johnsen and whispered hoarsely into the microphone, "And it's a plan my opponent rejects!"

He glared balefully at those gathered in the room. "If we do not act to protect ourselves, this city will suffer!" he thundered, seeming more than ever like an Old Testament prophet.

Old George grunted. "Kimble's just shot himself in the foot," he whispered to Digger.

Johnsen looked like an earnest Boy Scout as he sat smiling before he addressed the audience in a folksy tone. "Like I said before, I care about everyone here in Las Vistas. I care about the cost of living and how much tax people have to pay. And Mayor Kimble's so-called plan is going to hit people's wallets."

Johnsen paused while a few heads in the audience nodded.

"Yes, that's right," he continued. "You get it, don't you? Families need to be able to feed and clothe their kids; our seniors need be able to buy prescription medicines to stay healthy. Raising taxes to pay for some scheme to fix a problem that we may never see again in our lifetimes is just going to hurt Las Vistas. Is that what you want, folks?"

Shouts erupted all over the room. Sally Jenkins was standing, shaking a fist at Kimble.

"We don't need your high-dollar drainage project! We can take care of ourselves. No more taxes!"

That's rich, Digger thought, *coming from the woman who was screaming for help when her house flooded last summer.* She sounded like one of those people who refused to evacuate before a hurricane and then demanded a rooftop rescue.

Al Jenkins took up the cry. "No more taxes!"

A third man sprang to his feet. Digger recognized him from council meetings as one of those who hated the drainage plan.

"Make those people in the flooded areas pay," he shouted. "You buy a fancy house on a dirt road, you're gonna have problems. They shoulda known better!"

The man next to him, his face screwed into a tight ball of wrinkles, stabbed a threatening finger at the mayor.

"Yeah, Mayor Kimble, we shouldn't have to pay to fix their problems!"

Chairs clattered to the floor as people rose in protest. An argument broke out in one corner as a woman shoved her way to the aisle.

"Ladies and gentlemen, order, please! Order!" Jolly Jim cried, but the shouting went on.

Kimble surveyed the chaos in disbelief. What were these people thinking?

Last summer they were begging for help. They just didn't understand the situation. Unless there was a real fix, it was going to cost everyone a lot more in the end.

Johnsen's mouth was wide open. For the first time, he realized he had a good chance at winning. It felt good. He saw his wife and daughter at the end of a row near the back and beamed at them.

Suddenly a voice called out from the back of the room. Maria stood on a chair, brandishing the "No Road" sign she waved at protest rallies.

"Councilor Johnsen," she shouted, her voice high and clear over the din. "Do you support the road extension project?"

A hush fell over the room. People recognized Maria as the woman who led the protests that disrupted rush-hour traffic.

Johnsen smiled confidently. "Why, yes, I do. I believe it will open up more of Las Vistas for development that will bring the things I think are good for the city—business and jobs."

"Is that all you care about?" Maria demanded. "How about

our culture? Our history? How about protecting our environment from developers who build in places that will be flooded, who sell houses to people who don't know any better?"

Johnsen looked bewildered, but before he could answer, the group around Maria began shouting, "No road, no road!"

"Get 'em outta here!" yelled a man Digger recognized as Raposa's golf course pal Danny Murphy. She scribbled notes, then pulled out her recorder to get quotes. Rex was everywhere, snapping photos as the confusion raged around them.

The microphone screeched, and she wheeled round to see Jolly Jim on his phone. He looked as if he was about to burst into tears, like a bullied child calling for his mom.

Moments later two police officers marched in. "Okay, folks, let's settle down!" they shouted, breaking through the melée. The noise quickly subsided.

Red-faced and sweating, Jolly Jim spoke hoarsely into the mic. "Well, our time is up. This has certainly been a lively exchange of views and sentiments about our community. That's why the chamber holds these forums. We all have a lot to think about before we cast our votes. I want to thank everyone for coming out tonight. Now please leave in an orderly fashion. We don't want any incidents."

Out in the parking lot, Digger looked for Maria. She spotted her getting into the old blue SUV.

"Hey, got a minute?"

"I thought you weren't supposed to be seen talking to me at places like this."

Digger grinned. "You spoke up at a public meeting. That gives me a legitimate reason." She leaned close. "Listen, I have to run and file something fast, but I wanted to give you a heads-up. After the way Kimble talked tonight, I think voters are going to be turned off. And you're right, Johnsen is getting a lot of money from developers like Raposa, so he's going to back that road project. If your group wants to stop it, they need to mobilize support for Kimble."

"Should you be telling me this?"

"Let's just say I'm passing on a friendly tip." Digger reached out and briefly touched Maria's shoulder. Maria gave her a grateful smile.

"Thanks," she said.

CHAPTER TWENTY-FOUR

DIGGER'S STORY RAN above the fold on the front page of the *Courier* the next day with a photo that showed the chaotic scene: angry faces, hands waving.

Kimble and Johnsen were there in the background, the mayor with an expression of bewildered disdain, his rival's face all lit up with happy astonishment.

But it was the opinion page that caused a sensation. That was where John Pfister, the *Courier*'s publisher, had chosen to tell readers of his plan to sell the newspaper. Digger suspected Thompson or one of the editors had been pressed into writing the piece, because no one had actually seen Pfister in about five years. The piece hit all the right notes, mentioning the decades-long history of the *Courier* in Las Vistas and including highlights of the newspaper's service to the community.

There was a hint of verbal hand-wringing in the way it explained the reason to sell, with references to changing conditions in the industry and the lack of an heir apparent to take over.

It wasn't long before the phones started ringing and the emails began flooding in. Some were outraged, most saddened.

Digger opened one email that began, "What are we going to do for news about the election?" She didn't recognize the writer's name, but it went on, "I couldn't make it to the candidate forum last night, so I was delighted to see your story today. Keep up the good work." Digger wanted to show it to Halloran but couldn't find him. She went back to her desk.

About eleven thirty, her cellphone sang out the bouncy salsa tune that indicated a call from Maria.

"So, when were you going to tell me?" Maria's voice had an unfamiliar edge to it.

"Tell you?"

"This news about the *Courier*. You must have known it, so why did I have to find out by reading the paper?"

The barely veiled anger was something new. Digger felt a chill grip her insides. She chewed on her lip, trying to figure out the best way to respond. Finally she asked, "Why are you so upset? I'm the one who could be losing a job."

"Why the hell didn't you tell me? I thought I could trust you."

Digger was shocked. Maria tended to be forceful, but she'd never felt that force directed at her before.

"We need to talk," Maria said. "Can you meet me for dinner at that place in Los Jardines?"

Reluctantly Digger agreed. She didn't like being pushed around.

Later, when she arrived at the restaurant, she sat for a moment in her car, remembering the blazing-hot day they had first met here last summer. Now the limbs of the cottonwood tree that hung over the coyote fence were bare of leaves. A dusting of blossoms still clung to a small ornamental cherry tree in the corner of the yard. Sheltered between the fence and the adobe, its dark, twisted branches had escaped the fury of the spring winds. Above, the sky was a thick, moist gray, a color so familiar to Digger from the near-constant rain and humidity of Houston.

Here in New Mexico, months went by with no rain. They didn't even call it rain: it was "precipitation." Digger recalled a morning in January when the sky had opened and she'd had to think for a moment before she remembered how to turn on her windshield wipers. It had been that long. Sometimes she ran the Subaru through the automatic car wash just to revel in the sight and sound of water pummeling the windshield.

While waiting in the restaurant parking lot, she rolled down the window to sniff the air, catching the smell of impending rain that only a desert dweller would recognize. Within moments the first drops splattered on the windshield, pattering then drumming on the roof of the car. She thought of the storm last summer and the way the water had clawed into the bare earth as if ripping flesh. Rain in the desert was a two-faced god, bringing life and destruction.

Maria's car pulled into the parking lot. They looked at each other through the fogged car windows, their faces distorted. Maria was the first to emerge, her clothes darkening as she splashed toward the doorway. Digger grabbed her backpack and made a dash for it. Inside, flames flickered in the corner fireplace, their light glimmering on the smooth-plastered walls. The same middle-aged waitress who'd served them before guided them to a table in the corner. Without even looking at the menu, Digger ordered a bowl of posole. It seemed like a night for chile-hot soup.

Maria, usually so confident, seemed tense and anxious. She ordered a single taco, then picked up the saltshaker and twirled it nervously in her hands. Digger waited.

"You know what I realized the other night?" Maria didn't wait for an answer. "I realized we could lose this fight."

Digger blew out a long weary breath. "Yeah. You could, especially if Johnsen wins."

Maria dropped the saltshaker. "I don't like Kimble either. I think he'd sell us out if it suited him. They're like all the rest of those people who came here from Ohio or New York or wherever. They don't understand the land. They just drive around it in cars, and that's what they'll do if that road gets built. Just drive right over the land and never feel it. You have to stop and get close to the earth and feel it to understand why it is important."

The waitress brought their food. Digger picked up a spoon and poked at the pale blobs of hominy floating in her soup, thinking.

"Change happens, Maria, one way or another, whether it's because of someone's greed, or a war, or a storm like we saw last summer."

Maria snorted angrily. "You sound like you're on their side."

Digger leaned back in her seat, closing her eyes. Suddenly she felt very tired.

"I guess I'm just looking at it the way I would for a story. Trying to see both sides. Whatever you think of the people who come to Las Vistas, they have their dreams too. If you think about it, the people who built the chapel, they were newcomers bringing a new culture—and they weren't exactly respectful of the Native American culture that was here before."

Maria was silent for a long time, staring at the untouched taco in front of her.

She seemed to be wrestling with her emotions. Finally she looked at Digger her eyes glistening.

"It's hard for me to admit—but what you say is right," she sighed, frustrated. "I get that Las Vistas will keep changing. More people will come here, and they'll want nice houses and shopping and all that shit. But can't Kimble or Johnsen, or whoever the hell wins this damn election, find another route for that road extension? If it goes through the way it's planned, the foundations will be practically on top of the historic site. It will be totally destroyed. People need to be albe to connect with the past, with what has been important to the generations before them."

Digger smiled. "Maybe that's the fight. If it looks like the road will be built, maybe you could at least get them to change the route."

Maria reached over and clasped Digger's hands in hers. "You do get it. That's what I like about you."

"Well, thank God. This is really hard for me too, you know."

They laughed. After a few bites, Maria set down her taco. "So, what is going to happen with you—with the newspaper?"

Digger shook her head. "I don't know. A couple of the old guys—friends of mine—they seem to think we young reporters will be okay, whoever buys the paper. But there's no guarantee the publisher will find a buyer these days.

Everyone in the business is very jittery now. My editor is a wreck. He's being ultra-cautious about stories."

"And you? What are you thinking?"

Digger leaned on her elbow, cradling her head in one hand. "I don't know. I just have to keep going. If it comes to it, I've got a friend in Houston who could maybe get me a job at the paper there." She looked up at Maria. "But I don't want to go. This is my home." There was so much more she wanted to say, but she couldn't risk it.

Maria reached for Digger's hands. "I'm so glad. I was afraid you'd just go."

"That's not part of my plan.

CHAPTER TWENTY-FIVE

THE JANGLING RINGTONE jolted Digger out of sleep. Groggy, she eyed the clock beside the bed. It was five in the morning. Who the hell was calling at this hour?

She reached for the phone. Wakened by the noise and sudden movement, Lady Antonia sprang into action, making a claw dive for Digger's feet under the covers.

"Ow!" Digger said into the phone. "I mean—hello?"

"Miss Doyle!"

An old man's voice. *Oh, that's right,* she thought. *Old people wake up this early.*

"Uh, what?"

"This is Alex Simpkin. Remember? You came to see me a while back."

Digger sat up, struggling to place the name and the voice. Oh yeah, the old guy with the oxygen tank and the farting dog.

"Yes, Mr. Simpkin, what can I do for you?"

"Well, I was having lunch with some of my old coworkers from the county treasurer's office," he began, in a chirpy tone. "We've been getting together every Monday at the Village Inn ever since I retired. Anyway, the subject of that settlement money owed to the county came up, and one of them let on that there's been some update on that. I thought it was important to tell you before anyone else got wind of it."

Digger grimaced. Lady Antonia had definitely drawn blood. She struggled to gather her thoughts. "Um, I thought it was still tied up in a lawsuit.

She climbed out of bed and stumbled to the living room to search for a pen and notepad. Lady Antonia followed, meowing a breakfast demand.

Simpkin went on, excitement in his scratchy voice. "My friend seems to think there's going to be an investigation. Apparently somebody must have found some documents and leaked them to law enforcement."

"Is Raposa involved?"

Simpkin was silent for a minute, and Digger could hear the hissing of his oxygen machine.

"From what I was told, money was funneled from his company to an out-of-state LLC to hide the assets."

Digger gasped. She was wide awake now. This was huge. "Look, Mr. Simpkin, is there some way you can point me to documents that confirm any of this?"

Again he was silent. *Pff, pff,* went the oxygen machine. Finally he breathed heavily into the phone and said in a conspiratorial tone, "I'll check with my contact and get back to you. If I haven't called by noon, call me back. Okay?"

"Sure. I'll be waiting."

Outside it was still dark. Swenson wouldn't go into the office until nine thirty or so. She wondered how early she could call him on his cell. He was not a morning person.

The next few hours were torture as she waited to hear from Simpkin, hoping he would call before she had a chance to talk to the editor.

She was pulling into the parking lot when her cell phone rang again. It was the old man. This time he sounded breathless.

"I have more for you. Can you write this down?"

He gave her the information she needed for making public records requests, painstakingly going over the details. He kept stopping and asking her to recite everything to make sure she had them right.

"That's all I can give you," he said at last. "And please, don't mention my name in any way."

"Of course. I can't thank you enough. Give Geraldine a pat for me, she's a sweet dog."

"You're too kind. Good luck."

Digger rushed to her desk and began work on the records requests. She worded them carefully, hoping county staffers wouldn't be able to find a reason to wiggle out of releasing the information.

Shortly after nine thirty she saw Swenson come in, shoulders slumped, battered knapsack on his back. He always brought his lunch and ate it at his desk. Digger gave him a few minutes to get settled and log in to his computer.

"What is it?" he asked, glancing up at her. "You look pretty pleased with yourself."

Words came tumbling out of her mouth as she told him about Simpkin's call, the possible investigation, the records requests.

Swenson gave a skeptical frown.

"You're right. It could be really big. But it'll take days to get those records, and unless you get confirmation from the county or some other source, we're nowhere. The election is just two weeks away, and we have to be careful what we run. We don't want it to look like we're deliberately trying to sway voters."

"Oh, come on! This is a county issue, and Raposa isn't running for office!"

"Yeah, but Las Vistas is the big kahuna as far as the county is concerned, and you've done enough stories to make it clear Raposa is a key backer in Johnsen's campaign."

"That's all the more reason we should do a story," Digger argued.

Swenson rubbed his forehead. He'd been looking more tired than usual since one of the assistant editors had quit, leaving him with a heavier workload. While they were talking, a couple of other reporters had appeared and were hovering around his desk.

"Look," he said, nodding wearily. "See what you can get from the county or anyone else. If it looks solid, we'll talk about it again. And if you see Dan Halloran, tell him I want to talk to him."

He turned to the other reporters. "Yeah, what?"

Digger went to find Halloran, expecting to see him snoozing behind the berm of files that surrounded his desk, but he wasn't there. She figured he was out meeting someone for a story, so she went and grabbed a snack from the vending machine. She'd missed breakfast because of Simpkin's call. She'd done the records requests and had other deadlines to meet. The last of the three campaign finance reports was due out this afternoon. The first two reports had showed Johnsen way ahead, with nearly $36,000 in donations. For a little-known candidate in a small-town mayor's race in New Mexico, that was significant. Kimble was trailing badly, with about $18,000. A lot of it was from private donors, a few bigger contributions from Las Vistas businesses, and the local police union had ponied up big-time.

She pored over Johnsen's reports. Raposa had been generous, and she noticed a big donation from Danny Murphy too.

She recognized a couple of other names as those of developers and home builders. There were also several individuals and companies she'd never heard of. She spent the next hour poking around on the secretary of state's online database of corporations, searching for the companies, names of registered agents, addresses. Maybe something would match what she hoped to get from the county.

"You hungry? Want to grab a taco?" Rex was standing beside her, but she'd been so engrossed that she hadn't noticed him.

"Sure. But I need to see if Halloran ever made it in. Swenson wants to see him."

When he still wasn't at his desk, Digger was worried. She told Rex about the conversation they'd had before he'd walked out— the last time she'd seen him.

Rex shook his head, looking grim. "Stubborn old bastard. Thompson's announcement was the last thing he needed. You know he was in the program; this place was about the only thing holding him together."

"What program?"

Rex rolled his eyes. "I forget you were born yesterday. The program, as in twelve-step program. Alcoholics Anonymous."

Digger thought of Halloran's remark about Mel being an old drinking buddy in the days before he'd gotten sober.

"I better go check on him." Rex hurried toward the exit door. Digger ran out after him.

"You know where he lives?" She called.

Rex was already opening the door of the Cherokee. Digger ran round to climb in on the passenger's side.

Rex held up a hand. "No. It's better if I go by myself."

"What?"

"Look, Halloran's been living in a hotel by the freeway for the past six months and he's not in good shape."

"But ..."

"No. I'll call you later."

Digger had no sooner returned to her desk when the phone rang. A man's voice she didn't recognize said, "I thought you ought to know there's a group holding some kind of protest in front of Bob's Car Wash. It's where the truck with Johnsen's campaign sign is parked."

Before she could ask any questions, the line went dead. Digger hurried to tell Swenson.

"Halloran still hasn't showed up," she told him first. "Nobody's seen him for days. Rex has gone looking for him."

Swenson frowned. She couldn't tell whether he was mad or worried.

She took a breath. "And I just got word there's some kind of protest going on. Sounds like it's targeting Johnsen."

The editor ran a hand through his sparse hair and looked at his watch. "Take someone from photo with you. We're sucking wind for the front page, and we could use some good photos. I've got to go to the morning meeting. Call me if you need to." He was gone.

Digger found Tom Miller, the photo editor, frowning over a daily schedule covered with scribbles and Post-It notes.

"Whatever it is, I can't help you," he said without looking up.

"But, Tom, there's a protest going on and Swenson wants something for the front page."

Tom pushed his frayed Cubs ball cap back on his head, freeing a tangle of frizzy gray curls.

"Dan's gone to the wreck on the freeway, Harry's on vacation, Tony's wife is having a baby, and Rex—Rex has gone AWOL. Until they let me hire another photographer, I haven't got anybody." He threw up his hands. "They gave you an iPhone, didn't they? So go shoot it yourself."

Digger backed out of the room. "Okay, then. Thanks for your vote of confidence, Tom."

—▶

Bob's Car Wash was a run-down self-serve facility with peeling paint and weeds growing in the forecourt. It sat near the corner of a busy intersection between a Jiffy Lube and a nursery that sold gardening supplies and enameled metal sculptures that passed for yard art. Digger had rarely seen anyone using the bays, but people often parked cars out front with "For Sale" signs stuck to the windshields.

The sight that greeted her when she arrived at Bob's was beyond anything she'd expected. Two figures dressed all in white were holding up a huge white banner in front of the panel truck that carried Johnsen's campaign sign. Their faces were hidden behind Guy Fawkes masks, the eerie white grinning goateed face made popular in the movie V for Vendetta. In the middle of the banner were the words "Illegal Sign!"

Out of the corner of her eye, Digger saw a police cruiser pull up behind her.

Josh Sanchez, the young officer who emerged, was familiar to her from the days when she'd worked the cops beat. He'd put on a few pounds and lost a lot of hair since they'd hung out at SWAT scenes.

About a dozen people were clustered around the banner in front of the truck. She pulled out her phone and started photographing the scene. She noticed Danny Murphy moving swiftly towards the masked characters. Suddenly he reached out and grabbed the mask off one of the banner holders, shouting, "Show us who you are, coward!"

"Get your hands off me, you asshole!" Digger recognized the pale acne-scarred face behind the mask as that of Dillon James, Kimble's campaign manager.

"Officer!" Dillon shouted. "Did you see that? That man grabbed at me.

That's battery!"

Murphy, red-faced, shouted back, "You've got no right to interfere with free speech. This sign is perfectly legal!"

Sanchez ambled over and stood towering over them.

"You!" he said, pointing to Dillon. "Put that banner away and clear off. I've been fielding calls all morning about people ripping up campaign signs, and I don't want any more trouble here. And you"—he swung around to face Murphy—"I'm going to let you off with a warning. Keep your hands to yourself."

Murphy folded his arms across his chest, looking furious. "This sign is perfectly legal. They have no right to—"

Sanchez held up a hand to silence him. "According to city ordinances, that sign is okay as long as you're driving around. You're not allowed to park it here unless you've got permission from the owner of this property. So until you can provide me or the city clerk's office with written proof of permission, someone needs to drive that truck away. Now!"

Digger darted around, noting names and taking comments as the crowd drifted away. When she looked around for Sanchez, he was leaning against his patrol car, his jaws moving rhythmically as he watched them go. Sanchez and his cinnamon Dentyne, some things never changed.

She strolled over to the patrol car. "Well, that was impressive. Want to give me a comment?" she asked. "Nope." He grinned. "But I do want to ask a question."

She leaned against the car beside him. "Yeah?" "What's this I hear about the *Courier* being sold?"

Digger rubbed a hand through her hair. "Pretty much what you read in the paper the other day. The publisher, Pfister, wants to retire. He hasn't got an heir who wants to take it on, so he figures one of the media corporations will buy it."

"You think that'll happen?"

Digger shrugged. "Beats me. You know how things are going for newspapers all over."

Sanchez said nothing for a moment, scratching the bald spot on the back of his head. "Well, if things don't go the way you hope they do, you can always apply to the force. You sure did a good job when we worked together. People noticed that."

Digger's eyebrows shot up and she took a step back. "Whoa! Didn't expect that! Well, since we're handing out compliments here, there's something you could maybe help me with."

He shifted his bulk, eyeing Digger as he waited for her to continue.

"A while back I got a tip that the county was still owed millions from the settlement over the failed Rancho Milagro subdivision. I did that story, you remember? Anyway, I just got another tip that law enforcement has maybe launched some kind of investigation. Know anything about that?"

Sanchez worked his jaws, repositioning the wad of gum. Finally he said, "I can tell you this: it's not us." Then he looked around and leaned closer. "You might want to check with the AG."

"The attorney general's office?" Digger asked, incredulous. In her experience, the AG's office didn't usually get involved unless there was a pattern of activity. Maybe there was more to Raposa's past than she realized.

Sanchez gave an almost imperceptibly nod.

"Can you give me a name?"

"I can, but you'll probably have to go through the usual channels. Okay?"

CHAPTER TWENTY-SIX

DIGGER HAD FINISHED an early version of the protest story and was about to post it to the paper's website when Tom came by her desk.

"Hey, I saw those shots you took. Not bad. You could crop that one, make it a little tighter, and it would really pop," he said, pointing at the photo she had inserted with the post.

Words of encouragement from Tom were few and far between. She smiled as she made the adjustment. Once he was gone, she switched focus to finish the story that would appear in print. Swenson wanted to see it within the hour.

It was mid-afternoon before she had a chance to think about her conversation with Josh Sanchez. His suggestion that she apply to Las Vistas police struck her as bizarre. If he only knew what she really thought of the police! But what he said about the Milagro investigation was odd. Weird that the attorney general's office would be the first agency to be involved instead of local law enforcement or even the FBI. Halloran would know—he'd been doing investigative stories so long he knew the ins and outs of every scandal going back to the '80s. But Halloran wasn't there, and she still hadn't heard from Rex. The thought of Halloran living in one of those tired, dilapidated hotels by the freeway that offered weekly rates—it was awful! She'd spent hours hanging around outside those places on the cops beat, the sad old dumps where drug deals and homicides happened. Was that what happened when you cut yourself off from everyone who could help you? A chill ran through her.

Predictably, Sanchez's contact at the AG's office said he couldn't talk and directed her to the public information officer. In the five years she had been with the *Courier*, she'd had few interactions with the attorney general's office. The PIO she'd dealt with in the past had been easy to reach and always helpful.

Unfortunately, he was history when the AG elected a couple of years ago brought in a new team. Melissa Wickham, the current information officer, was notorious in the *Courier* newsroom for being blunt, condescending, and slow to respond to requests from reporters.

Digger sat mulling the best approach—email or phone. She took a deep breath and punched in the office number in Santa Fe. To her surprise, Melissa Wickham answered after a couple of rings.

Digger introduced herself and explained the nature of her call as briefly as possible.

Wickham made an impatient clicking sound and exhaled. "You're sure of your information? That doesn't sound like something we would take on without it being referred to us by some other agency. I'll make some inquiries and get back to you. Are you on deadline?"

"Not daily, but I'd hope to get something from you soon."

"Well," she huffed, "today is pretty crazy, but I'll see what I can do. If I don't get back to you by the end of today, I'll be in touch tomorrow, by phone or email, to let you know what I find out. Okay?"

"Fine. If you don't reach me by phone, please email me. Thanks."

A gnawing in Digger's stomach reminded her that she hadn't eaten lunch. She was headed toward the café across the street when she saw Rex's SUV swing into the *Courier's* employee lot. She dashed to where he had parked and stopped short. Rex was hunched down in the driver's seat, his head in his hands.

She opened the car door and heard a stifled keening sound, like a dog in pain.

"What? What happened?"

He lifted his head. His face was red and puffy, and the skin beneath his chin sagged loose. He stared straight ahead, rivulets of tears coursing down his cheeks.

"He's dead," he said, his voice a hoarse whisper. "He'd been drinking, but I think his heart just gave out. I found him slumped in a chair. I don't know how long he'd been there. I called the police. They got someone from OMI."

The office of the medical investigator was always involved in the case of an unattended death.

"Oh, no! No! No!" Digger closed her eyes. Halloran dead. It was like the news of her parents' accident all over again. She fought the memories as if they were live things, trying to push them away.

When she spoke again, her voice was shaky. "How did you know about Halloran? I mean, where he lived, that hotel?"

Rex exhaled, the air puffing out his cheeks. "We used to have a beer together sometimes, back in the day before he got sober."

"What made him decide to quit drinking?"

"I think his wife threatened to leave him. That's the irony of this. He finally gives up the booze, then she leaves him anyway." He gave a bitter laugh. "After that he just kind of turned in on himself. We couldn't go out for a beer anymore. I found out about the hotel by accident. His car wouldn't start one morning and he asked me to go help jump it. Man, it was a sorry place!"

Rex got out of his car and they stood silent for a while. Then Rex turned toward the building.

"I need to go tell Swenson."

————▶

A pall of disbelief hung over the newsroom for the next few days. Halloran's quirky personality might not have made him the most popular guy; he was the newsroom dinosaur, and his technology-challenged tantrums were legendary. But he was someone whose presence carried weight. He was Thompson's go-to guy on all the big stories.

Apart from the newsroom staff, hardly anyone else showed up for Halloran's funeral, not even his ex-wife. It wasn't even called a funeral. Rex had enlisted Digger's help to track down Connell, the brother Halloran had occasionally mentioned, and he had flown in from Boston. They'd briefly discussed whether a service should be at St. Theresa's, given Halloran's Irish Catholic background, but Connell had instantly quashed that idea. "My brother was not a religious man," he'd told them. So Rex and Tom had hastily arranged what they called a "Celebration of Life" at Duran's Funeral Home a couple of blocks from the *Courier* offices.

Duran's Funeral Home was a beige one-story building surrounded by desert willow trees and yucca shrubs. Inside, on the table set up in the lobby, was an array of awards Halloran had won over the years along with framed photos of him on assignment: Halloran dressed in hard hat and Nomex fire-resistant clothing on scene at the Cerro Grande fire near Los Alamos, Halloran in New York after the attack on the Twin Towers, Halloran and Rex in New Orleans after Hurricane Katrina, Halloran at his desk deep in thought on an investigative story.

Halloran had always been proud that the publisher of his small-town paper believed it was vital to have a reporter covering the big news stories of the day. He'd been the hero of the *Courier*'s heyday.

Connell had brought one small photo that showed a side of Halloran none of his colleagues had ever seen. In the faded black-and-white print he was aged maybe fifteen and sporting a Red Sox cap and baseball mitt.

Several reporters were standing silently in front of the photos when Digger entered the lobby. She wore the dark suit she'd worn to the mayor's ball. Rex met her at the door and hugged her for a long time. He had on a dark blue sport coat and shirt with a silver-and-turquoise bolo tie. His eyes were red-rimmed and moist.

The service took place in a bland room with pale, creamy yellow walls and equally bland fake wood bench seating. Piped organ music played softly in the background as mourners trickled in, some singly, some in groups. A few minutes after the scheduled time, someone closed the doors and the music faded. Thompson ushered Connell to the front of the room, where a microphone stood before an immense floral display provided by the *Courier*. He was a small, pale man, younger than his brother and lacking Dan Halloran's air of sardonic confidence. He fished glasses out of a breast pocket, put them on, and peered uncertainly out at the ranks of *Courier* staff.

"I'm very grateful to you all for coming to honor my brother Dan." He paused, took a breath. "We hadn't seen much of each other in the last few years." He paused again, swallowing a couple of times before continuing. "Dan was the big brother I looked up to. He was the one who dared break the rules and always got away with it, with a smile and that incorrigible charm of his. He was the eldest of the four of us, and he drove our parents around the bend. But he had this thing about him that commanded loyalty and respect. That's probably what made him the great journalist he was." Another pause while he seemed to be struggling to control himself. "He had his disappointments and his demons, but I never forgot his kindness to me and my wife. He was our rock."

Connell then nodded at Thompson and walked back to his seat in the front row. Digger wiped her face on her arm, hoping no one would notice.

Thompson moved to the microphone, cleared his throat, looked around, and spoke stiffly, recalling Halloran's awards and his many years of service to the *Courier*.

Swenson spoke next. He had on an ill-fitting tweed jacket and outdated tie.

His face was pale and drawn. Yet somehow he managed to offer up a few anecdotes that drew polite chuckles from the gathering. A couple of other longtime reporters shared their memories. Rex gave an emotional account of an assignment he and Halloran had done in their early years together, covering a prison riot in the southern part of the state.

"I remember the two of us were standing there, just outside the prison gates, dozens of state police and National Guard guys all around us. There's smoke and sounds of gunfire from inside. I'd been on the job maybe six months, and this was way beyond anything I'd ever experienced. I was shit-scared. But Halloran just stood there watching, like it was a kids' rodeo at the state fair."

After the ceremony, a bunch of people drifted over to the Pioneer Saloon on Second Street. It was the default bar where journalists used to congregate late at night. The wood-paneled walls were hung with sepia-toned photos of cowboys and horses and an assortment of western saddles and bridles. Bo Sampson, the owner, was known for the colorful suspenders he wore to keep his pants from sagging below a generous paunch.

Digger ended up between Rex and Tom at a table with Vicky

Sandberg, the features writer. A waitress in a white cowboy hat brought the two men bottles of a local craft beer; Vicky had a glass of pinot grigio and Digger a bottle of Corona.

Tom looked around the bar, remarking on its tired decor.

"Remember when we used to come in here after the paper went to press?" he said.

"Yeah," Rex mused. "Makes me think about when we used to travel all over the state. Back then, before we went digital, I'd have to set up a darkroom in a hotel bathroom."

They laughed, chattering, sharing stories.

"When was it we had that story about the state representative embezzling from a school contract to feed his cocaine habit?" Vicky asked.

"Must be fifteen years," Tom said. "You remember that county election where they had to get a judge out of bed so they could do a recount on the absentee votes? Jeez, you can't make this shit up."

Vicky emptied her wineglass and waved to the bar for another order. She looked over at Digger. "What's with those stories you're doing on that road? I feel bad for those protesters. Seems like nobody's listening."

"That's exactly why I'm writing," Digger said. "I saw the chapel they're trying to protect. You know, we—I mean, we at the *Courier* —we always write about the stuff on the surface. It's like we don't care about the people who were here before all those subdivisions started going up."

Vicky laid a hand on Digger's arm. "Sweetie, haven't you got it yet?" Her voice was loose, her eyes unfocused. "You see those people at the council meetings, they have no idea about what New Mexico is all about—and you're right, they don't care. The *Courier* doesn't care."

She gave a lopsided smile. "You know, I did your beat covering city and county government for ten years before I got on to features. Sometimes I thought I was going to lose my mind.

The people you came across, so entitled! The nasty phone calls, the emails you'd get. I remember one time I did a story about a program where volunteers helped kids learn to read—these were kids from families with single moms, women who were really struggling. When the story ran, this woman called me up and said people like that had no business having children. I mean, for God's sake!"

She stopped, took a gulp of wine, and shook her head.

"Then there's those stories that just make you want to cry. One time this guy with some health care organization asked me to do a story about a family with a young boy diagnosed with a rare disease. They lived in this trailer on the edge of town. They were very Catholic, and the place was crammed with pictures of saints and statues of the Virgin of Guadalupe. They'd started a fundraising website to get money for the little boy's treatment. He was lying on the couch, smiling, but he could barely move. After the story ran, they called to thank me because they'd gotten hundreds of dollars in donations."

Vicky drank again.

"It's those times when you realize something you wrote made a difference in someone's life that makes this all worth it," she added, then began crying.

Digger felt humbled watching her. Vicky, with her blond highlights, flashy wardrobe, and beautifully manicured nails, had always struck Digger as a lightweight. They sat glumly, staring at their drinks, while a basketball game on the wall-mounted TV blared in the background.

Rex sighed heavily and downed his beer. "I'm going to miss him. He was a real presence in the newsroom. You know, somebody you went to when you needed to figure something out. He seemed so solid, but maybe that was just a show he put on for everyone else. God, you should've seen his place. It was such a dump. Jeez, ending up like that . . ." Rex shook his head. "It's like another light going out in the newsroom. Who knows what's going to happen now."

Digger looked around at her colleagues. They were all at least twenty-five years older than she. What was it like to spend so many years at the paper and realize it could be gone? What would they do? What would she do?

Vicky mumbled something about getting home and staggered to her feet.

Rex put an arm around her for support.

"Vicky, you shouldn't be driving. Let me call your husband."

"Don't need him. I'm fine, I'm fine," she said thickly.

Rex nodded at Tom and together they led her toward the door. They said their goodbyes and Digger watched them load Vicky, still protesting, into the back seat of Tom's Honda CRV.

As they drove away, she felt an ache of loneliness. Halloran— his raspy voice, his dry humor, his rough kindness—he was gone. How did a man she had looked up to so much get so far down? How come none of them had realized what was happening to him?

She knew. Halloran wanted it that way. He'd kept it all inside, for whatever reason, because he felt safer that way. Like me, she thought. Again she felt the chill.

She looked up at the sky. A line of pigeons hunkered on a power line beside the parking lot. Suddenly they took flight, wheeling in a fluttering pattern against the fading light. She wanted, more than anything, to call Maria. She took out her phone. She looked at the number. This was temptation. This was sneaking around the rules. She thought of Armando getting away with the accident. She couldn't call Maria.

Instead she called Lexi.

"Hi guys, I'm having a really bad day. Can I come over?"

"Sure. I'm not working tonight. We're just hanging, watching the game."

A nearly full moon shone fuzzily through a thin layer of cloud over Lexi and Susan's ramshackle farmhouse on the edge of town. The faint moonlight bathed the tin roofs of the sheds where Lexi kept a collection of old dirt bikes. When Digger stepped out of her car, she caught the smell of piñon smoke from the chimney. Nights were cold in the thin air of the high desert.

Susan answered her knock, motioned her inside, and held a finger to her lips, whispering, "Game's almost over."

She led Digger into the tiny living room, where the glow from the fireplace and the television provided the only light. Digger sank into an old brown sofa and held her head in her hands.

A roar from the TV signaled the end of the game. Lexi swung her head around, noticed Digger, and stabbed a finger on the remote to turn off the set.

"Hey, hey, hey! What is it?" she said, heaving herself out of her recliner. "What gives? I've never seen you like this."

For a long time Digger couldn't speak. She clamped her lips, fighting to hold herself together. Finally she was able to speak.

"I was just at the memorial service for one of my friends at work. He was a tough, cranky old guy—older than my dad would be now—but he always had time for me. He died all alone in a crummy hotel down by the freeway."

She shook her head slowly. "I didn't even know him very well. He helped me on some stories, and we ate lunch together a few times. He never talked about himself. It was always work. Seemed like it was his whole life."

When she looked up at her friends, Lexi's face had the same sad expression she'd seen when her old cat Bingo had died.

"You think I'm like that too, don't you?" Digger asked.

Lexi folded her arms. "Remember what I said to you at Frankie's that night?"

Susan put a hand on her shoulder. "Digger, I know you want to act like you've got it all together. Nobody likes a drama queen.

But it's okay to set your bags down sometimes and let somebody else carry the weight. If that's what you need."

Lexi nodded. "Like I told you in the bar, it's okay to open up."

Susan leaned in close, saying gently, "Just remember, we're here for you anytime."

Lexi got up and disappeared into the kitchen. Minutes later she came back with a bowl of popcorn and beers for the three of them.

"Here, I bet you haven't had anything to eat."

Digger realized she hadn't had anything since early morning. She gratefully gobbled fistfuls of popcorn. Susan and Lexi watched her. Their mundane domesticity touched her. There they were, the two of them sitting by the fire, watching a basketball game together. Lexi had asked Digger what she really wanted. Was it this?

Lexi caught her staring. "There's something else going on with you, isn't there? Is it that woman? I saw the way you were with her in the bar that night."

Digger munched her popcorn morosely, sipped her beer. "Her name is Maria. I wanted to go see her tonight. We really get each other. But if I'm going to write about her cause, I have to hold back. It's a moral line I can't cross. It's tempting, believe me. I could rationalize it in a dozen ways. But if I did that, I'd be just the same as the sleazebags I write about—trying to get away with something by hiding it."

Even as she looked at them, she could tell they really didn't get it.

"Do you want to stay here tonight?" Susan asked. "The cats are in the spare bedroom, but the sofa is very comfortable."

Digger had no desire to stay, but the beer bottles lined up in front of her held a warning.

"Thanks, guys." Their kindness was comforting, even if this wasn't where she really longed to be.

The next morning, Lady Antonia was very displeased at being kept waiting for her breakfast. She greeted Digger at the door with a pitiful yowling sound and proceeded to dig her claws into the carpet so vigorously that Digger worried she would lose her security deposit. The sound of the tuna can being opened only encouraged the cat's maddening meowing.

"Who's a jealous girl, then?" Digger said, setting down the food bowl.

CHAPTER TWENTY-SEVEN

ON MONDAY MORNING, Melissa Wickham from the attorney general's office called Digger back with a bizarre equivocation that didn't really answer her question. She said the AG's office was "looking into" allegations about the Milagro Millennium development's accounting, but she stopped short of confirming there was an investigation. She spoke in the measured, official tones that might as well have been a robotic voice for all the honesty they conveyed.

Digger tried asking the question half a dozen different ways, but the answer was the same bland version of official bullshit.

"So, 'looking into the allegations,' is that like a preliminary to an actual investigation?"

Wickham answered curtly, "I'm okay with you saying 'looking into,' but that's as far as I can go today."

Digger knew when she'd squeezed as much as she could, so she thanked her and hung up. Damn! She pounded her desk. So far she'd only gotten about half the documents she'd requested from the county, along with an email requesting an extension on producing the rest. The election was just over a week away.

Swenson reluctantly agreed to let her do a story that confirmed the AG's office was looking into "possible accounting irregularities" related to the failed Rancho Milagro development. Documents she'd gotten from the county showed millions of dollars still owed on the settlement. She called Raposa on his office and cell phone numbers seeking comment, but even after she left multiple messages about the story she planned to write, he didn't return her calls. She included that in the story. It wasn't the powerful "gotcha" piece she'd hoped for, but at least she was able to show Raposa's connection to the development. It was a start and she was sure it would go a lot further.

→

Johnny Raposa was staring at the almost-empty cocktail glass in front of him and wondering who to call. He kept thinking over the details of the *Courier* story about Rancho Milagro. He thought he'd managed to keep a lid on it by refusing to comment. But the way it had been written—especially the words "accounting irregularities"—made him nervous, really nervous. He didn't need that kind of distraction right now, especially with the Arizona investors getting twitchy.

Maybe Fabrizzi could help. He ordered another cocktail, then fumbled for the phone in his pocket and punched in the councilor's number.

Nico Fabrizzi was in his garage, working on a model of a B-17 like the one his dad had flown in World War II, when he got the call from Raposa asking him to meet at a new cocktail bar he'd discovered. Fabrizzi ground his teeth. What the hell does the guy want to talk about? He had plans with his family. He hadn't talked with Raposa since he'd decided not to run for reelection. It wasn't like he could do anything for the guy in his last few weeks on the council. But Raposa was insistent, so he finally gave in. Raposa could be a pain in the ass but he'd been helpful in a lot of ways while he was on the council. Fabrizzi felt he owed him.

The Oasis Lounge had recently opened in a renovated space

on the top floor of a downtown hotel. Its windows had a panoramic view of the mountains and the vast high desert landscape.
Blue neon lights glowed above the bar counter. Tall tables flanked
by steel-and-leather stools stood randomly around the room; low-
slung couches hugged the walls. Fabrizzi felt out of place among
the patrons, most of them looked like they were in their twenties.

As Fabrizzi approached the bar, Raposa gave him a loose
smile. Fabrizzi suspected he'd been there for a while.

"Nico, my man! What'll you have?"

"A beer. Whatever they got on tap."

"Ah, come on," Raposa scolded. "This is a cocktail bar."

Fabrizzi considered, then ordered a vodka martini. The bar-
tender, a young man whose muscular forearms were tattooed
with Celtic symbols, rattled off a confusing list of vodka choices.
Fabrizzi shrugged and accepted his recommendation. Raposa
emptied his glass and ordered what he called a Sazerac. "You gotta
try one of these. It's a famous New Orleans drink. It's got cognac
and rye whiskey in it. Mmm-mmm."

Fabrizzi smiled and waited while the young man busied him-
self with glasses, bottles, ice, and cocktail-related paraphernalia.
When his drink was ready, he sipped it carefully, wondering what
Raposa wanted to talk about.

He didn't have to wait long.

"So, you're planning to move back East pretty soon after the
election?" Raposa said, opening the conversation.

"Yeah, we're going back to Long Island. My mom, she's not
doing too good, and my brother has been on my case. He feels
like he's doing everything 'cause I'm out here. That, and my wife,
she wants to be near the grandkids. You know how it is."

Fabrizzi was happy to talk about his family, but he knew
that wasn't why Raposa had invited him. Raposa always had an
agenda. He waited.

"The guy Caulfield that's running for your council seat—think we can count on him to support the road extension?" Raposa asked.

Fabrizzi sipped his drink, nodded. "Yeah, no problem. He's running unopposed. I talked to him last week and he's all for it. Real excited."

Raposa swirled his Sazerac, took a drink, and licked his lips. "What about the other council seat—Johnsen's?"

Fabrizzi thought a minute. "Well, it's between those two women. I don't know much about 'em, just what I read in the paper. One of 'em works for that out-of-state corporation that makes car parts or something. The other one is retired from some insurance company. I figure they'd be in favor of anything that would be good for business and bring the city money. Anyway, there's state and federal funds already approved for the road. There's just a couple more steps the city has to do to get it going."

Raposa didn't answer, just stared at his drink. Fabrizzi looked around at the young people in the bar. The lights and the music made him uncomfortable. He was thinking about making an excuse to leave when Raposa suddenly spoke again.

"You know, I don't get Jack Kimble. It's like he doesn't have anything else to think about besides that damn drainage project. I heard he's trying to work some contacts at the state to repurpose the money approved for the road so he can use it to help pay for the drainage."

Fabrizzi raised an eyebrow. He couldn't believe Kimble would entertain such a dumb idea. "I don't think there's any way he can do that, Johnny," he said patiently. "There's rules you gotta follow."

Raposa's glass was now empty. He thumped a forefinger on the counter. "I'm worried about this. If Johnsen wins the election, he'll get the road project going. But if it goes Kimble's way and he can get council support to push his stupid drainage project instead of the road, I'm screwed."

"Whaddaya mean, Johnny? You got lots of things going for

you." Fabrizzi was both disbelieving and irritated. "Why did you really ask me here tonight, Johnny? It's not like I can pull any strings for you on the council."

Raposa rounded on him. "Did you see that story in the *Courier* this morning? That damn reporter, that Doyle gal, she's been poking around. Stuff that happened years ago. I could have big problems. I've got investors that have put up money for the shopping center I'm planning to build next to Los Sueños—folks I worked with in Arizona—and if the road doesn't go through, they'll probably bail on me."

So that was it.

"Ah," Fabrizzi said. "You want me to back you up if that reporter woman calls, that it?"

"You bet I do. You and I go way back, remember?" Raposa's eyes were bleary, but there was no mistaking the menace in his voice.

Fabrizzi set down his drink and wiped his mouth with the back of his hand. "Look, Johnny, I helped you with a few votes, but Milagro was a county deal. I'll do what I can for you, but if the reporter calls me, the best I can do is refer her to the county people. We'll both be on safe ground there."

Fabrizzi looked at his watch. "You know what, it's getting late and I promised my wife I'd be back in time to watch a particular show with her. It's a thing with us. See you around, Johnny."

Fabrizzi slipped off the barstool and headed toward the door. Raposa watched him go, fists clenched in silent fury.

Jack Kimble stared out the window of his city hall office, surveying the expanse of the city, the mountains, and the desert spaces in between. He could see the arroyos, those dry rivulets carved through the sand that became raging torrents when the summer rains struck. The land was sere and dry now; there had been barely enough recent snowmelt to transform the Rio Grande from a patchwork of sandbars into a real river again.

The election was just days away, and he knew his campaign wasn't going well. Raposa had never come through, not a penny in contributions after all the cooperation they'd had over the years. Then there was that article! It sounded as though Raposa had swindled county taxpayers out of millions.

Kimble worried. All those people living in the homes on the dirt roads that had flooded last summer. If he could win and get support for the plan he'd worked out, it could make such a difference. They just didn't understand. It reminded him of the Old Testament stories of God warning his chosen people against disaster and them ignoring Him, over and over again. Kimble believed he had a duty to save Las Vistas from the scourge of the desert storms. But would the people trust him? Would they believe? And if he lost the election, what did he have to look forward to? Imelda's Tuesday-night meatloaf?

He turned away from the window, discouraged.

———➤

Dave Johnsen enjoyed Saturday-morning breakfasts with his family. On Sunday mornings they usually went out to breakfast after Mass, but Saturday was the day Connie made her special blueberry pancakes. He loved the smells of sizzling bacon and frying pancakes, loved listening to Mary chatter about her school friends, loved seeing little Jimmy's syrup-smeared face.

It was the last Saturday morning before the election, and Johnsen was feeling particularly elated. All the feedback he'd been getting indicated he would win. He felt proud of himself as he looked around the table at his wife and kids. Mary was doing well in second grade, and Jimmy was loving the preschool they'd found for him. And Johnsen had another reason to be joyful this morning: last night, as they were cuddling in bed, Connie had told him she was pregnant again. He planned to call his mom with the news right after breakfast.

At the thought of delivering news, a tiny cloud sailed over the bright horizon. That article he'd seen in the *Courier*. He'd read it while waiting in the barber shop. It had mentioned Raposa in connection with some subdivision and money still owed to the county. Johnsen had read and reread it as a twinge of discomfort began to nag at him. It was still there. He wondered if he should feel guilty about accepting Raposa's donations. It was all part of politics, wasn't it? What he wanted was to be able to do things for the city.

He decided he should go to confession before Mass tomorrow. Maybe that would help him feel clearer about everything.

CHAPTER TWENTY-EIGHT

ELECTION DAY IN Las Vistas dawned bright and cloud-free, like ninety percent of New Mexico mornings. Digger pulled on her running clothes and hit the foothills trail. Spring was still new, but already the mornings were warmer. She sucked in deep breaths of clear air. Lost in the rhythm of her feet springing along the foothills trail, she could blot out worries about the election and the fate of the *Courier*.

Reality came crashing back when she walked into the newsroom and saw. Swenson in Thompson's office. The editor's office had interior windows that looked out over the ranks of desks, and she could see Swenson with his back to the door, his shoulders slumped. His face, when he emerged, was grim. Digger decided to go find a cup of coffee before approaching him.

By the time she came back, Swenson was impatiently juggling phone calls and questions from reporters. She waited until he was free.

"I wanted to let you know what I'm planning for election coverage," she said.

"Okay, shoot," he said without looking away from his computer screen.

"I thought I'd hit a couple of the polling places, see what turn-out is like, talk to some voters. Polls close at seven. Turnout is usually pretty low, even when there's a mayoral election. The city clerk told me results ought to be available by eight or a little later. I'll get some comments from whoever wins, Rex will get photos. The usual kind of thing."

Swenson nodded. "Okay. Just give me a heads-up if you expect to run late."

Digger leaned over his desk. "So, any news from Thompson about where we stand?"

Swenson let out a deep sigh, almost a groan. "Nothing good."

"And?"

His features tightened. "I can't say any more at this point," he said crisply.

Digger walked back to her desk, a knot clenching at her stom-ach. She wondered if Rex knew anything.

Her first stop was the Las Vistas Senior Center, where morn-ing turnout was typically brisk. Half a dozen elderly people were waiting in line at the entrance. More were clustered around the door, waiting for a man with a walker to shuffle out. When he did, Digger put on a cheery smile and approached him.

"Hi, I'm with the *Courier*. Do you have a minute to talk about the election?"

"If you expect me to tell you who I voted for," he sneered, "you're wasting your time. Your paper is just a scandal rag."

"Thanks for your comments," Digger said, shoving her note-book into her back pocket. She bypassed the line and headed inside, hoping for a friendlier reception. The presiding judge was more accommodating. She and the other poll workers had been busy all morning. No problems with ballots or voting machines, she said.

Next Digger swung by Olson Elementary School, where she

waited outside, watching as voters trickled in and out. A plump woman in swirly pink-patterned yoga pants came by, pushing a chubby toddler in a stroller. The mom stopped and asked Digger if she was in the right place to vote.

Digger introduced herself and launched into her spiel. The young mother was happy to talk, on and on. She planned to vote for Dave Johnsen. She wasn't sure what he stood for or why he was different from the other guy who was running for mayor—what was his name? She had picked Johnsen mostly because he was young and she liked his smile. She liked that Johnsen had kids and seemed to understand what city families needed. She'd only been in Las Vistas a few months and didn't know much about New Mexican history or culture. She hadn't heard about the proposed road extension.

When Digger explained, the woman thought a minute and then ventured, "Um, if it made it easier to get from the stores to my subdivision, that would be great. We bought a house in Los Sueños, you know, and right now I have to drive all the way around the south end of town. It's really inconvenient."

How about Kimble's drainage plan? The question drew a blank from Yoga Pants. Digger gave her the Cliffs Notes version of the damage caused by the summer storm.

"Really, some people live on dirt roads in Las Vistas? Wow, I didn't know that. But it hardly ever rains here, does it? That's what one of the moms in my daughter's playgroup said."

Digger smiled and moved on. Sometimes she wondered if anybody ever read what she wrote.

By late afternoon she'd talked to more than a dozen voters. They were roughly split between the two candidates, but she had a niggling feeling that the election would go Johnsen's way. She made a couple of calls to make sure she'd be able to reach each of the candidates as soon as the results were available.

Johnsen was planning to meet with supporters and friends in a party room at the local Holiday Inn. Kimble said he'd be at the Denny's.

For now it was a waiting game. She called Rex to coordinate meeting later for the victory speeches.

"Hey, I've got an hour or so before I have to be at my next assignment," he said. "Want to grab a coffee at that little place down the street?"

TwoJay's was a tiny coffee shop with dark wood-paneled walls and 1950s-era Formica and steel tables. A black-and-white photo of two men in bow ties—the original owners, brothers named Joe and Jim—hung beside the kitchen door. The young man behind the counter had dreadlocks bound up in a crocheted cap that made him look as though he had a wasp's nest on his head.

Digger stirred creamer into her coffee and eyed Rex. "Swenson was in Thompson's office when I came in this morning. I figured it was about the sale of the paper. I asked him about it, but all he would say was that things aren't looking good. You heard anything?"

Rex shifted in his chair, took a sip of coffee. "Not much." He grimaced. "I was talking to that security guy—you know, the tall one that looks like he could bench-press three hundred pounds—turns out he's dating a woman in the executive office. Anyway, what she heard was that there was some interest from one of the big media companies, Gannett or some such, he couldn't remember exactly. But it sounds like that's fallen through."

Digger rolled her eyes. "I figured you'd know something. How come you were talking to the security guy?"

Rex laughed. "Turns out Mr. Fitness has a fondness for nicotine. He was out back vaping."

"Sounds like a useful habit for news gathering. Maybe I ought to take it up."

"Not unless you want to end up like Halloran."

"Smoking didn't kill Halloran."

"Naw, it was just a contributing factor." Rex shook his head. "I talked to his brother Connell when he was here. They grew up in a rough home. Dad was an alcoholic, abusive. Mom was very Catholic, afraid to leave him. All the old clichés. Dan was smart in school and got a college scholarship, and he became a damn good reporter."

Rex paused and stirred his coffee. "Sorry for being so flip about it, but you know how this business is. You end up pretty cynical."

"No shit."

"Yeah. Anyway, all that, and he was drinking hard for a lot of years. I kinda think that's why his wife left him. He started on the program after that, but her leaving ripped the rug right out from under him." He looked at his watch. "Well, the polls close in a little while. How do you think the mayor's race is going to go?"

"Before today, I thought Johnsen had it wrapped up," Digger said. "But quite a few of those I talked to voted for Kimble. If he gets back in, you know he's going to do everything he can to push that drainage plan. That's his baby. If it's Johnsen, he'll just fall in with the developers. They backed him big-time. That means the road extension will probably go ahead, and Raposa will do a happy dance."

"How come that's such a big deal for him?"

"Right now, people who buy homes in his Los Sueños subdivision have to drive forever to shop, so sales are sluggish. On top of that, Raposa bought a chunk of land zoned for commercial development right next to the subdivision. He's carrying a ton of debt. Plus there's that thing the AG's office is looking into, with the money that was never paid to the county. If Johnsen wins and the road goes through, you can bet Los Sueños and the commercial development will take off.

But if Kimble gets in again, the tax to pay for the drainage plan will make houses way more expensive, and Raposa will be in a world of shit."

"Well, I guess we just have a couple more hours to find out."

Rex's phone buzzed. "Yeah, Tom, what's up?" He listened for a minute, then answered, "Sure, I'm just hanging out with Digger, waiting for the polls to close. We can run over there right now."

He ended the call and shoved the phone into his pocket. "Swenson just got a call. There's some group holding a demonstration outside city hall. He thinks it's about the road extension. Come on, we can go in my car."

Digger felt a prickle of anxiety. If it was about the road project, Maria was bound to be there.

It was the border time of day, on the cusp of late afternoon and early evening, when commuter cars edged wearily toward the freeway. City hall rose sheer and stark from the desert landscape like some alien spaceship. Shards of light glinted off the glass-and-steel walls. Around the building, the brown earth glowed in the ebbing light, reminding Digger of the adobe bricks surrounding Abuela's hearth. City employees emerged from the doorway at the front of the building, headed home at the end of their work day. They glanced with curiosity at the small crowd of people milling around in front of the building.

Sure enough, there was Maria, a bright red scarf round her neck. She was waving a brightly colored banner that read "Protect Our Heritage—No Road!"

An SUV from the local TV station had beaten them to the scene. Digger recognized the hulking cameraman and the pert blond reporter she'd seen on the day the candidates had officially announced. Evidently the reporter favored form-fitting outfits and exaggerated heels. The shoes she was wearing today brought the top of her head just level with the cameraman's shoulders. She was looking around uncertainly. *Wonder if she needs me to tell her what the protest is about?* Digger thought.

Rex remained in the Jeep, watching the scene. "You've got to admire those folks, coming out time after time to protest that stupid road that'll probably be built anyway," he said. "Most of the time, people just roll over and let the developers do whatever the hell they want." He studied them for a while longer, seeming in no hurry. Then, almost as if on a whim, he nodded toward Digger and said, "Check out that one in the red scarf! Think she'd be your type?"

Digger blushed to the roots of her hair. She turned to respond, but Rex was already out of the Jeep, slinging camera gear over his shoulder. She grabbed her notebook and followed him toward the waving banners.

Rex was dodging around, snapping photos of the protesters. Digger hung back, watching Maria talk to the TV reporter. How tall and proud she looked. To think that someone like Rex, that consummate cynic, would have admiration for the cause Maria stood for. Digger's heart stirred. Could you sympathize with a cause and not betray your integrity as a reporter? Could you have feelings for someone and cover their cause fairly?

The petite blond TV reporter and her companion with the big cameras moved on. Digger approached Maria.

"Nice scarf," she said.

Maria whirled around, took in Digger's stance, the notebook in her hand, and gave a knowing grin. "This is the moment you've been dreading, isn't it?"

"Yup." Digger nodded.

"Well, we can get through this, can't we?" Maria gave her a mischievous smile. "I'll just stick to my talking points the way I did with that TV reporter."

Digger laughed. "You're something else!" she said. She pulled out her recorder, held it toward Maria, and put on her reporter's voice.

"Your group has held many rallies to protest this road extension, so why here and why now, on Election Day?"

Maria grinned and launched into her speech. "We've been trying to draw attention to the cultural treasure that would be destroyed if this project goes through the way it's currently planned. We're hoping the new mayor—whoever that'll be—will consider a different route for the road so that the people of Las Vistas will still be able to access the historic church and appreciate it. As it is right now, some of the foundations for the new section of road would damage that treasure."

"Have either of the mayoral candidates or those running for council seats given any indication that they're willing to consider your request?" Digger asked.

"At this point, no. But we will not stop trying until we are heard. We are the voice of the people who are sidelined every time there is a new development— people like my grandmother. She is nearly eighty years old, and she has seen the land torn up by people who don't understand it. People who don't understand the history and culture or what water means here in the desert. We are the ones who don't have money to buy votes. So, if they won't listen, we'll take action to make our voices heard. If you don't keep trying, you get nowhere."

"Do you have any more actions planned?"

Maria pointed at the other banner-waving protesters. "We'll keep fighting as long as it takes," she said.

Digger nodded, clicked off the recorder, and shoved it into her backpack.

Then, leaning close, she said, "I really hope all those voters out there will understand why this is so important." She paused. "But I have to tell you, it's not looking good. From what I'm hearing,

Johnsen is almost certain to win, and he's been making all kinds of positive noises about the road project."

Maria bit her lip and gave a defiant shrug. "Like I said, we'll keep on making our voices heard as long as it takes. Now go! Your photographer's looking at us."

Digger wheeled around. Sure enough, Rex was heading their way. Was that a smirk on his face?

CHAPTER TWENTY-NINE

CHEERS ERUPTED IN the brightly lit hotel ballroom. The results were unofficial, but Johnsen had a such a commanding lead over his rival that there was no point in postponing the celebrations. The mayor-elect stood on a platform at one end of the room, flanked by his wife and two young children. A spotlight shining on him glowed halo-like on his blond head. He beamed at his supporters, holding up his hands to quiet the crowd.

"Thank you, thank you! This has been a great day. I'm so excited to take on this new responsibility. I have such a bright vision for Las Vistas, and we are all going to work together to make it an even better city than it is. I want to give special thanks to my wife, Connie, who put up with the crazy hours I had to keep during the last few weeks. Also to those who donated to my campaign and volunteered their time."

The clapping was so loud Digger barely heard her phone. The call was from Swenson. "Hang on, it's really loud in here," she said. She ducked into a hallway. "You're at Johnsen's victory party now?" he said, but didn't wait for an answer.

"I got the stuff you sent earlier about the polling process and the turnout, but I need you to send me a few paragraphs with some color from the celebrations. A few happy quotes, you know the kind of thing."

"Sure. I just did a quick interview with Johnsen. I can have it to you in thirty minutes, okay?"

"Right. I'll be waiting—and tell Rex, if he's still there, that I need his photos as soon as possible. Tell him to send them over and Tom will do any editing that's necessary, got that?"

Digger looked around and spotted Rex on the other side of the room. She made her way through the crowd.

"Hey, Swenson just called. He needs you to send him something pronto." "Yeah, yeah," he said, not taking his eyes off the platform. "Well, would you look who's here!"

Digger followed the direction of his gaze and made out the tall figure of Raposa not far from the platform. He must have just come in. Danny Murphy stood beside him.

"He must have come to gloat," Rex said. "Johnsen's win is like him cashing in at the slots."

Raposa was a few feet away. It was an opportunity she couldn't miss.

"I need to go talk to him. He's been avoiding my calls. Tell Swenson I've got one more interview to do and may be delayed a few minutes."

Rex gave a thumbs-up sign. "I got it. Go for it," he said.

Digger made her way around the edge of the room so she could approach Raposa from behind. He seemed startled when she called out his name. A beach tan—or was it a salon bed tan?— showed off his heavy eyebrows and dark eyes and the radiant white teeth he flashed at her.

"Oh, Miss Doyle, always on the scene."

Raposa was sporting a navy blazer. A thatch of black chest hairs peeked over the open neck of his white dress shirt. His close-cropped hair was receding at the temples, with a small patch in the center on top. His cheeks were fashionably dark with a two-day beard growth. His dark eyes sized her up.

Digger folded her arms across her chest. "It's my job," she said flatly. "You must be pleased about the election results. You gave generously to the Johnsen campaign."

Raposa glanced over at Johnsen, who was talking enthusiastically to a group of young women. "I consider it my civic duty to support candidates who show promise," he said, flashing that smile again. "As a businessman, I see it as an important way to look out for the future of the city."

I'll bet you do, especially when you can smell money.

Aloud Digger said, "In the past you've been a strong supporter of Mayor Kimble. Why the change this time?"

Raposa didn't appear fazed. "I think Mayor Kimble has been great for the city, but it's time for a younger man. Las Vistas is growing, and maybe we need new energy."

"Is it true you and Mayor Kimble disagreed on his plan for infrastructure improvements that would help prevent flooding like we saw last summer?"

"Oh, I wouldn't say that," he answered smoothly. "That's a priority for him, but a lot of people in the city aren't on board with it."

"How about the proposed road extension that would connect your Los Sueños development with other commercial areas of the city? Dave Johnsen has indicated he'd support it. Is that why you backed him?"

"Miss Doyle!" He seemed irritated. "I've already given you my reasons for supporting him. But I will say this. I've got big plans for Los Sueños, and Danny here is going to be closely involved with those plans going forward."

Murphy had been silent up to this point, but now he interjected himself into the conversation.

"Yeah, Johnny and I have worked together in the past, and

now that I've been here a few months and know my way around, I'm going to get involved so he can focus on some other areas."

"Can you be more specific?"

Murphy just shrugged. "It's still being worked out."

Digger turned back to Raposa. "What about Millennium Milagro and the Rancho Milagro settlement money that the attorney general's office is looking into?"

Raposa's face hardened. "I've already told you, I can't comment on that because of pending lawsuits. Now, if you'll excuse me, I have to go and congratulate Dave and his wife."

Digger had read the cases. A couple from California and two families from Seattle had each paid deposits of about $15,000 to buy homes in Rancho Milagro. They had sued, but the cases were still winding their way through the legal system. The district court was notorious for its glacial rate of progress.

Raposa turned his back on her and disappeared into the crowd. As soon as he was gone, Murphy eased himself away from the table he'd been leaning on and took a step closer, close enough that Digger could smell his cologne. He gave her a broad smile that was something between an ingratiating smile and a leer.

"You play golf, Miss Doyle?"

Digger backed away. "No, thanks. I gotta go."

She shuddered as she walked toward the door. Glancing at her watch, she realized she'd be a few minutes late in filing. Swenson would fume, but it was worth it to get face to face with Raposa. His remark about Murphy getting more involved in the business had struck her as odd. Something must be brewing.

CHAPTER THIRTY

JACK KIMBLE SPREAD his long fingers on the windowsill of his city hall office and gazed at the mountains. A faint green haze clung to the lower slopes thanks to melting snow and the few spring showers they'd had. Leafy buds were showing on several of the trees planted in the graveled areas around the building. He couldn't remember what those trees were called; they didn't have them in California.

The thought of California made him wince. Now that he'd lost the election, it would fuel Imelda's infernal whining about going back. But her homesickness wasn't going to bring in more money each month. Without his job as mayor, they were going to have to live on their Social Security somehow.

He looked down at the dry landscape gouged by erosion, feeling bitter. The rain they needed so badly was always a two-faced friend, bringing fertility and destruction. Apparently Johnsen and the developers who supported him—thinking about Raposa gave Kimble heartburn—had convinced themselves and a majority of Las Vistas residents that the city would never see another rainstorm like the one they'd had last summer. Well, they were wrong! He'd done the research. An El Niño weather pattern was brewing, warming the waters of the South Pacific.

According to the weather experts, that naughty child would bring moisture to the parched Southwest. That moisture usually hit New Mexico in the form of thunderstorms and torrential rain. Kimble smiled to himself and cracked his knuckles.

The door behind him opened.

"Mayor, Dave Johnsen is here to see you," said Carol, the city manager's assistant.

Kimble sighed and turned around. "Fine. I was expecting him."

Johnsen came in, smiling confidently. He stopped, rested his hands on his hips, and looked around. "Nice office! Great view!"

Kimble gritted his teeth and managed a tight smile. "Yes. I've enjoyed it, and now you will."

He eyed Johnsen's broad shoulders and athletic build, noting the way his shirt stretched taut across his muscular chest. Then he looked back to the window, taking in the city sprawl.

"I think I've done a good job here as mayor," Kimble said, "but apparently the people of Las Vistas think it's time we had a change, someone younger, obviously. I wish you good luck."

Johnsen reddened slightly. He hadn't expected Kimble to take it so personally.

"Well, I plan to carry on a lot of that good work. I think we all want to do what's best for the city."

Kimble shrugged. "I've cleared out my desk. Everything is in those boxes over there. Someone will be here in a minute to carry them downstairs to my car."

"Oh, heck, I can carry them for you," Johnsen said, bending to grab a box. "They're quite heavy," Kimble said, but evidently the subtle warning he had meant to convey was lost on Johnsen. The younger man answered brightly, "It's no trouble, really. I'm happy to help."

Happy to help kick me out, thought Kimble. *Oh, the humiliation!*

"No, please!" he said. "I've already arranged for someone to pick them up.

Now, if you'll excuse me, I have to go down to HR and complete some paperwork."

Kimble walked straight down the hall to the elevator and punched the button for the ground floor. He didn't need to see the human resources director; he'd done all that the morning after the election. He just wanted to get out of that office, away from Johnsen's naive, smiling face. Exiting the elevator, he crossed the lobby, nodding goodbye to the receptionist, and emerged into the warm spring sunshine.

He walked to his aging tan Buick and leaned against it. He would wait for his boxes to be brought to him.

Thank God it wasn't Tuesday; at least he wouldn't have to endure meatloaf tonight.

➤

On the following Wednesday, Dave Johnsen and the two new city councilors were sworn in by the municipal court judge. After the brief ceremony, Johnsen took his place on the dais to preside over his first city council meeting as mayor.

He sat in the middle seat, flanked by the councilors on either side of him. It was also the first meeting for the two new councilors: Jordan Caulfield, who had been elected to Johnsen's former seat, and Fabrizzi's replacement Bettina Aragon.

"I'd like to welcome our new councilors," Johnsen began, but Adam Fletcher, the city manager, gave him a stern look and nodded toward the American flag near the dais. Johnsen stood up, embarrassed, and led those assembled in the Pledge of Allegiance.

"You'd think he'd remember that at least," Old George murmured, standing next to Digger.

Johnsen quickly recovered his composure and plowed on, introducing his new colleagues. Jordan Caulfield was a short man whose balding head and weathered expression reminded Digger of a walnut. He was an Air Force veteran from Indiana who'd spent some time stationed in New Mexico and decided to retire in Las Vistas. The other new councilor, Bettina Aragon, was a plump, dark-haired woman who'd grown up in Las Cruces, attended the University of New Mexico, and landed a job with an aircraft corporation that had a plant in Las Vistas. She'd been a frequent commenter at city council meetings over the past two years. She'd been clamoring for an ordinance requiring pet owners to neuter their animals. She had a real problem with dogs fornicating in public.

Johnsen nodded at the councilors and said, "I'm very excited to be working with this great team and looking forward to the work that we will be doing together."

They reacted with smiles and happy comments. Watching, Digger wondered how long this general sense of bonhomie would last. Public meetings were a form of theater. She'd seen the shifting alliances, the subtle—and sometimes not so subtle—digs, the dramas. Tonight's drama would probably be the presentation on the new road project. She'd tipped off Maria as soon as she'd seen it posted.

When they reached that agenda item, Josh Bebs, the public works director lumbered up to the lectern to speak. He faced the council, his back to those assembled, revealing a rumpled shirt that hung over low-slung, creased pants.

Bebs laid out the road project details and sources of funding in a high-pitched, jerky voice, pausing occasionally to run his hands through his thinning red hair in nervous little grooming movements.

After Bebs finished, Johnsen invited comments from the public. Raposa was first up to the lectern, welcoming the mayor and the new councilors. Then he launched into a brief speech.

"The extension of Paseo del Valle through the cliffs will provide critical access for residents of a growing new development to the rest of the city. There is also potential to bring in more badly needed tax revenue to Las Vistas. I'm hoping you will quickly move ahead on this project."

Of course you are, Digger thought, *because you stand to make a bundle if the road goes through.*

A couple more people who said they lived in Los Sueños came up and spoke in favor of the project. Then Maria appeared. She must have come in quietly, Digger thought, while everyone's attention was focused on the new councilors. She stood before the lectern, long hair loose, silver bracelets glinting on her brown arms as she she planted them on her hips, and faced the council.

"I am Maria Ortiz," she said. "And I am here today, as I have been here before, to ask the council to reconsider the plan to extend Paseo del Valle. As it is planned right now, the route will cut right through an area of great historical and cultural importance to people who have been living here for many generations. We families who have our roots here—not in other states, like so many people in Las Vistas—we want our voices to be heard just the same as you listen to the developers. All we want is for you to consider a different route for the road—and maybe to think about the water that will be needed if you keep going ahead with all these developments. You can't make more water no matter how much you want the city to grow."

The councilors appeared taken aback by Maria's passion, glancing uncomfortably at one another. After a brief silence, Johnsen leaned forward with a sympathetic smile.

"Thank you, Ms. Ortiz. We really appreciate your concerns." He turned to Bebs. "Josh, have you looked at any route alternatives for the road?"

Bebs heaved himself to his feet and returned to the lectern. "Yes, Mayor, we did that in the early stages of planning. We considered taking it south of the currently proposed route. This would be about a quarter mile away from the sites Ms. Ortiz mentioned, but it would add roughly a half mile to the length of the road and contribute significantly to the cost."

Caulfield immediately jumped in. "How much more? What kind of money are we talking about here?"

Bebs consulted the papers in front of him. "As it is, the project is expected to cost $10.4 million. We estimated the alternative routing would add about $3 million."

"Did I hear that right? $3 million?" Caulfield barked. "And how many people visit this cultural site we just heard about?"

"We don't have any figures on that, I'm afraid," Bebs said.

"What about the tax revenue that the city expects to get from the new commercial development proposed next to the Los Sueños subdivision?" Caulfield persisted.

Bebs looked at a loss.

"Anybody?" Caulfield looked around.

Adam Fletcher broke in. "The land is zoned commercial, but at this point any tax figures would be entirely hypothetical, so I prefer not to say."

Caulfield snorted. The noise seemed to goad the councilor sitting next to him, the normally somnolent Tony Apodaca, into action. He shot Caulfield an angry look and cleared his throat.

"As one whose family roots in this area go back generations," he said, "I think we should put more value on our heritage. Maybe we should get those figures so we can truly weigh the alternatives."

Councilor Larry Martinez, the former deputy mayor, broke in. "Yes, I remember my grandfather taking me to see the Spanish chapel. We really have a treasure there."

The discussion continued back and forth for about twenty minutes before Johnsen intervened, asking Bebs and Fletcher if they could come up with some numbers by the next council meeting.

"However," Johnsen said firmly, "I understand city staff have been evaluating bids for the contract on this work, and I would hope we can vote on this in two weeks."

CHAPTER THIRTY-ONE

WHEN SHE GOT home later, after filing the story, Digger called Maria. "You really made them listen tonight."

"Yeah? You think they'll pay any attention to what I said?"

Digger hesitated, skeptical but not wanting to spoil the conversation. "Councilors usually hate it when it sounds like something will cost more money," she said. "But the way those two spoke up, sounds like they're in your corner on this."

"Thank God. I need some positive news." She paused. There was anxiety in her tone.

"What is it? What's wrong?"

"Abuela isn't well. She's been in bed all day, says she feels dizzy. I'm worried. I think I'll take her to urgent care in the morning."

Digger was alarmed. Abuela, the tiny woman with the strong spirit, had deeply touched her heart.

"If you need me to, I'd like to help in any way I can," she said.

The next day dawned bright and warm, the warmest day of the year so far. Digger drove to work with the window down, music from a country station blaring. About half an hour after she arrived in the newsroom, Maria called.

"We just got back from the doctor. He thinks it's just a form of flu, but they want her to see a cardiologist as soon as possible. He said she should rest. I'm not teaching any classes this afternoon, so I'm taking the remainder of the day off from school to stay with her."

"Would it help if I came over?"

"If you can, maybe later this afternoon, that would be great." Digger heard the hesitation in Maria's voice. This was the first time she had asked a favor.

"Don't worry. I'll find a way."

Around four thirty Digger saw an opportunity to slip out under the pretext of going to the district court to search for documents. Instead she headed toward Los Jardines. The day had continued to warm up, unseasonably so for the end of March, and in the narrow street beside Abuela's house, she could feel the heat radiating off the adobe walls. Maria greeted her at the door with a hug.

"Thanks for coming. She's in her room," she said, gesturing. "I was just going to make something to eat. You hungry?"

"Always."

Maria busied herself in the kitchen, Digger pushed Abuela's bedroom door open and stepped in quietly. The room faced west and the late afternoon sunshine poured in, soaking the brick floor with light. Abuela was sitting in an armchair beside the bed, a crocheted blanket over her lap. Her eyes were closed and her breathing was quick and shallow. Digger sat down on the bed and studied her, noticing again how dark her hair still was, just a few strands of gray and a feathering of white around the temples. How old was Abuela? Maria had said she was nearly eighty. Digger sat listening to her breathing, aware of the tick of the clock on the bedside table, the sounds of Maria in the kitchen.

Looking around, she took in the dark wood of the furniture, the dresser marred with old cigarette burns and water stains. A mirror propped atop the dresser had a crack in one corner. On the wall opposite hung a faded black-and-white photo of a couple standing stiffly in their wedding clothes, the man with a big dark mustache, his wife with her hair gathered up under a lacy, draped veil.

The sound of a yawn drew Digger's attention. "Abuela, are you awake?" she asked gently.

The old woman's dark, deep-set eyes opened slowly and she gazed about as if uncertain where she was.

"Is that you, cowgirl?"

Digger smiled. "Is that what you call me?"

Abuela's brown, wrinkled face split in a grin. "That's how I see you, with your jeans and your boots and a big hat."

"I don't wear a hat."

"No matter," Abuela said. She regarded Digger for a few moments as though she were studying her for a portrait. "I see you like one of those pioneering women that came to New Mexico a hundred years ago," she said. "Women who wanted to learn about the land and its history. Not like these people who come here now. They don't care. All they want is their big house where they can look at the mountains. They talk about freedom, but it's only *their* freedom, *their* way." She paused to take a sip of water from a glass on the bedside table, cleared her throat, and went on. "What do you think about that road that Maria is trying to stop?"

Digger sighed and leaned her head closer to Abuela. "I don't know. From what I saw at the council meeting last night, it could go either way. Some people support her, but there's a man out there who's willing to spend a lot of money to make the road happen, because he stands to lose a lot if it doesn't."

Abuela stared toward the window, lost in thought. Finally she said, "Do you know how the chapel came to be there?"

Digger shook her head. She'd been wanting to ask Abuela about the chapel and how it got its name.

"The story told to me when I was a little girl," Abuela continued in a soft voice, "is that a group of settlers was on their way north to Santa Fe from New Spain—that's what Mexico was called three hundred years ago—and apparently they got lost. They were hungry and exhausted and desperate to find water. Their leader, a young man named Lorenzo Tafoya, prayed to the Virgin Mary and San Lorenzo, the saint he was named after. That night he and several others in the group had a dream that they would find water soon. The next day they came upon a spring at the base of a cliff, and all the people and horses were finally able to get water. Tafoya was so grateful that he promised to build a chapel beside the spring and name it for the Virgin. That's the chapel Maria is fighting for."

"That's a beautiful story. But I didn't see the spring when Maria took me there," Digger said.

Abuela shook her head. "No, you wouldn't. It only flows if there's heavy rain, like that storm last summer. But I've seen it. The water just gushes up out of the ground. It must have seemed like a miracle to those people long ago."

They sat quietly for a few minutes, then Abuela's eyes narrowed and a bitter look came over her face. She shook her head slowly.

"When I was young, we heard about Cesar Chavez and what he was doing for the farmworkers. I used to tell Maria stories about him when she was a little girl. I think that's where she got the inspiration for what she's doing. I've seen a lot of change here in my lifetime, and I know it's just part of life, but it's not always for the best."

Her voice had gradually sunk to a whisper, and her breathing was becoming labored. Digger reached out and clasped her hands, warming them with her own.

Maria appeared at the door. "Dinner's ready. Are you okay, Abuela?"

Abuela roused herself. "I'm going to be all right, *mija*. Digger, can you help me up?"

Digger stepped to the side of the chair and slid an arm behind Abuela's back, carefully supporting her till she had her feet firmly on the floor, then helped her to stand. With Maria on one side and Digger on the other, they helped her walk the few steps to the kitchen, where they settled her at the table.

Maria served them bowls of posole and homemade tortillas. "I made this a while ago and froze it," she said. "I hope it's okay." Digger hadn't realized how hungry she really was until she began eating.

"Wonderful," she murmured between spoonfuls. "I don't cook much for myself. I've got one of those George Foreman grills, a microwave, and an electric can opener."

Maria rolled her eyes. "Your grandmother never taught you how to cook?"

Digger grinned sheepishly. "Um. She wasn't that kind of grandmother. She and my grandfather were always running a business. We ate out a lot when I was growing up."

Abuela cast her a pitying look. "*Mija*, you can teach her how to make posole."

"Aie! Abuela! You must be feeling better if you're telling me what to do!" Maria said. "When do I have time to give cooking lessons? We're always working." She looked over at Digger. "Talking about work, have you heard anything about the paper finding a buyer?"

Digger shook her head. "Not yet. I'm trying not to think about it. I want to see how the vote goes on the road contract, and that's likely going to happen in a couple of weeks."

After the meal, while Maria cleaned up, Digger helped Abuela back to her room. She eased the old woman into her chair and refilled the glass of water that had been on the table beside her. Abuela closed her eyes as if the effort of talking during dinner had exhausted her. Digger sat on the edge of the bed, watching her anxiously. Abuela's fierce spirit had touched something deep

within her. What was it? A yearning for strength, permanence—
something like the sensation she had felt in the chapel, where she
was wrapped around by adobe walls that were almost like living
flesh, walls that seemed to both protect and nourish.

"Abuela," she said, softly, "I have to go home now."

The old woman's eyes opened slowly, and she smiled. "Cowgirl, you always have a home here too."

Maria was waiting for her in the kitchen. For the first time
since Digger had met her, she looked frightened.

"I didn't tell you this before, but the doctor said she has an
irregular heartbeat. That's why he wants her to see a cardiologist.
I'm really worried. I don't know what I'd do if I lost her."

Digger put her arms around Maria, her thoughts racing. What
could she say that didn't sound shallow and trite?

"Abuela is a strong woman, and she knows you care for her,"
she said at last. "I care for her too. I have to go now, but I can come
back any time if you need me."

CHAPTER THIRTY-TWO

SHE COULDN'T SLEEP, tossing and turning as Maria's concerns about Abuela ricocheted round her brain. Digger finally threw back the covers and got out of bed. Lady Antonia immediately assumed it was Tuna Time, darted into the kitchen and began meowing in the insistent tone that said, "I will not be ignored!" Digger fed the cat, turned out the lights, and stood looking out her living room window. A nearly full moon hung yellow above the mountain crest that cut a serrated line across the sky.

She had her own worries too. On and off she'd been wracking her brain wondering what she would do if the *Courier* closed. Last week, when she'd made her regular call to Grandma Betty, she'd let slip that the paper was being sold. That had unleashed the usual suggestions. *Why don't you come back here? There are so many more opportunities in Houston. You could stay with us. You have friends here.*

Do I? Digger wondered. Going back to Houston and staying with Grandma Betty? She appreciated the offer, but she'd been out on her own too long.

Houston—that whole city environment, feeling like an insignificant microorganism amid a forest of glass and concrete towers, driving on traffic-clogged, rain-pelted freeways divorced from human contact, walking outside and being assaulted by thick, humid air that wrapped itself around your face like a wet wash-cloth—it was too depressing.

What if the paper did close? It could happen next week, next month. She sighed. It was time to get serious about working on the resumé. Other papers in New Mexico might be hiring, or maybe TV—God forbid—or a PR job.

But, if the paper closed . . . she could be with Maria. She sighed again and continued staring at the moonlit landscape, the con-tours of the foothills just visible, boulders, juniper bushes, the hint of a trail. She thought about the day Maria had taken her to see the old Spanish chapel: the marigold flowers placed in front of the statue by an unseen hand, someone who still cared.

As the thoughts percolated, the story she'd been wanting to write formed in her mind: Las Vistas, the place of aspirations. A small town that became all things to all people who came there— and the land that ceased to be what it was as they carved their desires into the earth heedless of the impact.

Abandoning thoughts of sleep, she went to her laptop and began writing: "A road to a burgeoning subdivision that would destroy access to a centuries-old cultural site is pitting newcom-ers to a fast-growing New Mexico city against families who have lived there for generations . . ." She worked on into the wee hours, poring over her old stories, searching the internet for additional information. By four in the morning, she had a 1,000-word arti-cle she felt proud of. Exhausted, she tumbled back into bed and finally fell into a deep sleep.

She woke around eight, showered, grabbed coffee and toast, and headed to the office. Once there, she read through the piece twice more, then searched her phone for the photos she had taken of the chapel. She made a printout of the article and four of the photos, then waited for Swenson to appear.

As soon as he arrived, she took the printouts to show him.

"Morning," she said, beaming a confident smile.

Swenson pulled a thermos out of his backpack, unscrewed the cup, and poured himself some coffee. On his second sip he nodded at Digger. "Well? What is it, or are you just going to stand there?"

Digger grinned, handing him the story printout and the photos. "I think I've got your Sunday centerpiece. Wanna read it?"

Swenson took another gulp of coffee, grabbed the papers from Digger, and sat down. She stood by while he read, glancing every few seconds between the photos and the printed pages.

Finally he set the papers down but kept eyeing them, moving his jaw around as if something were stuck between his teeth.

"This is good as far as it goes," he said. "In fact, it's some of the best writing you've done. But you're letting your sympathy for these protesters show. You ought to know better."

He stared hard at her for a few moments. Disappointment pricked. She swallowed. She'd tried to be so careful. Swenson picked up the printout and pointed at the bottom of the first page. "Right here I want to see more from the developer angle. Can you talk some more to this guy Raposa, really probe whether he had any concerns about the way the land was being used? And here you've got Kimble talking about the whole drainage thing, but you need to get more. I know a lot of these decisions were made before he was mayor, but he's the one that's had the come-to-Jesus revelation about the whole flooding issue. If you can get those elements in the story, I promise I'll find a place for it."

Digger returned to her desk, heart thumping. That had been a close call, but the outcome was better than she'd hoped. She just had to figure out a way to get Raposa to talk frankly. Every time she'd managed to reach him by phone or in person, he'd dodged around, citing legal issues. The guy was as slippery as a wet fish. She stared at her computer, brain whirling. It took maybe five minutes for an idea to jump into her head. She shoved a notebook into her backpack, then slipped her recorder into a hip pocket for insurance; sources often tried to deny stuff they'd said. She jumped into her car and tore out of the parking lot, headed for Raposa's office. Somehow she was going to get that arrogant jerk to talk.

Raposa's business, now called Cielo Development, was located in an office park close to downtown. The buildings were low and boxy-looking, set among grassy areas landscaped with flowerbeds and desert willow trees. It was about ten thirty when she drew up outside the entrance. With any luck, Raposa would be there. If not, maybe someone in the office would be willing to tell her where and when she could find him.

She had just slung her backpack over a shoulder when she noticed the front door starting to open. She got out of the car and hurried toward the entrance. At first she couldn't see who was coming out because of the sunlight glancing off the door. Then there they were: Raposa and—surprise, surprise—the yoga teacher ex-wife, Phyllis Lynton.

What the hell is she doing here? Last time we talked, she hated this guy.

Phyllis flinched at the sight of Digger, but Digger gave no indication they'd ever met before.

"Oh, hello, Mr. Raposa," she said. "I just wanted to ask a few questions about Los Sueños and the Paseo del Valle project."

Raposa did not look happy at finding Digger outside his office. "Miss Doyle, I've told you before—"

Digger cut him off. "Yes, I know, you've been saying you can't comment about the Rancho Milagro subdivision because of a lawsuit. But I'm not asking about that. I'm asking about the road project that the council is expected to vote on in a few days and about how that will affect your subdivision."

Phyllis looked at him as though she expected him to answer the challenge. "Well, Johnny, that subdivision is all you've been talking about for the past three months."

Digger slid a hand into her pocket, felt for the recorder, and pressed the "record" button.

Raposa glanced angrily at his ex-wife, then at Digger. "Look, you were there at the council meeting. I told them the road extension would be critical for residents of Los Sueños."

"Is it true," Digger asked, "that sales there have been slow because of the lack of direct access to shopping areas?"

"Let's just say that the homes in Los Sueños appeal to the kind of people that want to be able to get to a grocery store without having to drive five miles out of their way."

"How many homes have you sold there since it opened last year?" "You're the reporter, you can find that out," Raposa said, his tone edged with sarcasm.

"I understand you've also bought the land beside the subdivision and you're applying for it to be zoned commercial."

"So? That's no secret."

"At the last council meeting, a Ms. Ortiz asked the council to consider an alternate route for the Paseo del Valle extension, one that would not prevent access to the historic sites she mentioned. What do you think about that?"

"What do I think about that?" he scoffed. "I think it would be a complete waste of money. Nobody goes to the place she's talking about. Until Ms. Ortiz and her crowd started protesting, nobody even knew about it."

"It seemed as though Councilors Apodaca and Martinez were familiar with the chapel."

Raposa made a snort of disgust. "That's just two guys. There is plenty of support for this road just the way it is, without spending an extra $3 million because half a dozen people have a bee up their ass about some old deserted chapel."

Digger took a different tack. "How did you come to develop the Los Sueños land if there wasn't good access to shopping? Seems like it would have been better to find a place closer to existing commercial centers."

"Look," he said, "the land became available, the price was right, the views are amazing. It's what people want when they come to Las Vistas."

"But did you do any research on the impact of the access road?"

"We believe in the free market here. People can choose where they want to live."

"It sounds like you're saying access to Los Sueños wasn't a factor in your decision to build there."

"Like I said, in a free market people can choose where they want to live." "Even if the houses you build are on unstable land? Isn't that what happened at Rancho Milagro? Seems like you have a pattern here."

Raposa glared at her. "I've told you before, I'm not commenting on anything to do with Rancho Milagro."

"That's okay," Digger said. "There's plenty of information in the court filings, which are all public record."

"We're done here, Miss Doyle."

Raposa steered his ex-wife past Digger and toward his BMW. Digger waited until he'd driven away, then fished the recorder out of her pocket and hit the stop button. So much for Raposa.

Now for Kimble.

CHAPTER THIRTY-THREE

DIGGER PUZZLED OVER the location Kimble had chosen for their meeting. Instead of his home, a café, or even the *Courier* offices, he'd cited a specific intersection, carefully spelling out the street names. She plugged it into the app on her phone and followed the blue line. It wasn't until she passed an ostentatious house with a mushroom-shaped turret that it struck her he wanted to meet on one of the dirt roads that had flooded last summer.

There he was, sitting on a rock at the side of the road. Digger parked a few feet from Kimble's ancient Buick. He greeted her, and they stood looking out over the bare earth of the arroyo. Its deeply gouged sides looked like the flexed tendons of some great tawny animal. She let the silence stretch out, waiting for him to speak. She had waited like this for tribal leaders to initiate a conversation.

Kimble seemed to have aged even in the short time since his election defeat.

Finally he held out an arm, pointing at the arroyo.

"You probably know the background, but this land, on this side of the city, was part of a large ranch. The owner got into financial trouble about thirty years ago and sold it to a consortium of developers. They platted it out on a grid system with no regard to the land—its shape, the way the water drained from here down to the river—just plots that could be sold for home building."

He glanced at her. "I've done a lot of research recently. As you know, I have a lot of time now." His angular face twisted in what she took for a smile, thin and neat like a surgical cut.

"Back then city leaders were eager to expand the size of Las Vistas, figuring it would bring in more revenue. Does this sound familiar?"

Digger nodded. "Was Johnny Raposa part of the consortium?" Kimble shook his head. "No, there was a Mr.—Bester? Brewster?

Something like that. They made a lot of money. Raposa came later, but the story is the same. He sold a lot of people on the Los Sueños dream. You know, 'sueños' means 'dreams' in Spanish."

Digger nodded. "Weren't there ever any environmental studies? Public meetings? Did anyone ever raise questions about how the building would affect the land?"

Kimble waved a hand dismissively. "The records I've found showed only a very cursory analysis. You can find them in the city archives. There were some public meetings. However, the records show no concerns about drainage or how building would affect water flow."

"What about this road extension that's sparked these protests?"

Again the thin smile. "The initiative started before I became mayor. Raposa was close with state representatives, people in Santa Fe who could approve money. Things slid by."

A thought occurred to Digger. "Are you bitter about Raposa because he didn't support your reelection? He gave generously in the past, right?"

Kimble grimaced. "I was naive and I wanted to be mayor, same as that young fellow Johnsen. He'll see."

He turned toward his car. "Now, Miss Doyle, I have to go. My wife is expecting me home for lunch. She gets anxious easily."

Digger reworked the story, adding the new material from Raposa and Kimble. She reread it. Something was still missing. She
needed someone who had decades of experience watching the
way the weather took a toll on this land.

Someone like Abuela.

She called Maria and explained the story.

"Do you think she'd talk to me? Is she strong enough?"

"The cardiologist put her on some medication, and she's doing
much better.

I think she'd be happy to talk to you. I'll make the arrangements."

The old lady was waiting for Digger on the broken-down bus
seat outside her front door, the place where they had first met.
She wore her signature faded brown corduroy pants, checked
shirt, and wide-brimmed hat. She patted a rusted blue metal chair
beside her.

"Come, sit. I'll make you coffee if you'd like." Her breathing
was still labored, but she seemed much stronger.

"Maybe later, thank you." Digger explained the story idea
again and launched into a series of questions, probing Abuela's
memories about her childhood, the growth of Las Vistas, how it
had affected her and her neighbors. At length the old lady reached
out and put her hand on top of Digger's notepad.

"You remember the night you came here a few weeks ago, the
night we talked about your family and what happened to them?
Do you remember what I said to you then?"

Digger looked at her, puzzled.

"We survive," Abuela said. Her dark brown eyes glistened with
tears, but her voice was strong. "We find new ways of living. Yes,
there have been changes we didn't like, but we adapt. How can we
not? I am glad Maria is fighting so that people will know about
the places that were sacred to people long ago. The city will keep

on growing, but perhaps her fight will mean that others learn to adapt as we have."

"You mean those who come here from elsewhere?"

Abuela nodded. "Now I think you have all that I can say. Now we should have coffee."

The day the story ran, Digger came in to work early and grabbed a paper from the stack left out for reporters. There it was, her story, front page, above the fold, just as she'd hoped. She turned on her computer and checked email to gauge reader reactions. About a dozen emails referred to the story. She read them and then listened to a slew of messages on her desk phone. Most were from Los Vistas residents who said they'd never heard of the Spanish chapel. Some suggested the historic site could be moved to be out of the way of the road extension. Digger sighed. This was not the reaction she'd hoped for.

A little while later, Swenson called her over to his desk.

"I know we didn't really see eye to eye on this piece when you first proposed it," he said, sounding genuinely contrite. "But I'm glad you did it. The extra reporting really made it. That said, I got a bunch of phone calls and emails, and Raposa went ballistic. You'd better call him right away."

Great, Digger thought, *just great.*

She went back to her desk and dialed Raposa's number. He answered on the second ring.

"Johnny Raposa."

"Hi, this is—"

"I know who this is. What the hell were you thinking with that story? I never said those things."

"Uh, yes you did, Mr. Raposa. I have my notes—"

"Oh, sure you do. You reporters just make stuff up."

"Actually, no, we don't. And I also have a recording."

"*What?* You recorded me without my permission? I'll sue your sorry paper."

"On what grounds, Mr. Raposa? New Mexico is not one of the states that requires two-party consent to a recording. I always record interviews as well as taking notes, to ensure accuracy. The words I quoted were exactly what you said."

The line went dead.

That evening Digger had a hard time finding a parking spot outside city hall.

She walked in to find the council chambers packed. Maria's group was ranged against the back wall. Luckily, Old George was there as always and had saved a seat for her.

"That's so kind of you, George."

"Anything for you, Miss Doyle," he said. He gave his naughty wink.

"Uh, thanks, George."

Dave Johnsen was better prepared for his second meeting as mayor. He ran briskly through the fluff items: a high school basketball team's success in the state championship, an honor for a Las Vistas veteran returned from Afghanistan, and a Las Vistas Fire Department fundraiser to benefit children with cancer. Then he got down to business.

Digger waited impatiently as the councilors debated a couple of zoning requests and considered allowing backyard chickens. Finally they got to the road project item: "D.42, advice and consent to award a contract for a 2.7-mile extension to Paseo del Valle in the amount of $10.4 million, to XJB Construction Co., Inc."

As soon as Johnsen invited comment, Maria rushed to the lectern.

"Mayor Johnsen, councilors, I'm coming before you because I'm asking you again to consider an alternative route for this road extension. If it could be moved just a few hundred yards, then people would be able to get to the cliff face to see the site. The chapel dates to the eighteenth century. Don't you think Las Vistas should honor this 'treasure,' as Councilor Martinez called it at the last meeting?"

Several more people whom Digger had seen at the protest rallies said more or less the same thing. Then a tiny woman edged her way down the aisle with the help of a cane and stopped before the lectern, her chin barely level with it. Digger noticed a small bunch of yellow flowers in her hand. At the sight of the flowers, Digger recalled the day at the chapel and the vase by the statue of the saint.

"*Señores y señoras,*" she said in a soft voice, "I have been going to the Chapel of Nuestra Señora de los Sueños every week for many years to put flowers in front of the statue of Saint Francis in memory of my husband, who was killed fighting for his country in Korea. I promised him I would do this as long as my feet would carry me, and I want to keep my promise."

The councilors nodded at her sympathetically but said nothing. She bowed her head toward them, turned, and shuffled slowly to the back of the room.

Digger expected Raposa to make his pitch next, but it was Danny Murphy who appeared, striding confidently down the aisle, head thrown back, white hair bouncing as he walked.

"Good evening, councilors, really good to see you here tonight. I think we all understand the need to remember our fallen heroes. We owe a debt of gratitude to our veterans—those who gave their lives for this fine country."

He looked around the room as if to give everyone a moment to appreciate the sentiments. Then he continued in an upbeat tone.

"But I am here tonight to talk about the future—a bright future for Las Vistas and everyone who lives here. My colleagues and I are so excited about this proposed road extension. I mean, this is going to bring a world of opportunity, not just to the residents of Los Sueños but to everyone in Las Vistas. Just think of it. One short piece of roadway will open up a new subdivision to the commercial center of the city. It will also give the rest of the city's residents access to a new shopping center next to Los Sueños that's already being planned. This is something that we shouldn't miss, something that we should go ahead with while we have the chance.

"Councilors, it's up to you. I'm looking forward to this opportunity happening as soon as possible so citizens of Las Vistas can benefit from a choice of high-end homes in this great new subdivision and from the shopping experience in the stores we plan to bring to the new commercial center."

The councilors nodded in a ho-hum kind of way, as though they'd heard it all before. Johnsen smiled and thanked Murphy, then invited the public works director to give the report he'd asked for at the last meeting.

Josh Bebs waddled up to the lectern. His shirt was still half untucked, hair mussed.

"Good evening, Josh," Johnsen said. "I hope you have some news for us about the cultural sites that we talked about at the last meeting."

Bebs looked flustered. "Well, my staff and I did a lot of research, and we came up with some historical data about the chapel," he said, "but we pretty much struck out when we tried to get statistics on the number of visitors to the site. It's just not something that anybody tracks."

Councilor Apodaca frowned. "Well, who did you talk to? After the story that appeared in the *Courier* this morning, I had a lot of calls from people who said they used to go to that chapel."

"That's just it, Councilor," Bebs said. "Anything we got was just anecdotal, no hard numbers."

"How about the cost of taking an alternative route? Anything more definitive on that?" Johnsen asked.

"As I said at the last meeting, the alternative we looked at— which would take the road about three hundred yards east of its currently proposed track— would cost about $3.4 million more than if we stay with the bid request."

"Are there ways that we could find that money?" Martinez asked. "Like Councilor Apodaca said, a lot of people reacted to the article in the *Courier*, particularly our senior population. Some of them are really concerned about this."

Bebs smoothed stray hairs over his shiny scalp. "Right now the money is coming from state and federal sources. We could look at city finances; maybe we could reduce expenses somewhere else, cut some programs, figure something into the upcoming city budget. But it would also mean delaying the project for several months, if not longer."

Bettina Aragon suddenly broke in, the first time she'd made her voice heard on the council. "I had an email from someone in my district suggesting the chapel could become a place of pilgrimage. It could become a real tourist attraction, and that would bring in money to the city."

Caulfield burst in. "Oh, did something miraculous happen there? Las Vistas's very own Lourdes? Are we going to see crutches lined up outside the door? You turn it into a tourist attraction and you're going to have to put in a parking lot and Porta-Potties and have someone to clean it up. That would cost a lot more."

Linda Raccaro shot Caulfield a nasty look while Aragon practically shrank into her seat.

"You know," Raccaro said, "just a few months ago, we were all talking about the great drainage plan, but as soon as everyone found out how much it would cost them, suddenly nobody wanted it. Nobody likes to spend money if it comes out of their own pocket, but if state and federal money is going to pay for this road, I say we should just go ahead with it the way it's planned."

Caulfield leaned forward on his elbows and said, "I appreciate the concerns of those who revere these historic sites, but I'd like to point out that they do not live in Las Vistas. Ms. Ortiz and the others live in Los Jardines and rural areas outside of the city. Since this road is of utmost importance to the residents of Las Vistas, I move to approve the contract with XJB Construction as it is." He looked at the other councilors.

"Second," Raccaro said.

Johnsen glanced around, then called for the vote. Caulfield, Raccaro, and one other councilor were in favor. Martinez, Apodaca, and Aragon voted no. A tie meant it was up to the mayor to cast the deciding vote. A hush fell.

Dave Johnsen looked out at the crowd in the room. He'd never expected to be in this position. He saw the faces of the people out there: the beautiful young woman who had pleaded so passionately, the Korean War widow with the flowers, Murphy with his talk of new shopping opportunities and growth for the city. He heard Raposa's voice in his head, telling him he could lead the city to a better future. He remembered Kimble's bitter defeat.

Digger watched Johnsen's face as he wrestled with the decision. The seconds ticked by. Everyone in the room was staring at him. Finally, Johnsen squared his shoulders, looked out at the crowd, and spoke.

"I vote for the motion."

CHAPTER THIRTY-FOUR

THE NIGHT AFTER the council meeting, Digger ran into Maria at Frankie's. It was quiet at this hour, just a couple of women shooting pool and a small group in the corner with their eyes glued to a basketball game on the TV. Digger sat beside Maria at the bar, trying to think of something to say to lighten the mood. Maria just sat staring at the Corona in front of her, shoulders slumped, eyes not really seeing.

Finally Maria sighed deeply and said, "I don't know what I'm going to do now. I really believed we could persuade them. I really thought those people on the council would listen. I thought your story would make people understand why it was important to protect those places from the developers." She looked over at Digger. "What kind of reaction did you get, anyway?"

Digger took a sip from her own beer and shook her head. "I got a lot of emails, mostly from people who said they'd never heard of the chapel."

Maria shrugged and rolled her eyes. "That's Las Vistas for you!"

Digger laid an arm on Maria's shoulder. What could she say? Right now she had her own worries. People were starting to desert the sinking ship that was the *Courier*. Last week the education reporter had given notice; she was going to Los Angeles. Another reporter had announced his retirement. She'd been scouring internet job sites, but everything she'd seen was out of state: a business publication in San Diego, a daily in San Antonio, another in Orlando. She'd sent out resumés, but she wasn't hopeful. She wanted to talk to Maria about it, but now was not the time.

————➤

Jack Kimble stopped his Buick at the spot where he'd seen the protesters a few months back. There was just enough room to pull off the road beside a pathway that led into the woods beneath the cliffs. He wanted to see for himself the site they were so passionate about—not that it mattered any more, he was just an ordinary citizen now. He sat for a while, listening to the engine ticking. He'd been looking back over his life the past few days, wondering what was left. It seemed like he'd done everything he'd hoped for and all he had to look forward to was the final decline toward the inevitable. But, of course, there was Imelda. She needed him, and for now that kept him going.

He opened the car door and stepped onto the soft earth. He looked down at his feet. He was wearing the brown punched-leather lace-up shoes he always wore to the office. They weren't the right shoes to go walking through the woods, but he had nothing else to do for the rest of the day, plenty of time to clean shoes. He set off, his steps crunching on the sandy path through the trees. The cottonwoods were fully leafed out, big gnarly trees with thick, twisted branches. They looked strong, but that was just an illusion—the branches were notorious for breaking under the onslaught of spring winds. *Just like some people*, Kimble thought. That Dave Johnsen, for all his youth and his strong body, he'd crumbled like cheese when Raposa put the pressure on. Kimble knew all about Raposa's tactics. He was your friend when it suited him, and when it didn't, his money was on a different horse.

After about five minutes, he spotted a low adobe building with a sort of belfry at the front. That must be the chapel. He walked slowly up to it, noting the way its brown walls seemed to grow directly out of the earth as though they hadn't been made by human hands. At the door he paused as if waiting for permission to enter. A breeze rustled the leaves above him, and he took it as a sign. He pushed the door open and stepped inside.

Filtered through the dust-caked, broken windows, the afternoon light cast fuzzy shadows on the floor. He stepped ahead carefully, fearful that the sagging floorboards might give way. Halfway to the altar he stopped and sat on one of the benches propped against the wall. He stared around, feeling like an intruder in this Catholic place with its statues and paintings of saints. His eyes came to rest on an image of Mary with the child Jesus in her arms. The baby was looking out at the world with a benign but serious expression, as if he were looking far into the future, as if he could see an old man in scuffed brown leather shoes staring at him. Kimble bowed his head and let the tears trickle down his cheeks.

After a while he got up, left the church, and headed back to his car. He had to clean his shoes and study the weather reports. He had to follow El Niño.

———➤

Johnny Raposa was drinking a rum and Coke at the golf club bar. It was his third, and he didn't feel like moving. He knew he ought to be relieved that the council had voted to go ahead and award the contract for the road project. That would get things going at Los Sueños. He'd been sweating the past few months as sales stalled. He couldn't afford another Rancho Milagro, and he still wasn't sure if the Arizona investors would come through with what they'd talked about for the shopping center. Thinking about that fiasco and the AG's investigation kept him awake at night.

But that wasn't the only thing keeping him awake. After all the bitter words they'd said, Phyllis had suddenly come back into his life. He'd forgotten how hot she was—that toned yoga-teacher body! He remembered how hard he'd fallen for her after his Michigan divorce. He just wanted things to go back to the way they were before all that Rancho Milagro shit happened. But they weren't the same.

There was something weird about the way she wanted to be with him all the time, even when he was at work. Like the other morning when she'd showed up at the office and the odd way she'd reacted to that reporter. Thinking about his conversation with Digger made him furious all over again.

➤

Dave Johnsen stood in the middle of the mayor's office, his office. He looked around, marveling that he really belonged here. After all his mother's skepticism, the move to New Mexico had been good for him. She'd even sounded impressed the night he'd called to tell her he'd won the election. Connie seemed glad too, although it was sometimes hard to tell with her. Right now she was focused on the baby that would come in a few months.

He walked over to the window and looked out. The land sloped gently down to a ragged green line of vegetation that bordered the river. Beyond it the mountains leaped up toward the sky. Over to one side, he could just make out the edge of Los Sueños, cut off from the main part of town by a broad, deep gully and a steep escarpment. The road extension they'd voted on the other night would go somewhere across that divide.

Thinking about it troubled him. He believed that projects like the road and the new business centers were the right direction for Las Vistas, but he didn't feel good about the way Raposa had steered him through the election campaign. The bitterness in Kimble's voice when he'd handed over his office had stuck with him. Kimble had said he wanted to protect the city from future floods, but people had protested his plan because they wanted to keep their dirt roads. They had their vision of what life in Las Vistas should be, and they didn't want change. Was that so different from the people who didn't want the road extension? They wanted to keep the symbols of a way of life.

He closed his eyes and saw again the beautiful young Hispanic woman, heard her voice speaking so passionately. She was beautiful. He realized he was on the verge of having impure thoughts. No, they were impure thoughts. Father Heaney's words about temptation popped into his head. *Stop, stop, stop,* he told himself.

The click of the door opening snapped him back into the present. The city manager's assistant had come to remind him of a meeting.

"Dave, it's almost ten o'clock. Adam is waiting for you in the conference room."

Johnsen panicked. He'd barely started to prepare, and he'd already found out Adam Fletcher was a tough taskmaster.

"Tell him I'll be there in a minute."

CHAPTER THIRTY-FIVE

NICK ROEMER CURSED the weather. All month long they'd had one delay after another. They'd begun work by tearing down trees to clear a site where they could stage equipment for the job. The crew had made a good start when a freak storm dumped several inches of snow, halting work for a couple of days. Once the snow melted, the bare earth was a morass. Soon after that, the weather shifted back to the usual spring winds, blowing grit everywhere. Today the wind was out of the northwest, and the sky was brown with sand blown from the cleared land. It was nearly mid-May, they were days behind schedule, and the contract contained penalties for missing deadlines.

Now they were busy ripping out a wide swath of trees to clear a path for the equipment to access the site. Then they could dig and pour the foundations for the supports that would carry the road to the top of the escarpment. Nick had heard the controversy about the project, how a group of protesters wanted the road to follow a different route so they could protect some historic landmark. He'd seen the alternative plan; privately, he thought it made a lot of sense. The route this project would take meant a nearly seven percent grade, which was pretty steep for a city connector road. The other route would mean a more gradual ascent, but it would involve more rock blasting, and that was expensive. He knew from experience that the guys who made the decisions were all about the money. So who was he to complain, as long as the paychecks kept coming? In a few months he'd be on another project in some other state.

On that windy morning, Rex wasn't happy about the weather either. He had to shoot photos at the ground-breaking for the new strip mall next to Los Sueños, and the blowing sand would make it a nightmare.

"How come you're doing this story?" he asked Digger. "I thought somebody from business usually got stuck with the golden shovel routine."

Digger slung her backpack over a shoulder and climbed into the Jeep.

"Biz didn't have anybody. They're down two people now. So they figured if the mayor was going to be there, it was my gig."

Rex was loading his gear into the back. "I don't know why they're in such a hurry to break ground on this. From what I heard, the road project is way behind on schedule."

"It's probably a prestige thing for the new mayor and Raposa."

Rex climbed in. "Yeah, that guy is everywhere. It bummed me out when they voted to go ahead with that road. That protest gal ought to run for office. What's she doing now? You still in touch?"

"She's a teacher, and now that school is out she's been going up to Santa Fe talking to people at state agencies to see if she can get any support to stop the project."

"Not giving up, huh?"

"She's that kind of person—has to have a cause."

Rex shot Digger a meaningful look. "Be careful, Digg.

Swenson's suspicious of the way you've been handling the protest stories. The *Courier* may be going down the tubes, but there's other places, and you've got a great future in front of you."

Digger looked away, uncertain whether to thank him or tell him to mind his own business. Instead she changed the subject. "You know what I really want to do? I'd like to nail Raposa. Everything I've found shows he's ripped off a lot of people. He thinks he's going to get away with it, and I am not going to let that happen."

"Okayyy," Rex said slowly. "You got some history with this guy, too?"

"No, not him." She shook her head. "Let's just say I have personal experience of a cover-up. I don't trust the justice system. As soon as I get a few more documents I'm going to do that story on Raposa."

"Well, you may be running out of time."

Digger glanced at him in alarm. "No! What have you heard?"

"I'm hearing a rumor that the publisher is losing patience and if a buyer doesn't appear pretty soon he'll probably just close us down."

"Shit!" Digger stared out the windshield, letting Rex's words sink in. "What are you going to do?" she asked finally.

He rubbed his chin. "Well, my wife's an RN, so we'll have one income. My son's got a part-time job. Me, I thought I'd try going out on my own—you, know, weddings, real estate photos, advertising, whatever. What about you?"

"I've been looking—replied to a few job postings, but they're all out of state, and I kind of want to stay in New Mexico."

"You got someone keeping you here?"

"Come off it, Rex, I know when you're fishing for information. Let's go. We're going to be late."

"Oh, definitely touched a nerve with that one. Like I said, be careful. Know what I mean?" He started the engine.

———▶

The ground-breaking site was about a quarter mile from the nearest house in the Los Sueños subdivision. Sand swirled up in wisps from a small patch of land that had been cleared for the ceremony. Half a dozen vehicles were parked along the road next to the site.

Rex drew up behind the local TV station van. While he unloaded his camera gear, Digger sauntered over to a group of men huddled together with their backs to the wind. She made out the bulky shape of Councilor Larry Martinez.

"Good morning," she hailed the men.

Martinez turned and gave her a long-suffering look. "It'd be better without this wind."

Digger recognized the others in the group as city staffers. She stepped in close to Martinez and ventured a question. "So, Councilor, what do you think about this road project? I hear work is behind schedule."

Martinez shrugged. "You were at the meeting, you know I didn't vote for it. I think it would have been better all around if they'd at least discussed the alternative route a little more. But there you are: money makes things happen around here."

A white SUV bearing the city's parks and recreation department logo arrived at the site. A man got out and unloaded a folding table and a half-dozen shovels from the back. He opened the rear door and produced several white hard hats. Rex and the TV cameraman wandered around taking photos. Martinez looked at his watch.

"They should be here by now."

As if on cue, Dave Johnsen drew up in a dark blue Ford Escape. Behind him was a silver BMW with Raposa at the wheel. The woman who emerged from the passenger's side was Phyllis Lynton.

Martinez looked toward them and glowered. Digger made her way over to Johnsen and Raposa and asked about the development. Raposa seemed in an upbeaat mood, as though he'd gotten over his ire at Digger for recording their last conversation. When he smiled, his teeth showed eerily white against his dark beard, which was now full-grown and neatly trimmed. Phyllis stood silently beside him, slim, fit and elegantly aloof. But as Digger was about to walk away, Phyllis shot her a look and jerked her head toward a couple of Porta-Potties that stood on the edge of the site.

What kind of game is she playing?

The parks and rec employee handed out the shovels and hard hats. Officials mugged for the cameras as each pitched in and tossed a shovelful of dirt. Johnsen made a brief speech about the benefits of free enterprise, business, and jobs and how more retail development would be good for Las Vistas. Raposa smiled and talked about his great partnership with city officials, blah, blah, blah.

As soon as the speeches were over, the TV cameraman moved in to get comments from Johnsen and Raposa. Digger decided she needed to answer a call of nature so she headed for the Porta-Potties; she was sure Phyllis had been trying to say something with that odd look. She went into one of the stalls, waited, then heard footsteps. When she opened the door, Phyllis was standing right in front of her.

"I need to talk to you. Go around the back, I don't want to be seen," Phyllis said.

Digger followed her behind the toilets, where they were sheltered from the wind and out of sight of the others.

"You didn't do very much with all that stuff I gave you before," Phyllis said harshly.

Digger was taken aback. "You mean the stuff about the divorce, how Raposa got money from his first wife? I don't know what you expected. It was good background, but—"

Phyllis cut her off before she could finish the sentence. "That was just a teaser. I wanted to get you interested. I talked to my old friend Alex Simpkin and suggested he call the paper about Rancho Milagro. You're looking into it now, aren't you?"

Digger's mouth fell open.

"Yes, that was me." Phyllis smirked. "I used to work for the county too, you know."

"No, I didn't know."

"I was there when Johnny came to the county with his plans for it," Phyllis said. "I met him in Arizona and he charmed me into moving here. That's when I got the job with the county. I was with him all through that Rancho Milagro—that fuckup. He swore he'd lost everything on that project. That was his excuse when he went back to Arizona after that woman—and left me with nothing. Nothing!"

Phyllis looked as if she were about to explode. She grabbed Digger's arm and got right in her face.

"Have you ever been jealous? Do you know what it feels like?" She didn't wait for a response. "I'll tell you what it feels like. It feels like fire eating at your insides. I knew he was lying to me. He made the mistake of sending me a text that was meant for her. It hurt so bad I really wanted to make him suffer. But I was smart enough to bide my time."

She nodded archly. Then she reached into the big leather shoulder bag she was carrying and pulled out a thick manila envelope.

"Here. See what you can do with this," she said, thrusting it into Digger's hands. "You didn't get this from me. Got it?"

Digger studied her for a moment, puzzled. "Last time we talked, you were really angry at Raposa. You still sound mad. So what are you doing with him?"

Phyllis's lips twisted. "I spent a long time planning how I could do the most damage. He always thought I was just a nice body. Well, I know a thing or two, and I figured it was easiest to get back at him if I was closer. I could make him believe I still cared about him. Nice way to turn the tables. Besides, I'm not making much of a living teaching yoga." She turned abruptly and marched off.

OMG. The woman's even crazier than I thought.

———

Rex was on the phone and the officials were dispersing when Digger got back to the ground-breaking site. He waved when he saw her, flapping an arm to show he was in a hurry. As soon as he finished the call, he shoved the phone into a pocket and started toward the Jeep.

"Where've you been? Tom called. There's been a crash on the freeway— blowing sand, semi driver couldn't see."

"Sorry. Stomach trouble. Bad burrito. Believe me, a Porta-Potty is not the place you want that to happen."

———

When Digger got back to her desk, she banged out a perfunctory piece about the ground-breaking, then switched attention to the envelope Phyllis had given her. She pulled out a sheaf of papers and began going through them one by one. She found an email thread between Raposa and someone in Scottsdale—the name wasn't familiar—detailing the transfer of substantial assets from the development company in New Mexico to an Arizona company. Further checking revealed that the listed address was evidently a rented mailbox in a UPS store. She couldn't find any more information under the name of the registered agent. Several invoices showed payments the Arizona company had made to an architectural consultant, tens of thousands of dollars.

The kicker was a handwritten note with a date and a reference that Digger recognized as a federal filing in bankruptcy court. So that was the money trail! Raposa had funneled assets of the Milagro Millennium company to the shell company in Scottsdale, then declared bankruptcy to get out of paying the settlement money. At least that's how it looked. Phyllis must have hacked into Raposa's records somehow. What was she hoping to get from exposing him? Just revenge, or something more?

At this point, Digger didn't care. With these documents and what she had from the county, she had two legs of the stool. Now if only the AG's office would respond.

CHAPTER THIRTY-SIX

Saturday morning; Digger stretched, luxuriating at the thought of two full days ahead, pregnant with possibilities. Lady Antonia took Digger's movement as a cue to come sit on her chest, where she began a loud, rhythmic purring. The phone buzzed. Digger reached for it, dislodging the cat. It was Maria.

"Did I wake you?"

"I'm about halfway there. What's up?"

"I'm really happy! Abuela is feeling so much better with the new medication. It was touch and go there for a while. Anyway, she wants to make tortillas. She thinks it's a skill you might want to learn."

"Are you serious?"

"Of course not. It's just fun to watch. Come for breakfast."

The sun was already hot by the time Digger arrived, and Abuela's front door was open. She could hear music from inside. Abuela kept her radio tuned to the local Spanish language station that played cumbias, rancheras, and Mexican polka tunes.

The old woman was at the kitchen table, busy measuring flour into a large mixing bowl. Maria was stirring something on the stove and moving to the music. Digger stood for a moment in the open doorway, feeling awkward. Then Abuela looked up and caught sight of her.

"Ah, it's my cowgirl! Come in! Come in!" She beckoned Digger with flour-covered hands.

Maria gave Digger a hug. "Here, have a seat. I'll get you some coffee. We can talk while we cook."

Abuela had made a remarkable recovery. She looked much stronger than on the day of the interview. Her eyes were bright behind her glasses, her hands deft as she added a chunk of lard and worked the mixture.

"*Mija,* get me some hot water, will you?" she called to Maria.

Digger sipped her coffee while she watched as Abuela poured in the water slowly, her brown fingers squelching the sticky dough, absorbing the flour and drawing it together. She plopped the dough onto the table and continued pinching, squeezing, punching, over and over, humming along to the music as she worked. Gradually the dough became smooth and elastic under the relentless assault from Abuela's practiced hands.

Digger finished her coffee, took the mug to the sink, and joined Maria at the stove. She was stirring a pot of green chile stew. Chunks of pork floated in the chile broth. Digger leaned over Maria's shoulder, feeling the warmth of her body as she breathed in the meaty, smoky aroma of the stew.

The radio DJ announced a *cumbia.* Maria grabbed Digger's arm and steered them around the kitchen, laughing as they danced. Abuela watched them, patting the dough into balls, letting out little whoops of excitement. Digger shut her eyes, moving to the music, feeling Maria's arms around her, hearing Abuela sing. She thought of Abuela's words. Maybe someday this could be her family, someday they would get beyond the obstacles.

Later Abuela set a plate with a stack of freshly made tortillas on the table and Maria ladled the stew into bowls.

"Okay, this isn't really breakfast, but it's hot and it's good," she said. Digger ate hungrily, tearing off pieces of tortilla to dip in her stew. "Abuela, these are so much better than store-bought," she said.

The old woman's face split in a grin. Maria beamed.

All morning Digger had been wondering what had lifted Maria's spirits. The past few weeks she'd been in such a funk it was hard to talk to her, but now things were happy, easy. It was more than just Abuela's health improving; she was sure of it. Finally she ventured a question. "So, did you have any luck with anybody in Santa Fe?"

Maria set down her spoon. "No. Everyone I talked to passed me off to someone else. They were mostly very polite, but not very helpful. Each time I hit a wall, someone would say, 'Oh, you should try over at the Environment Department,' or the Department of Transportation, or whatever. It was really frustrating."

Digger watched her, chewing on a piece of tortilla, waiting for more. Finally she said, "So, what's next? You seem pretty happy for someone who's hit a brick wall."

Maria leaned forward, her eyes shining. "I have a plan. I've been talking to my group, and they're on board with the idea. Have you been down there where they've started work on the road?"

"Yeah, I've been by it. It's pretty bad."

"It's awful. They've ripped out trees—beautiful big cotton-woods—and completely torn up the land with their equipment. It looks terrible. I heard they're supposed to start construction in ten days. So this is what I've decided. We're going to go to the site early in the morning, before the workers get there, and we're going to form a human blockade to stop them bringing in any machinery."

Digger stared at her, mouth open, trying to find a polite way to respond. At last she said, "You're not really going to do that. Please tell me this is a joke."

Maria's eyes flashed. "Of course it's not a joke. We tried all the other ways to stop this thing and no one would listen. We're not going to give up till someone pays attention."

"You could get arrested. That could get you fired from your job."

Maria stared at Digger defiantly. "I don't care. Right now, this is more important to me."

Digger shook her head. "I know you care, but you don't want to get police involved. That won't solve anything. Can't you try an appeal with the environment department?"

Maria stared at her as if she couldn't believe what she was hearing. Her eyes blazed with fury. "I've already told you I tried that. I feel like I've been wasting my time. I'm doing this my own way, and I don't need your help. What is it with you? Why are you always on the fence? Don't you ever care enough about anything to stand up for what you believe in? It's like you just hide behind that job of yours."

Digger banged her spoon on the table. "How can you say that?" she snapped. "I believe in what I do. This is not an easy job! People give me shit all the time. I don't expect it from you. I told you I'd write about your cause, and I've really stuck my neck out. What more do you want?"

Maria pushed her chair back so hard it fell over. She stormed out of the room and slammed the door. Moments later the RAV4's engine roared, there was a grinding of gears, and the car screeched away.

Digger's eyes fixated on her plate. Silence settled thickly over the table.

After what seemed like hours, she became aware of Abuela's

breathing, slow and regular. She looked up. The old woman was looking at the fallen chair. Tears slid down the grooves on her cheeks.

"She does that because she's fallen in love with you, and you are out of reach," Abuela said.

Digger let her breath out slowly, as if her chest were being squeezed by a giant weight. "I know, and I feel the same way about her, but I don't know what to do. Right now it looks like I'm going to lose my job. I might have to leave the state. I want to do the best for her—I guess I'm just scared."

Abuela looked up with a sad smile.

"When I was a girl," she said, "there was a young man here in the village— aie! He was so handsome! We used to walk back from Mass sometimes. He used to read to me. I had dreams that we could be together." She paused, sighed. "He wanted to be a priest. One day I got mad at him, just like Maria did with you now. I told him he was only doing it because his parents wanted a priest in the family. But I was wrong. It was his own heart that wanted it."

Abuela fell silent. Sounds from the outside leaked into the tiny house: dogs barking, a motorcycle, the rooster next door. Digger waited, wondering if she should leave. She was about to stand up when the old woman's voice rasped again.

"I used to go to the chapel to remember him. I took Maria with me when she was a little girl. That's how she came to know that place. It has memories for all of us for different reasons."

She looked up at Digger. "I think you have many memories too—memories of the ones you have lost. Sometimes memories create a wall around us. We think we are safe inside that wall, but all we are doing is keeping those who love us now from getting inside."

Digger backed her car into the street and drove off. She drove aimlessly, barely paying attention to where she was going. She found herself on the winding road that led to the Crest. She kept going, tires squealing on the curves, upward higher and higher.

The road ended in a parking lot next to a small picnic ground. Groups of tourists were milling around the souvenir shop beside the path that led to the overlook. Digger got out of the car, uncertain what to do. She felt jittery and depressed. She walked through the parking lot past the store and clambered up the rocky path. She stopped by the iron railing at the edge and looked down. From there, the city was just a small patch in a vast expanse of dun-colored desert, bounded by mountain peaks.

Maria's words stung. Was she right that Digger was just using her job as an excuse not to get involved? Was Abuela right that she was just staying safe behind her own walls? Was it worth it, always holding back, never saying what you really thought? Was it worth staying at the paper till the ship went down? What did she have to gain, when she had so much to lose?

Digger stared for a minute at the stark landscape. She knew some people found it hostile, but she loved the vast space, the ever-changing play of light on the mountains. This was the land of her childhood, of the time before the accident.

There was no way she was going to leave.

CHAPTER THIRTY-SEVEN

REX WAS SITTING alone on the bench outside the newsroom door, cigarette in hand. He looked up as Digger approached.

"It's not the same without Halloran, is it?"

"Nope," he said. "I sure miss that old guy."

Digger slung down her backpack and, with a sigh, sat down beside him.

"What's up with you?" he asked. "You look like your cat died."

She blew out a long breath. "You were right, you know. The protest woman, Maria, and I, we were kind of . . ."

"Yeah, I guessed," he said, taking another drag on his cigarette, not looking at her.

"She's pissed at me. I thought I was being careful, but it's hard to draw a line."

Rex shot her a glance, shifted on the bench as though thinking how to respond. Finally he said, "If Halloran was here, he'd tell you not to beat yourself up." He paused a while. "You know, this can be a tough business. My wife used to ask me why I stuck with the *Courier* when the pay was so lousy. My neighbor used to wave the paper in my face and tell me it was a worthless rag." He paused again, his smoker's voice catching. "But when my son was in grade school, he'd want me to come talk to his class, and he'd be so proud. I remember her holding up the paper, saying, 'My daddy took that picture.'"

He put the cigarette to his lips, then exhaled the smoke in a thin stream and nodded as if continuing some inner dialogue. "I think I have the best job in the world. Every day I come to work, I get to do what I love doing. Okay, maybe sometimes those ground-breaking ceremonies make me want to slit my throat, but that rush of being there when stuff happens, seeing people's faces, hearing their stories—there's nothing like it."

Digger just sat staring at the parking lot, trying to think what it would be like if the paper closed. What it would be like not to come to this place every day, not to see the familiar faces, hear their voices? Out of the corner of her eye, she noticed movement. A roadrunner strutted jerkily out from between two cars just a few feet away. The bird stopped, and she could see the flash of blue and orange behind its eye under the jagged crest feathers. It seemed to be studying them, long tail feathers wagging. Then, just as suddenly, it took off running and disappeared into the shrubs beyond the cars.

"Those weird birds. Till I came to New Mexico, I thought road-runners only existed in the cartoons," Rex said. He crushed the cigarette butt with his boot and looked around at Digger. "I should tell you, I've been offered some steady work by a home-building company. It's a national outfit that's coming into Las Vistas. The guy I've been talking to mentioned they'll be looking for some-one local to do PR. Thought you might be interested."

"Oh, Rex! A home-building company? What was that you said a minute ago about slitting your throat?" she said, pained that he was considering something so alien to him, yet touched at his offer of help.

He shook his head. "Hey, I just thought I'd mention it. You know, if you get desperate. Here's the guy's card. You can drop my name."

He handed her the card and went inside. Digger stuffed it into her backpack, sat a moment hoping to see the roadrunner again, then followed him into the newsroom.

The papers Phyllis had given her were still spread all over her desk. She sat down and pored over them again. She wished she could talk to Halloran. She forced herself to dial the attorney general's office and leave another message, hoping to get more out of Melissa Wickham. She was sitting there, head in hands, when she realized someone was standing next to her desk.

Manny Begay, the cops reporter, had a wispy mustache and a shock of spiky black hair bleached orange-blond at the tips. He brandished papers in one hand, grinning broadly.

"You're going to love this," he said, waggling his thick eyebrows. "You've been following Johnny Raposa's real estate deals, haven't you?"

Digger looked up at him. "Yeah?"

"Guess who got stopped by the cops last night?"

"No way!"

"Check it out," he said, laying the papers on her desk.

Digger skimmed quickly through the police report, catching phrases: "ignoring a red stoplight," "high rate of speed," "slurred speech," "strong smell of alcohol," "performed poorly on sobriety tests," "refused a blood test." She'd read dozens of reports like this. But this wasn't about some random person. This was about Johnny Raposa.

"Holy shit! I've been digging into that guy's shady dealings for months and hitting brick walls. Then he goes and does something like this! He refused a blood test! That makes it an aggravated charge and jail time!" She shook her head, incredulous. "How did you get this so quick?"

"I've got my ways," Begay said archly.

"Who else has this?"

"Just me and you, babe," he said, pointing a finger at her. "Don't worry. You can still put the rest of his shit out there. Just look at this as the icing on the cake."

Digger jumped up, sending her chair shooting back behind her. "Come on. We've gotta get something out there. Let's go talk to Swenson."

The city editor was on the phone, engaged in one of his legendary verbal meltdowns. They were almost a daily occurrence now as the future of the paper became more uncertain and morale sank.

"I don't know where you're calling from, sir," he was shouting into the phone, "but you obviously haven't been reading the *Courier* very long. We've covered those issues extensively for the past year at least."

Whatever the reaction was, Swenson didn't like it. "You know what, we're done here!" He slammed down the phone.

Digger looked at Manny, rolling her eyes. "You talk to him."

The cops reporter ran a hand through his spiked hair, cleared his throat, and said, "Hey, Swenson, got something new here. Johnny Raposa, the developer, was stopped for driving under the influence last night. I got the police report, and I don't think anyone else has it yet."

"No shit? Gimme that." Swenson skimmed over it and let out a harsh laugh. "Put something online as fast as you can. See if you can get comment. Digger, what about you?"

Digger outlined the documents Phyllis had given her. "They back up what I've been told. They show how he hid assets so he could avoid paying the county."

Swenson frowned. "Sounds good, but wasn't the AG's office looking into this?"

"Yes, but they haven't confirmed whether it's an investigation. I've been dogging them on this for days."

Swenson tugged at his mustache, frowning. "Okay. Here's

what we'll do. You check with every source you can on those
documents. We've got to move fast on this. We might not have
a lot of time."

Manny and Digger stared at him in alarm.

"What do you mean?" Digger asked.

Swenson shook his head, showing frustration and deep sad-
ness. He didn't need to say more.

Jack Kimble was sitting on a fallen log, watching the road crew
wrestle with a tree root jammed against the wheel of their truck.
Ever since the first time he'd visited the Spanish chapel, he had
felt drawn to the place. He'd bought himself a pair of hiking boots,
cargo pants, and a big hat.

He'd discovered a way to walk through the woods so he could
reach the chapel while avoiding the construction traffic. Almost
every day for the past couple of months, he'd spent some time
there. He usually sat on the bench against the wall, listening to
the sounds of the doves cooing and lately to the faint noises of
construction activity. Often he stared at the painting of the Virgin
Mary holding the baby Jesus, as if he could find meaning in his
own life in the image of that ageless little face.

One day, about a week after he began coming regularly, he
heard the door open behind him and turned to see a tiny old
woman. Despite the heat, she was wearing a dark sweater and
skirt and a black, lacy head covering. She made her way slowly
toward the altar, her shoes scuffing along the floorboards. If she
saw Kimble, she gave no sign of it. She stopped in front of the
statue and set down the woven bag she had been carrying over
one arm. She picked up the vase from the stand and emptied
the faded flowers into her bag. Then she pulled out a paper cone
of bright gold marigolds and a bottle of water. She put the new
flowers in the vase and filled it with water. She knelt then, giving

a little groan. Kimble could hear the breathy murmur of her voice as she prayed, head bowed. After a few moments she rose stiffly, gathered her bag, and turned to leave. As she passed Kimble, her dark eyes met his. She gave the slightest nod but said nothing. He saw her many times after that, always engaged in the same silent ritual.

He sat now surrounded by the cacophony of machines and men working. He was near enough to hear them shout to one another and to pick up tidbits of gossip. The men did not look happy in their work. Every now and then, the guy he took for the crew chief would show up and shout. He seemed frustrated. Things kept going wrong; machines broke down, guys didn't show up for work, supplies were late.

Once he heard someone say it seemed like the whole job was jinxed.

CHAPTER THIRTY-EIGHT

DIGGER ARRIVED EARLY for the council meeting, something she rarely managed.

She took the opportunity to gaze around the room. When Old George arrived, he made a point of sitting in the seat next to her.

"I really wanted to congratulate you," he said in a breathy whisper, leaning close. "I loved your article about Johnny Raposa. That scoundrel belongs in jail. Hiding money he owes the county! That's our taxpayer money! And then he gets caught drinking and driving. Serves him right."

His breath tickled her ear and she shifted uncomfortably in her seat. "Thanks, George. I'm always glad to hear that people actually read what I write."

He leaned in again. "We're going to miss you, you know, when the paper closes."

Digger stared at him in alarm. "Is that the rumor going around? It's out there?"

He nodded, patting her shoulder sympathetically.

"Thanks," she said. "We don't know anything for sure. No dates. It's still officially for sale, but buyers aren't exactly lining up with offers. We'll see." She shrugged.

All the councilors were seated and waiting when the mayor arrived. Dave Johnsen took his place, looking flustered and upset. Digger wondered how he'd taken the news of Raposa's arrest. After all, the developer had pumped a ton of money into his election campaign.

During the public comment period at the beginning of the meeting, Sally Jenkins marched up to the microphone. After being a regular fixture at meetings, she'd been noticeably absent for the past couple of months. *She must be thrilled to have found something new to complain about,* Digger thought.

Sure enough, she got straight to the point.

"Councilors, I live on a street downwind of that road project they've been working on for the past few weeks, and the dust is terrible, terrible!" she said in her grating, nasal voice. "I mean, this is spring in New Mexico, and you know the wind blows all the time. Everything in my house is just covered in dust. I don't think they should be allowed to work when it's that windy. They're creating a public nuisance."

Councilor Larry Martinez interjected, "Mayor, if I may comment?" Johnsen nodded.

"As you may know," Martinez said, "my district covers the area where the new road extension is being built, and I've been getting calls from people who live around there, complaining about this fugitive dust."

"'Fugitive dust'? Is this some kind of joke?" Councilor Caulfield snapped.

Martinez gave him a long-suffering look and proceeded to explain as if he were talking to a young child.

"Fugitive dust—for those of you not familiar with the expression—is an air quality term. It refers to particulate matter flying around in the air, like sand and dirt from construction sites, that can be a health hazard. The city regulates this stuff, and when you're going to do a construction job, you're supposed to get a permit." Martinez paused, letting his words sink in. "Well, after I got those calls I did some checking, and it turns out the city didn't issue a fugitive dust control permit for that project. Somebody goofed."

Caulfield's face darkened, the wrinkles tightening, making him look more than ever like a walnut.

"This is ridiculous!" he said. "You're just trying to stall the project because you were against it. This city needs that road and the new business it will generate. We don't need people using petty regulations to obstruct progress."

"Order, Councilor, order!" Johnsen said. "Let's hear what the public works director has to say. Josh, could you come up here, please?"

Bebs lumbered up to the lectern. "Councilor Martinez is correct. City regulations say any project that's going to disturb more than a quarter acre of soil requires a fugitive dust control permit. After the councilor raised the issue, I looked into it and found out that no permit was issued for this road project. I'm not sure how it escaped our attention, but sometimes these things happen, I'm sorry to say."

"What does this mean for the project?" Johnsen asked.

Bebs ran a hand through his tousled hair. "They just have to apply, and they'll have to take some remedial measures. It won't mean a significant delay."

Caulfield's face twisted into a smug smile, as if he felt vindicated in his outrage.

As the meeting dragged on, Johnsen found his attention drifting. He and Connie had argued in the morning over the way he did the laundry. Wanting to be helpful, he'd dumped everything in together and started the machine. Connie had been furious. Always particular, she'd become almost obsessive during her latest pregnancy. It wore on him like heartburn.

Then there was the news about Raposa. He'd thought the developer's talk about business and jobs for Las Vistas aligned so well with his own free market principles. But after reading the story in the *Courier* about the way Raposa had used shell companies to hide assets, Johnsen felt duped. If that weren't bad enough, now there was the drunk driving arrest. Johnsen wondered when people were going to start asking why he'd accepted campaign money from a guy like that. He'd wanted to be mayor, but sometimes he felt out of his depth.

"Mayor?"

Martinez's voice drew him back to reality. He had a meeting to run.

The next morning Digger was seated at her desk, drinking coffee and wondering if she should try to call Maria. She hadn't heard from her in days, not since the explosive scene at Abuela's. Every time she picked up her phone to call, she saw their faces again—Maria furious, Abuela pale with shock. Why had she questioned Maria's plan? Wasn't it obvious that Maria honestly cared about her cause, cared so much that she was willing to risk being arrested? And why had she yelled back at Maria? Blame it on the frustration of holding her feelings in check. No, it was the way Maria questioned her loyalty to her job. She wanted to write about the chapel, she wanted people in Las Vistas to see what development was doing to the area. That was why Maria's accusation had hurt so much.

The phone on her desk rang.

"Is that Elizabeth Doyle?"

"Yes."

"This is Joan Moore from the New Mexico Department of Cultural Affairs. Do you have a minute?"

"Uh, sure."

"Secretary Julia Montoya asked me to call you because she was very impressed with a recent piece you wrote about a historic site in Las Vistas. Would

you have time to meet with the secretary this week? She has some time available at nine thirty on Friday."

"Yes, of course. That would be fine. I'll be there." Digger had no idea how she'd make time for the appointment, but you didn't say no to a cabinet secretary.

"Good, I'll put it in her calendar. Thank you for your time." Click.

Digger's mind was reeling. Montoya was impressed with the article, really? Maybe something had been wrong? But no one had contacted the *Courier* asking for a correction. Friday was the day after tomorrow; she had to hurry and find out as much as she could about Montoya and the Department of Cultural Affairs.

Meanwhile, she'd better alert Swenson.

"The secretary of the Department of Cultural Affairs wants to meet you?" He looked incredulous.

"Yeah, her assistant—or whoever she was; I need to check her title—called and said Secretary Montoya was impressed with the story I did about how the controversy over the chapel and the road is polarizing folks in Las Vistas."

"Yeah, yeah. Well, you better go see what she wants. I just hope it's not trouble." Swenson waved a hand and went back to his computer.

———

Digger resurrected her dark suit from the back of the closet for the trip to Santa Fe. The Department of Cultural Affairs was in the Bataan Memorial Building. A brass plaque outside explained that it was named after the Bataan Death March in World War II, during which thousands of Filipino and American prisoners of war—including many New Mexicans—had died during a forced march on the Philippine island of Luzon.

Digger walked in and gave her name to a receptionist. Moments later, Joan Moore came to the lobby to escort her to the secretary's office. Digger was nervous, still fearing some unforeseen backlash from the story. She'd read it over multiple times in the past two days, and she was sure all the research and facts were solid.

Julia Montoya was a petite woman with impeccably cut blue-black hair and a face with the kind of bone structure featured in fashion magazines. She wore a dark, silky blouse with short sleeves that showed off her tanned arms. Digger noticed a generous-sized diamond ring on one hand. Around her neck was a gold chain with a Kokopelli pendant.

She came forward to greet Digger, holding out a hand and smiling. "Thank you for making time to come here this morning. I know you reporters are always on a deadline."

"It's a pleasure to meet you."

"Sit, please," Montoya said, indicating one of the chairs in front of her desk.

The secretary put on a pair of glasses, opened a folder on her desk, and began to read aloud. "'A road to a burgeoning subdivision that would destroy access to centuries-old cultural sites is pitting newcomers to a fast-growing New Mexico city against families who have lived there for generations.'"

She looked up at Digger. "I was very impressed by this story. You obviously know the community well, and you'd clearly done a lot of research to back up your arguments. What you say in this piece gets at the core of some of the issues we see in our work throughout the state. I take it you've familiarized yourself with what we do here at the department?"

"Yes. I've been doing a lot of reading since Wednesday."

"Good." Montoya removed her glasses and leaned over the desk toward Digger. "There is a delicate balance between the value of the unique blend of cultural and historic traditions we have here and the obvious need to accommodate to change that can benefit the people and the economy of the state. From reading this piece, I think you get that, and that's why I asked you to come here today."

Digger leaned forward, rubbed her hands on her thighs, then looked up. "I'm . . . I'm glad you understood what I was trying to say. A lot of the time I wonder if people really bother to read what I write. I started to look into this a few months ago when I met the group that's been protesting against the road extension—the one I mention in the story."

She hesitated, uncertain whether to go on. Montoya nodded encouragingly so she continued. "I was born in New Mexico, but I had to go live with my grandparents in Houston during my teens. It was important to me to come back. I think that being away and then returning to this culture gave me a special appreciation. That's why I understand how people like Maria Ortiz are disturbed by the impact that Las Vistas has had. It's like people from other states come here for their version of the American Dream and they believe they're entitled to it without ever appreciating the place they've come to. Does that make sense?

The secretary nodded, but said nothing for what seemed like an eternity. Digger waited. Finally she said, "I suppose you're wondering why I asked you hear today. I've been hearing rumors that the *Courier* may be ceasing operations soon. I understand that no buyer has come forward."

"I'm afraid not."

"In that case, you may be looking for another job. Is that right?"
Digger nodded.

"Well, we could use someone with your experience and passion for a position we're creating to do outreach to cultural organizations and at historical sites around New Mexico. I'd like to invite to you to apply. Would you be interested?"

Digger stared at her, mouth open. "Well, Miss Doyle?"

"I—I—uh—would I be able to talk about the kind of stuff I've just been saying? I mean, the cultural issues? I really believe in this. I want people who come here to understand New Mexico."

Montoya nodded, smiling. Digger could barely breathe. If Montoya really meant what she said, it would solve so much. She had a future if the paper closed . . . and maybe she and Maria did too. So many possibilities!

The secretary was getting to her feet. "I'll have Joan send you more information, and of course we can discuss salary and other details in the coming days. I just wanted to gauge your interest."

Digger realized she was being dismissed. She shook Montoya's outstretched hand and left. As soon as she was out of the office, she phoned Maria, but the call went to voice mail. Digger decided not to leave a message. They still had things to work out.

CHAPTER THIRTY-NINE

DAVE JOHNSEN HAD agreed to meet Raposa at Denny's. He thought it ironic they were meeting at the same spot where the developer had first suggested he run for mayor. Back then he'd been flattered by the suggestion. He'd been, frankly, a little in awe of Raposa. The guy seemed to have the Midas touch: doing all kinds of deals around town, getting support from influential councilors, speaking at chamber of commerce events. He'd thought Johnny Raposa was a great guy, the kind of guy who could get things done, the kind of guy you'd want in your corner.

Yeah, well, he'd been there all right, saying all the right things so he could get his own project through. When that story in the *Courier* had come out, Johnsen had a hard time believing it at first. Then he remembered that niggling feeling of doubt he'd felt even before the election. The feeling that he was being used.

He saw Raposa come through the door, look around, then flash a smile of recognition. He was wearing tan slacks and a dark shirt and blazer. If his arrest experience had ruffled him, he didn't show it. Johnsen wondered whether the developer's sleek silver BMW was sitting in the parking lot or whether he'd had his license revoked.

Raposa approached the table, hailing him with the familiar,

hearty, "My man!" and a fist bump on the shoulder. Johnsen felt soiled at his touch.

"Good to see you, Mayor," Raposa said.

Johnsen merely smiled and ordered coffee from the waitress who appeared beside the table. Raposa wanted a glazed donut with his coffee.

"I have the worst sweet tooth." He grinned.

Johnsen wasn't in the mood for pleasantries. "Johnny, I have to say I was really concerned when I read about the Rancho Milagro situation. How could you be involved in something like that?"

Raposa blew him off with a wave. "That reporter gal, she's just had it in for me. I'm talking with folks at the county level and we're working this thing out. Besides, my lawyer back then gave me legal advice on all the business dealings related to Rancho Milagro, and he assured me it was all above board." He turned to beam at the waitress as she brought the coffees. "Oh, thanks, honey. Gimme a couple extra creamers if you would, please." Without pausing, he switched his focus back to Johnsen. "Believe me, Dave, that's the problem. If you're successful in this town, that shitty little rag of a paper will go after you. It's probably a good thing it's gonna close soon."

Johnsen watched Raposa peel the tops off three tiny cream containers and dump them, one after another, into his coffee. His own cup sat untouched in front of him. He didn't want any coffee. He didn't want to be sitting here with this man who, for all he knew, had deliberately swindled home buyers and the county out of more money than he, Dave Johnsen, was likely to see in a lifetime. He hated himself for being sucked in by Raposa's lofty talk about how Los Sueños and the new commercial center he was going to build would bring jobs and revenue to Las Vistas. Sure, the developments would probably bring money into the city, but at what cost? He thought about the beautiful young Hispanic woman—what was her name? Maria—and the sincerity in her eyes when she had spoken to the council about the historic chapel. He'd ignored her pleas and let the council go ahead and vote, and now the road was under construction, benefiting Raposa.

"Hey, Dave?"

The developer had already eaten half his donut while Johnsen's thoughts were elsewhere. He leaned toward Johnsen.

"There's something I wanted to talk to you about. That's why I asked if you could meet me." He paused. "It's like this. I think you understand that my support, both financial and in terms of contacts in the community, played a pretty big role in getting you elected mayor, wouldn't you agree?"

Johnsen's stomach lurched. He said nothing.

Raposa leaned closer, his chest nearly touching the half-eaten donut.

Johnsen could see sugary crumbs sparkling in his beard, could smell the man's coffee breath. "What I wanted to say was, as mayor, maybe you could help me out with this DWI business. You know, talk to somebody . . .?"

Dave Johnsen thought for a moment. Then he laid his hands on the table and looked Raposa straight in the eye. "Johnny, I took an oath when I became the mayor of Las Vistas. I swore to uphold the duties of the office for the safety and welfare of the people of this city. I'm also a religious man, and what you're suggesting is wrong. If you want help with your situation, maybe you should go back to the lawyer you used for the Rancho Milagro deals. Now, if you'll excuse me, I have to go. Goodbye, Johnny."

Raposa's face fell and his whole body seemed to collapse in on itself. There was a glint in his eye that looked like fear.

Digger eyed the newsroom clock nervously, hastening through the concluding paragraphs of her story to make deadline. She'd just sent the story off to the city editor when Manny Begay dashed up to her desk.

"Digg, come quick, you gotta see this!" He beckoned. She followed him to the bank of televisions blaring the evening newscast. He pointed to the TV on the left. Digger's jaw dropped. There was the pert blond reporter she kept running into. She was interviewing Maria. They were standing in front of the Spanish chapel.

The blond reporter was saying, "You led the protests against the road extension that will block access to this beautiful old church. Now that the road is under construction, I understand you're planning to continue your protest. Could you tell us about that?"

Maria looked straight at the camera, her jaw lifted confidently. "Work may have started, but my team and I are not going to give up our protest efforts. We had the support of some city councilors, and we believe that if we continue to make our voices heard, we can get this stopped."

"Could you talk about what further action you plan to take?" the blond asked.

"We will be taking further action in the near future, but we're still in the planning process, and I'm not at liberty to discuss any details yet."

Digger stared at the screen in shock.

"I don't believe it," she said. "She told me all this, but she made it sound like she didn't want me to write anything more. Then she gives an interview to TV! Shit!"

Begay looked sympathetic. "Yeah, it sucks when you think you've got a good source and they do something like that. Well, now it's out there. You better call her quick and follow up or Swenson will be pissed."

Digger sat listening to the blood pulsing in her ears. How could this happen, just when it looked as if there was a way forward? Last night she'd tried Maria's number again to tell her about

Montoya's offer, but there'd been no answer. She picked up her desk phone, connected the recording device, and took a few more breaths to calm herself.

"Hello?" Maria answered.

"It's me."

"Oh . . . hi."

"I understand you're planning to continue protests against the road extension, even though it's under construction. What are you planning to do next?"

"Why are you talking to me like that?"

"Because I'm interviewing you," Digger said. "Why didn't you call me before you went to that TV reporter with your story? I've been working with you on this for months, and you turn around and give her the scoop?"

"You sound jealous."

"I'm doing my job."

"Oh yeah, the job, always the job."

Digger took a slow breath. "My job is what I believe in, and right now my job is to write what you care about." She said the words slowly, her heart pounding. The ensuing silence lasted so long she thought she had lost the connection. Then she heard Maria exhale.

"I'm glad to hear you say that. After we had that fight, I thought I'd lost you over this."

Digger's shoulders slumped with relief. "I know. I'm so sorry. Listen, I've got some other news, but I can't talk now, I've got my boss all over my case for missing the story. What can you tell me about what you and your team plan to do next?"

"You heard what I said at Abuela's."

"You were talking about forming some kind of human chain to stop the machinery from getting to the site. Is that still the plan?"

"I don't want you to publish that. We can't let them have advance warning: that would ruin what we're trying to do."

"Can I at least say you tried getting help from state government agencies in Santa Fe but they turned you down? That hasn't been reported yet."

Maria sighed. "Yes. Okay, that's fair. I'll tell you which ones I approached and what the response was. Is that enough?"

"Sure, fire away. I'm already pushing deadline, and I'll have to call a couple of them to get comments. Thanks for this. I'm glad we talked."

Maria gave a quick overview of her experience with the state agencies and agreed that Digger could say that the group was still planning more protest actions.

After the interview, Digger put the phone down and left the newsroom. She needed to breathe and to think. From force of habit, she headed to the café down the street and ordered a latte. She sat outside under an umbrella and stared back at the *Courier* building.

Thoughts swirled through her head: the interview with Julia Montoya, the job offer. It was tempting, but how would she keep reporting on Maria's campaign? Then there was Maria accusing her of sitting on the fence. All this time, she'd thought she was doing the right thing by trying to stay objective. But maybe that wasn't really who she was. Images flashed through her mind: the walls of the old chapel, the women around Abuela's table on Christmas Eve, Maria's face.

Digger set down her mug. For now, there was a story to finish. She walked back to the office and began to type.

CHAPTER FORTY

DIGGER WAS SITTING on her cramped balcony sipping coffee as she looked out at the mountains, Lady Antonia on her lap. The slopes were slate blue, the air pleasantly cool. As the sun climbed over the mountain crest, she knew, the colors would change and the temperatures rise. Already the freshness of spring was gone and the vegetation had the dusty dullness of summer. The truly hot days were not far away, the days when the sun was so bright it hurt your eyes even with sunglasses on. Desert heat might be dry, but it was still hot. People in the old villages would be holding ceremonies to pray for rain.

Her phone buzzed, startling the cat, who scampered into the apartment.

Digger glanced at the screen; the caller was Maria. The only contact they'd had since the blow-up at Abuela's had been that stiff phone interview. She wanted to tell Maria about the job possibility with Montoya, but she wasn't sure how that news would be received. Also, she felt if she said it out loud, it would be more real—and leaving the *Courier* meant letting go of the world she knew. After a moment's hesitation, she answered.

"Hi, Maria. Um, I have to leave for work in a few minutes. Can I call you in a half hour?"

"Please, I'll be quick. In that story you wrote, what was the name of the woman who complained to the council about the dust from the road construction?"

"Sally Jenkins. Why?"

"I was thinking: If she and her neighbors are upset about the road, maybe I could get them on our side. They have neighborhood meetings where they talk about this kind of stuff, don't they? I could go there and talk to them. Right now they probably think I'm just this weird woman who shows up at protests. If I could talk to them, maybe they would understand that this place is more than just sunny skies and pretty mountain views where out-of-towners can buy their dream houses. Maybe they could understand that the place where Las Vistas has grown has been home to generations of families who worked the land, families who paid attention to the seasons and revered the Earth. Maybe they can understand that it's important to keep doing those things, and that's why that road is bad for all of us."

Digger was glad Maria was trusting her again, but she wasn't optimistic about Maria's chances of gaining more support. People who went to neighborhood meetings in Las Vistas usually had their own agendas, and those didn't include revering the Earth. Still, anything was worth a try. "I say go for it, girl. You've got nothing to lose."

The meeting room at the senior center was more crowded than Digger had ever seen it, even during election campaigns. Maria had persuaded someone on the neighborhood association board to allow her to give the featured presentation. She was sitting in the front row, close to Sally and Al Jenkins and some of the other people Digger saw at council meetings. Digger picked a seat near enough to the front to hear what was said but sufficiently inconspicuous to note who was around her without attracting attention. Councilors Larry Martinez and Tony Apodaca had showed up, and there was Old George, and that skinny young guy with acne—wasn't that Kimble's campaign manager, Dillon James?

Shortly before the meeting started, she spotted the former mayor sitting in a back row near the door. She hardly recognized him. Kimble had obviously quit caring about his appearance. His beard was thick and bushy like a Santa Claus cartoon, and his woolly gray hair nearly touched his shoulders. Instead of the tweedy jacket and tie she was used to seeing him in, he was wearing a rumpled olive green shirt with bulging pockets. As she looked around, trying to estimate the number of people attending, the door at the back of the room opened and Mayor Dave Johnsen slipped through.

This was not going to be an ordinary neighborhood meeting.

Sitting in the back, Jack Kimble was surprised to see the association chairman introduce the tall young Hispanic woman as the featured presenter for the evening. He recognized her as the leader of the protest group that had tried to stop the road extension. It was from her he'd learned about the historic chapel that had become a place of almost daily pilgrimage for him. Did she really think she could persuade this audience to care about a place they knew little or nothing about?

He'd come to the meeting to try once again to show them the folly of doing nothing to protect the city from the destructive power of the rains. He'd seen it with his own eyes. They'd seen it too, the way the gushing water sliced through the sandy soil, washing away roads, ripping through fences, drowning pets. As mayor, he could have helped them. But they hadn't listened. How had he gone wrong?

Money. It always came down to money. Fixing the problem was going to cost them money, and they'd rather listen to that fast-talking salesman Raposa and that naive young idiot Johnsen, who'd been here five minutes and still thought Las Vistas could be like his hometown in Ohio. Bitterness welled up in Kimble.

Dave Johnsen was sitting near the back of the room, where he couldn't take his eyes off Maria Ortiz. Normally he didn't come to neighborhood association meetings, but he'd heard she was going to speak. There she was, tall and imposing, with those piercing black eyes and that gleaming curtain of hair.

"Hello, everybody," Maria began. "Your chairman graciously allowed me to come and speak to you tonight. I am Maria Ortiz, and I represent a group that is trying to preserve access to two historic sites that are part of the heritage of this area. These sites are threatened by construction of the Paseo del Valle extension, which began recently. I hope to draw your attention to the cultural value of these sites to Las Vistas and to what it would mean if residents of this city no longer had access to them."

She asked for the lights to be dimmed and began a brief slide-show with pictures of the old Spanish chapel and the volcanic cliffs nearby.

"This is the Chapel of Nuestra Señora de los Sueños, Our Lady of the Dreams. It was named that because of a legend that Mary, the mother of Jesus, appeared in a dream to the leader of a group of Spanish settlers. His family built the chapel on land they farmed near here in the 1700s. All of the family members gradually died out or moved away, and the chapel hasn't been used regularly for services in many years. But many people still visit it to pray and to leave offerings for those who have passed away. Councilors Martinez and Apodaca remember it." Here she nodded toward the two councilors.

Johnsen became aware of a noise to his left. He glanced around. An elderly couple were leaning close together, whispering loudly.

"Who is this woman? Does she live in the neighborhood?" the man asked.

"Never seen her," the woman replied. "She looks Mexican, doesn't she?" "Who does she think she is, coming here to lecture us?"

Johnsen was incensed. He turned to the old couple and held his finger to his mouth. "Shhhh!" he hissed.

"Well, excuse me!" The woman pursed her lips.

Slideshow over, the lights went back on. Maria faced the audience.

"I have opposed the building of this road because the chapel has very special meaning for me and my family and others in our community. When I was a child, my grandmother used to take me there with her. For me, it was a place where I could find refuge when life seemed tough, like when my brother was deployed to Iraq. I prayed for his safe return there, and he did make it back safely."

Hearing the emotion in Maria's voice, Digger remembered the Christmas scene at Abuela's when Maria's mother had appeared and what that had done to Maria. She'd had lots of reasons to visit the chapel.

Kimble's throat constricted as he listened to the young woman speak of the solace she'd found in the simple little church that had become his refuge too. He thought of the elderly lady with the marigolds and the silent communion they shared in that secret spot. He hoped no one noticed the tear that slid into his beard.

Johnsen glanced at the other people sitting in the seats around him, trying to gauge their reactions. Was she winning them over? Did they care? He wanted to rush to the front of the room and wrap his arms around her protectively. He gripped the metal frame of the chair to steady himself.

Maria was concluding her presentation. "I hope that by seeing these pictures you can understand that the area where Las Vistas is growing has a long and diverse cultural history. As a teacher in the Las Vistas school system, I believe having access to this site is of value to everyone here, especially our children.

That's why I hope you will join me in opposing the building of this road. If you are interested, you can pick up a leaflet with my contact information on your way out."

The association chairman rose, thanked Maria, and invited questions from the audience. Someone in the front row stood up: Sally Jenkins, hair frosted in a spiky halo, red sweatshirt stretched tight across her broad behind.

"This is all very well," she began, her voice heavy with sarcasm, "but I live right near the construction, and it's been a living hell since the day it started. There's noise and dust like you wouldn't believe. And we just found out that the company that's building it didn't get a permit for the 'fugitive dust.' I wanna know what's being done about that."

Maria clearly wasn't prepared for this reaction. She stood for a moment as if in thought, then peered around the room, her eyes finally alighting on Johnsen.

"I see the mayor is here. I think he'd be the best one to answer that question. Mayor?"

Dave Johnsen sat transfixed. He hadn't expected to be called out like this.

He'd just wanted to come and hear this beautiful woman talk. Now she was reaching out to him, but in a way that made him distinctly uncomfortable. He stood up, smiling awkwardly.

"I—uh—yes," he said, stumbling over his words. "We discovered recently that the city had not issued a specific permit to the construction company that's building the road. Unfortunately, according to our public works director, things sometimes get overlooked on a big project like this. But it's all been cleared up now, I can assure you."

Sally piled on. "What other permits did the city 'forget' to issue? How many other shortcuts did that company take? Is this road even gonna be safe?"

Johnsen could feel the audience growing hostile. The old couple he had shushed were now glaring at him. He looked at Maria standing at the front of the room. Her eyes seemed gentle, her face benign like the image of the Virgin in the stained glass window behind the altar where he had served at Mass as a boy.

"Mayor?"

He smiled back at her. He wanted to say, *I'm the good guy here, please believe me.* Instead he said, "We are looking into this. I will be talking with city staff, and every effort will be made to ensure that all the required permits were issued and the proper procedures followed."

Sometimes he really hated his official voice.

CHAPTER FORTY-ONE

NICK ROEMER RUBBED the stubble on his shaved head and grunted. He read the email from his boss again, seething. What next? The city was asking for a review of all permits for the Paseo del Valle project. Did those idiots have any idea what a pain this would be, on top of all the delays they'd had? Already the days were getting hot, and that was hard on men and machinery. He pounded his desk again, wincing at the pain in his fist. Sometimes working for the company that had won the low bid just wasn't worth it.

———

Kimble had found a new path to the chapel along a ditch bank that flanked an acequia, part of a historic network of waterways constructed by Spanish settlers to irrigate the fields. The purling sound of the water soothed his anxiety. He stopped in the shade of an immense cottonwood tree, its thick, grooved branches reaching sideways and upward in a yoga-like pose. Light filtering through the leaves created a speckled pattern on the earth around his hiking boots. Here in the shade, stillness cloaked him. Out there, under the full glare of the sun, heat lurked like a predator waiting to pounce.

Day by day the temperatures crept up. He still followed the meteorological reports. El Niño conditions had appeared in the Pacific as expected in April, but now he feared the summer rains might be delayed. Maybe they wouldn't come at all, just those teasing clouds and virga—moisture trails that evaporated before reaching the earth. Perhaps that was the way of the future. There would be no rains, but Raposa and his like would keep on building more and more homes, sucking up all the water. The underground aquifer and the river would dry up, the people would move away, their houses worthless white elephants abandoned in the desert.

Then it struck him. The contractors had already built the section at the top of the escarpment that would connect the Paseo del Valle extension to the existing road to Los Sueños and the new shopping center. He'd walked along it, noting they'd included gutters on each side to channel water. When the rains came, if they came, he doubted the gutters would be sufficient to handle the volume of water in a big storm. That quarter mile of paved asphalt at the top would act like a giant collection point, channeling sheets of water over the edge. Where would the water go? It hit him that he'd seen no evidence of drainage ponds when he'd walked around the site at the bottom of the escarpment, where the foundations were going in.

He heard voices—probably some of the road crew. Over the weeks of coming here, he'd learned to move almost silently through the bosque. When he was close enough to make out their words, he stopped, hiding behind a low branch. Even if they saw him, they'd probably just think he was one of the homeless people who often camped out in the woods. His wife couldn't understand why he'd let himself go—she complained about his hair, his beard—and he wasn't sure either. He'd lived his life, been the preacher, the husband, the father, the mayor of this town that had rejected him. It just didn't seem to matter anymore what he wore or how he looked.

At first Kimble had trouble understanding the men. They were speaking in the singsong accent of northern New Mexico. They sat leaning against the back tire of a dump truck.

"I heard we might not work for a couple days—heard the city wants to check permits," said one man.

"They gonna pay us for them days? Man, I got bills, I got rent."

"They gotta pay us. It's in the contract, no?"

"I don't trust that guy Roemer, man. He acts all happy in front of us, says everything is cool, but you know what, a few days ago I heard him talking on his phone, he was telling somebody he thought the road shouldn't be going in here— said he saw some engineer report that said the ground was all wrong."

Kimble emerged from the trees and walked toward the men, intending to ask them about the drainage.

"Good morning."

They looked at him, wide-eyed. Kimble realized they might be afraid of him, this strange figure appearing from the forest with shaggy hair and unkempt beard.

"I'm interested in the road. Do you know if they're going to build drainage ponds over there at the base of the cliff?"

Their expressions changed to a mixture of puzzlement and pity. They probably thought he was demented.

"Ain't no ponds 'round here, mister. If you wanna go fishin', you gotta go down to the river."

His companion guffawed. "Man, you hungry? You wanna sammich or something?"

"It's okay, thanks. I've got food at home." Kimble smiled grimly. Today was Tuesday, meatloaf day.

———

Digger had just ordered a tall latte at Mojo's on her way to the office when Maria called.

"You said those people wouldn't care—well, guess what? I got *nine* of them interested in helping me."

"That's amazing. I really didn't think they'd go for it after the way they jumped on the mayor."

"I think they're mostly like that fat lady, just mad about the dust and noise. But as long as they're against the road and willing to do something about it, I'm happy to have them."

"So, what's next? Are you really going to do that blockade?"

Maria was quiet for several seconds.

"You know I can't tell you right now," she said at last, "because if I tell you, you're going to want to report it. I can't let that happen just yet. You understand?"

Digger gave a dry laugh. "So, you get what I've been up against all along— why it's been so hard for me to be with you and write about this. Yes. I understand. Let me know what you can when you feel okay about it."

"Okay. Soon. Let me get this set up and I'll call you." Her voice softened. "You know Abuela wants to see you; she was really upset by what happened between us."

"I know. I'm sorry. Tell her I'm ready for another tortilla lesson."

Digger picked up her coffee and walked back to the office. The tension hit her as soon as she walked into the newsroom. Swenson and the business editor were in Thompson's corner office. She saw Swenson throw his hands in the air and shake his head. She went straight over to the photo room to find Rex.

He was crouched over his laptop.

"What's going on?"

Rex looked up, cast his eyes around, then said, "I need a cigarette. You coming?"

"Sure. I love your secondhand smoke."

She followed him out the back door to the bench overlooking the parking lot. Rex took his time, pulling a crumpled pack of Marlboros from his shirt pocket, shaking out a cigarette, lighting it, and blowing out a stream of smoke. Digger waited. He would talk when he was ready.

Finally he said, "There's been an offer."

"For the *Courier*?"

He nodded.

"That's good news, isn't it?"

"Maybe—but probably not." He shrugged. "It's one of those corporations that's buying up small papers around the Southwest. They come in, get rid of half the staff, concentrate all the ad sales and production operations in a central spot out of state, and you're left with something that isn't even a local newspaper anymore."

"Is that what Swenson's so mad about?"

"Probably. Thompson will likely meet with the publisher and the financial people this week. We could get a decision pretty soon. They'll likely call a meeting."

His head slumped between his shoulders, his eyes on the ground as though reality were staring back at him: the end of his career and the job he loved. Digger wondered again how old Rex was. Today the creases on his forehead seemed deeper, his hair grayer.

The newsroom door burst open and Manny Begay rushed out.

"Oh, there you are!" He sounded panicked. "There's a fire east of the mountains, and Swenson wants us to cover it. We've gotta hurry."

Rex leapt to his feet and hustled inside. Digger sat still, feeling the heat radiating off the asphalt in front of her. Moments later the two men emerged, clambered into Rex's SUV, and sped away.

Of course there was a fire. It hadn't rained in weeks, and everything was paper dry. The air sucked the moisture right out of your body. Even the lawn around the office had that water-starved bluish tinge. If the rains didn't come soon, there would be more fires.

She hadn't told Rex about her interview with Julia Montoya. Right now it seemed like bad timing. Rex, a real estate photographer? He would so hate it.

Joan Moore had gotten back to her from the cultural department, and Digger had a letter with the formal job offer and salary details in her backpack. It had arrived yesterday. If she said yes, it meant a new career, an opportunity to follow what she cared about. But would there still be time to write the rest of Maria's story? They needed to talk.

CHAPTER FORTY-TWO

JOHNNY RAPOSA'S PHONE pinged with the reminder to rate the Uber driver and add a tip. He didn't feel like adding a tip. He felt like smashing the phone on the ground right there in front of his office. He ground his teeth and shoved the device into his pocket. The receptionist smiled as he came in and offered Raposa coffee.

He shook his head. He didn't want coffee. He wanted a stiff drink. He went into his office, shut the door, sat down, and listened again to the voice mail from his attorney.

"This isn't going to go away, Johnny. I got a call from the AG's office, and someone in their litigation division is really interested in the money you were supposed to pay back under that settlement with the county. As you know, you benefited from taxpayer money when you were building Rancho Milagro. There are ways we can fight this, Johnny, but it doesn't look good. I'm just saying."

Raposa closed his eyes and clenched his fists. Why had that worthless lawyer assured him everything would be okay? Just when he'd gotten a mayor elected who could make sure sales at Los Sueños took off. This would spook the investors for sure. Murphy would probably desert him too. And Phyllis! He burned at the thought of her.

Last night, when he'd listened to the voice mail for the first time, it had taken his breath away. They'd been sitting on the back patio drinking wine. Things were, he thought, going well between them. He thought she'd forgiven him for that fling in Arizona. She asked for more chips and he went inside to get some. That's when he saw his phone on the kitchen counter and noticed the alert. He came out with the phone in his hand and no chips.

"What?" She looked at him.

When he told her about the message, she just smirked and held up her glass as if she were toasting him. Then she got up and went inside. Stunned, he didn't move for what seemed like a long time. Finally he got to his feet and went looking for her. She was in the bedroom, packing a suitcase. He stood in the doorway gaping at her. That's when it hit him.

"It was you. You gave information to that reporter," he said. She folded her arms across her chest and met his gaze.

"Yeah, Johnny, it was me. You deserved it. You ripped off those people at Rancho Milagro; you ripped off the county; you ripped off your first wife and you ripped off me. You deserve whatever happens to you."

With that she turned around, slammed the suitcase shut, heaved it off the bed and marched out, pushing past him as she left.

Now Raposa slumped over his desk, forehead pressed into his fists. He'd thought she really wanted to get back together, but it was just a way she could get revenge. His head hurt—he hurt all over. He wished it would all go away.

The phone in his pocket jangled. He answered automatically, without thinking. "Hello?"

"This is Elizabeth Doyle from the *Courier*—"

"I know who it is. No comment." He stabbed the round red icon to end the call. That damned reporter!

Digger grinned to herself. Melissa Wickham had finally called back to confirm the AG's office would be investigating Raposa.

She filed her story and earned a brief smile from a harassed-looking Swenson. After work she headed to Los Jardines, anxious to tell Maria about the job offer.

She found her in the kitchen chopping onions. She handed her a damp cloth to wipe her eyes. "Here, can I help you with that?"

Maria held up oniony hands and gave a quick smile. "Thanks, I'll be fine. Abuela wants to see you. She's out in the garden."

Digger decided to wait for a better moment to broach the news about the job.

She went outside and found the old woman kneeling in the middle of a row of zucchini plants, her head and shoulders hidden under an immense straw hat.

"*Hola*, Abuela."

The old woman looked up, pushing back the hat. A smile lit her face.

"It's my cowgirl! You came back!"

"Of course I came back." Digger squatted down beside her. "I'm so sorry about the last time. Maria and I, we—"

Abuela laughed. "Ha! You and Maria, you're two tough women. I told you she cares a lot for you. I know you care a lot about her too. Right?"

Digger sighed. "Yeah. I told you, it's complicated."

Digger looked beyond Abuela at the old adobe house, the stucco of the irregular walls like an old brown coat.

"That day when I was with you two, cooking, I felt like you were my family," she said.

Abuela's weathered face crinkled in a mischievous grin. "I don't mind having a Texan in the family—you know New Mexico and Texas don't always like each other—but you were born here, no?"

"Yeah, Albuquerque. I went to Houston after my parents—"

"I know, but you're here now." Abuela smiled. "Come, help me look for the squash bugs. If I don't get those rascals, they'll eat up every last squash. Here, see, there's one. Look at the underside of the leaves, that's where you'll find their eggs."

As they sat together, searching for the tiny orange clusters of eggs, a feeling of peace slipped over Digger like a warm blanket.

"I like doing this," she said, as she pushed a yellow flower away and peered under a broad leaf.

"You like looking for squash bugs?"

"I've never had a garden. I remember my mother did, though, and I used to help her sometimes when I was little."

Abuela laid a wrinkled brown hand on her arm. "This is healing work. You kneel on the earth and plant the seeds and new life appears. You take care of these little plants and they will take care of you. But"—she looked anxiously at the sky—"we need rain. I collect all the water for my garden in that cistern over there, and it's nearly empty."

They ate together, a simple meal of beans, tortillas, and salad.

Digger helped Maria clean up and then they went out to her studio. Inside, it was still hot from the blazing afternoon, even though the sun was sinking and the doors and windows were open.

"I wanted to show you this," Maria said, pointing to a half-finished canvas landscape painting. Digger recognized it as a stylized portrayal of the chapel in the bosque sitting at the base of the cliffs.

"I wanted to capture it as it is now, while I can."

They stood together silently. In the fading light, the painting seemed to come to life. Digger thought of the day Maria had taken her to see the chapel, of the light in the woods—of all the moments that had led them to where they were now.

"Do you remember the first time you invited me here?" Digger said. "Did you feel the electricity?"

"Of course I felt it."

Digger leaned in close, putting her arms around Maria. "I told you I had news."

Maria's eyebrows shot up, questioning.

"It's okay," Digger said. She took one of Maria's hands and brushed it with her lips. "It's good news. Remember that story I wrote?"

Then she told her about the interview with Julia Montoya. Maria said nothing. Her eyes searched Digger's face. Anxious. Finally she said softly, "Are you going to take this job? Leave the *Courier*?"

Their eyes met. Digger swallowed. When she spoke, her voice was barely above a whisper. "I didn't want to accept their offer until I talked to you. If I leave the paper, it would mean—"

She didn't get a chance to finish. Maria grabbed her shoulders, pulled her close, and kissed her as if she'd been crawling through the desert dying of thirst and Digger was cool water springing miraculously from the parched earth.

"Of course I want you to accept. I know you care about your job, but you have a heart too, you beautiful woman. Now don't give me any more shit about the blockade. We're going ahead with it. Just write the story and be done with it."

CHAPTER FORTY-THREE

MARIA'S CALL CAME two days later, just before eleven in the morning. Digger looked at the digital clock as she listened.

"We're doing the blockade today. We're going to be standing by the construction area that's closest to the chapel. It's near the base of the cliffs where they'll be working."

"Why so late? I thought you'd be going first thing in the morning to stop the road crew when they came to work."

"A cousin of mine is on the crew, and he said they'd be on a late start because of the city's permit investigation. He said that's where a bunch of them would be working today. If we get there before noon, we'll have our banners up and stop them."

"Are you going to call TV?"

"Yes. But I called you first. I promised I would."

"That's fair. I'll be there soon."

Digger looked around the newsroom, feeling sad. She'd called Montoya on the way to work and accepted her offer. Maybe that was why this place felt gloomier than ever. Yesterday, the publisher, the *Courier*'s financial officer, and Thompson had met with the corporate team to discuss the sale of the paper.

There'd been no word yet.

She walked over to tell Swenson about the protest. He looked worn out.

When she told him about the blockade, he just shrugged.

"Fine. Make sure you get some good photos." He looked away, distracted.

Tom, the photo editor, reluctantly agreed to let Rex cover the story with her. "You guys should ride separately, though. I'm going to need Rex later for a business story."

As Digger and Rex walked out together, he flung a glance back at the *Courier* building. "Today could be the day, you know."

She didn't want to hear that, not right now. "Come on, Rex, we've got a story to cover."

He was still loading his gear into the Jeep when she drove out of the parking lot. Up ahead she noticed a bank of dark clouds, the first she'd seen this summer. She hadn't thought to check the weather forecast.

When she reached the spot where she'd first met Maria's protest group, she found a vast staging area with a temporary worksite office, trucks, and heavy machinery. Land that was once thick with cottonwoods and salt cedar was now a broad slash of bare earth. In the distance she saw several men in orange vests and hard hats. She heard shouting. Maria's group must be up ahead.

Inside the worksite office, Nick Roemer was rereading another email request from the public works director that had set his blood boiling. His walkie-talkie crackled.

"Boss, we can't get to the site. There's people blocking the way. They got banners."

"What the hell?" he yelled. "Goddamn it, who are these people? What are they doing here?"

Digger was walking in the direction of the shouting when she saw a heavyset man burst out of the temporary building. Roemer shouted into his walkie-talkie, then started running toward the orange vests. Just then, Rex's Jeep swung in off the road. As soon as he opened the door, she called, "Hurry! I think the road crew's just found the protesters."

Rex grabbed his gear from the back of his vehicle. "For Christ's sake, have you looked at the weather?"

Digger looked up. The bank of clouds she'd seen earlier had moved in, the top huge and billowy like a pile of mashed pota-toes, the underside slate gray. No time to waste. She jogged in the direction she'd seen the men go, hoping Rex could catch up.

She rounded a bend and spotted figures ahead. The heavyset guy and the men with the orange vests had their backs to her. She saw Maria holding one side of an immense banner that read, "Save Our History: Stop the Road." A half dozen people stood on each side of her with arms linked, forming a human chain aroun a bulldozer. Digger recognized several faces from the neighbor-hood meeting and— surprise, surprise—Old George and Dillon.

Roemer was yelling, threatening to call the police. The protest-ers chanted back, "No road! No road!" A pickup truck suddenly appeared, bouncing along a track through the bosque. It stopped behind the protest line, and Councilors Larry Martinez and Tony Apodaca climbed out and stood watching the commotion.

Rex arrived, panting. "This is a goddamn circus! Have you talked to anybody yet? I saw the TV van right behind me."

Sure enough, the van rounded the corner. It stopped about fifty yards from where Digger and Rex stood. The cameraman emerged, shouldering his heavy gear. The petite blond reporter, in tight-fitting yellow dress and heels, picked her way awkwardly over the sandy ground.

Moments later, they heard a *woop-woop* sound and a police cruiser drew up, lights flashing, behind the TV van. Two officers jumped out.

Roemer shouted at them. "You gotta do something about these people! They're trespassing on my worksite!"

"No road! No road!" The chant nearly drowned his words.

As the officers moved toward the protesters, a dark blue Ford Escape arrived in a cloud of dust. Dave Johnsen got out, his face a picture of panic. He rushed forward to stand between the human chain and the advancing policemen. Digger followed him, recorder in hand.

Johnsen held out his hands to Maria, pleading. "This can be worked out. Please don't do this."

The policemen looked baffled.

Suddenly a gust of wind tore through the gap in the trees, swirling sand around them. Digger looked up at a charcoal gray sky. Seconds later it began to rain.

Rain pelted down, soaking their clothing, soaking the banner. The chanting ceased, Roemer shut up. Rain hissed all around them.

Johnsen seemed uncertain what to do. "Please, please! Miss Ortiz," he called, looking back and forth between the police and Maria. "Let's everybody go home. We're all getting wet. It's dangerous to stay out in this storm. We'll handle this another way."

Rex's phone rang. He pulled it out of his soggy pocket, looked at the screen.

"It's Tom." He listened for a moment, then put away the phone. He looked at Digger with a dazed expression. "The buyers walked away. The paper is closing, effective immediately."

Rex just stood there, rain dripping off the edge of his ball cap, fogging his glasses. She remembered the same stricken look on Halloran's face. She laid a hand on his shoulder.

"Rex—"

He shook his head. His lips trembled. "Thompson's called a meeting. We better go." He slung the cameras over his shoulder and turned to head back.

Digger didn't move.

The paper was closing. There would be no deadline. There

would be no story. The newsroom would be dark, the presses still. *How long do you keep silent? she wondered. How long do you listen to prejudice and bite your tongue? How long do you deny your heart?*

Rex called back to her, "Aren't you coming?"

She looked ahead at Maria and her small band, sheltering under the drooping banner, still defiant. She looked back at Rex and slowly shook her head. It was time to get off the fence. She had a new future waiting.

"Not this time, Rex. I've made up my mind. Good luck to you, my friend."

Digger stuck the recorder and notebook into her backpack and left him staring at her in disbelief. She walked past the road workers, the policemen, and Dave Johnsen. She walked up to Maria and put her arms around her and kissed her there in front of everyone.

"I'm here now, with you." Digger and Maria clung to each other fiercely as the rain poured down.

It fell in torrents, clawing deep grooves in the soft sand. Roemer and his workers hustled away. The TV cameraman and reporter rushed back to their van. Digger noticed the reporter was carrying her muddy shoes in her hands. Then the officers had to push the news van till it got traction. Then they too drove away, the wheels of their cruiser spinning on the slick soil.

Maria was thanking the bedraggled protesters when someone interrupted her.

"Look, up there!"

From the top of the escarpment, water sluiced down in two powerful jets, striking the base around the support structures. As they watched, the streams pounded into the sand, blasting holes in the earth. Within minutes the holes were the size of trash cans. At the same time, water suddenly spurted up out of the earth.

Digger's heart leapt. "It's the spring!" she said. "Abuela said the spring would come if it rained!"

Slowly, the concrete supports leaned inward and cracked as the earth beneath them caved in. Moments later, chunks of asphalt began toppling from above. They crashed, splashing the terrified protesters with mud and sand.

At that moment a figure emerged from the woods.

"It's Jack Kimble, the old mayor!"

Maria stared at him, then nodded at Digger, a smile spreading across her face. "Remember his warning?"

Kimble strode toward them, his wild hair and beard hanging like seaweed around his gaunt face, a dark green poncho clinging to his skeletal frame.

He stood before them, and as he watched the deluge, his eyes glowed. He raised his arms to the heavens.

"Behold the power of the rain!"

The End

CPSIA information can be obtained
at www.ICGtesting.com
Printed in the USA
BVHW071055090822
644142BV00008B/476